MW00777217

THE ACCARDI TWINS BOOK TWO

CRUEL KING
of *New York*

USA TODAY & WSJ BESTSELLING AUTHOR
SIOBHAN DAVIS

Copyright © Siobhan Davis 2024. Siobhan Davis asserts the moral right to be identified as the author of this work. All rights reserved under International and Pan-American Copyright Conventions.

SIOBHAN DAVIS® is registered as a trade mark at the U.S. Patent and Trademark Office and at the European Union Intellectual Property Office.

This is a work of fiction. Names, characters, places, incidents and dialogues are products of the author's imagination or are used fictitiously. Any resemblance to actual people, living or dead, or events is entirely coincidental.

This book is sold subject to the condition that it shall not, by way of trade or otherwise be lent, resold, hired out, or otherwise circulated without the prior written consent of the author. No part of this publication may be reproduced, transmitted, decompiled, or stored in or introduced into any information storage and retrieval system, in any form or by any means, whether electronic or mechanical, including photocopying, without the express written permission of the author.

This paperback edition © May 2024

ISBN-13: 978-1-916651-08-1

Edited by Kelly Hartigan (XterraWeb) editing.xterraweb.com
Proofread by Final Polish Proofreading
Research and critique by The Critical Touch
Cover design by Robin Harper of Wicked By Design
Cover imagery © depositphotos.com
Formatted by Ciara Turley using Vellum

BOOK DESCRIPTION

The boy I grew up loving is now the made man who broke my heart.

I had one primary goal in life: to marry Don Caleb Accardi, give him lots of babies, and live happily ever after.

Until he shattered my fantasy and destroyed my belief in love.

His playboy status isn't the issue. I learned to live with his womanizing while patiently waiting on the sideline for him to truly notice me.

But he never has. Not the way I want him to.

One promise. That's all I asked of him, and he couldn't even keep it.

Something inside me dies when I learn the truth, and I reach my breaking point.

This is the last time he hurts me.

I'm not saving myself for him anymore.

So, I cut him out of my life and begin dating.
Caleb sure doesn't like that, and a switch has flipped in his brain.

Now, he wants me. And he's pulling out all the stops to win back my heart.

Too bad it's too late—for him and for me.

Because Caleb has powerful enemies who are aware he loves me, and now I'm fair game.

Siobhan Davis
Stories with Heart

Note From the Author

This book should only be read after reading **Cold King of New York** as the mafia story continues from book one to two.

This is a dark mafia romance with mature content. For a full list of triggers, refer to my website. Please note this page contains spoilers.

Mafia Glossary

- Barone – Made men from New Jersey who are hired by other made men for jobs and contract killings.
- Bastardi – Bastards.
- Bastardo – Bastard.
- Bratva – The Russian mafia in the US.
- Capo – Italian for captain. A member of a crime family who heads/leads a crew of soldiers.
- Consigliere – Italian for adviser/counselor. A member of a crime family who advises the boss and mediates disputes.
- Consiglieri – Plural of consigliere.
- Cosa Nostra – A criminal organization, operating within the US, comprising Italian American crime families.
- Don/Boss – The male head of an Italian crime family.
- Famiglia– Italian for family.
- Famiglie – Italian for families.
- Five Families – Five crime families who rule in New York, each headed by a don.
- Made man – A member of the mafia who has been officially initiated/inducted into a crime family.
- Mafioso/Mafiosi – An official member of the mafia or a reference to the mafia in general.
- Principessa – Italian for princess.
- RICO laws – The Racketeer-Influenced and Corrupt Organizations Act, a federal statute

enacted in 1970. It allows prosecutors to seek tougher penalties if they can prove someone is a member of the mafia.

- Soldati – Italian for soldiers.
- Soldato – Italian for soldier.
- Soldier – A low-ranking member of the mafia who reports to an assigned Capo.
- The Commission – The governing/ruling body of Cosa Nostra, which sits in New York, the organized crime capital of the US.
- Tesoro – Italian for treasure.
- Triad – Chinese crime syndicate.
- Underboss – The second-in-command within a crime family and an initiated mafia member who works closely with and reports directly to the boss.

FIVE NEW YORK FAMILIES

GRECO	MAZZONE	DIPIETRO	ACCARDI	MALTESE
Massimo Greco Don & Commission President	**Bennett Mazzone** Current don	**Cristian DiPietro** Current don	**Caleb & Joshua Accardi** Current dons	**Fiero Maltese** Current don
Sons	Sons	Brother		
Cassio Greco	**Rowan Mazzone**	**Cruz DiPietro** Las Vegas don		
Armis Greco	**Rhys Mazzone**			
Rocco Greco				

ACCARDI FAMILY

- **Natalia Messina** (Nee Mazzone)
- **Gino Accardi** (Deceased) — **Married** — **Juliet Accardi** (Deceased)

Married

- **Leo Messina**

- **Caleb Accardi** — **Twins** — **Joshua Accardi**

Children

Step-siblings

- **Rosa Messina**

- **Leif Messina**

MAZZONE FAMILY

Bennett Mazzone (Ben) —— Siblings —— Natalia Messina (Nee Mazzone)

Bennett Mazzone — Married

Sierra Mazzone (Nee Lawson) — Sisters — Serena Salerno (Nee Lawson)

Natalia Messina — Married — Leo Messina

Children

Rowan Mazzone

Raven Mazzone

Rhys Mazzone

Joshua & Caleb Accardi (Stepsons)

Rosa Messina

Leif Messina

DIPIETRO FAMILY

Josef Di Pietro (Retired) — Married — Beatrice DiPietro

Cruz DiPietro
Current don

Cristian DiPietro
Current don

Sabina DiPietro

Married

Cousins

Anais DiPietro
(nee Salerno)

Alesso Salerno

Half-sisters

Catarina Greco
nee Conti

GRECO FAMILY

Maximo Greco (Deceased) — **Married** — **Eleanora Greco**

- **Carlo Greco** (Deceased)
- **Primo Greco** (Deceased)
- **Gabriele Greco**
- **Massimo Greco** Current don

  Married

  Catarina Greco nee Conti

  Children

  - **Cassio Greco**
  - **Armis Greco**
  - **Bella Greco**
  - **Rocco Greco**

MALTESE FAMILY

Roberto Maltese (Retired) — Married — Ingrid Maltese

Fiero Maltese Current don

Zumo Maltese

Sofia Maltese

Tullia Maltese

SALERNO FAMILY

Anais Salerno
(now DiPetrio)

— Cousin — **Alesso Salerno**

Married

ex-lovers **Caleb Accardi**

Married

Cruz DiPetrio

Serena Salerno
(Nee Lawson)

Children

Elisa Salerno

Romeo Salerno

Will Salerno

Aria Salerno

THE ACCARDI TWINS BOOK TWO

CRUEL KING
of *New York*

Chapter One
Caleb

"**G**ive the order, Massimo," I hiss through gritted teeth, keeping my rifle trained on the old prick in the chair. Our sniper team is a mile away. We are on the top floor of an abandoned building with a perfect vantage point and an unobstructed view of the shit going down by the ocean. Gia glances at me briefly from her position at my left side. Sheer terror is written all over her face and I share her concern. Cruz holds a gun to my twin's brow while Joshua presses the muzzle of his gun into that backstabbing *bastardo's* chest. Primo Greco—Massimo's brother recently resurrected from the grave—has just declared his intent, and our president needs to get his shit together and give the order, now.

I understand his shock, but delaying too long could cost us a lot of lives.

"Massimo." Fiero lifts his head from my right, staring his best buddy down. "Do it now before it's too late."

There are twenty-one sharpshooters on this roof awaiting instruction, and this team was always the ace up our sleeves. That and the additional one thousand men led by the four newly appointed dons to The Commission dotted around the battle scene. They are still in hiding, awaiting the call. If Massimo doesn't act in two fucking seconds, I'm intervening. I don't give a fuck about reprimands. We need to end this before we lose our loved ones on the firing line.

Gia and I share a look, and I nod, understanding we're on the same page without the need for spoken word. Girl has big lady balls, and I love the way she loves my brother. She is everything Joshua deserves and needs.

Don Greco snaps out of wherever he went to in his head, thank fuck. "The old man is mine. You take Primo." He stares at his buddy before swinging his gaze to me and Gia. "Caleb, you take Calabro. Gia, you've got Cruz. Don't kill him. He needs to be interrogated and punished accordingly."

Sometimes, I really hate all the bullshit rules. Who cares if he's a don and it's the one hard and fast rule? He has betrayed us, and he should die on that field. I'm tempted to riddle him with bullets myself, but today isn't the day to go rogue. There are too many lives at stake.

Massimo turns to face the rest of the men. "Marrone, watch McDermott. When he runs, stop him, but don't shoot to kill. Cascio, protect Don Mazzone and Don DiPietro. The rest of you pick enemy targets and take as many of them down as you can."

Gia briefly clenches her jaw, but it's the only sign she's affected. I'm guessing she wants to end Cruz as badly as me, and she wants Liam alive so she can exact revenge. I want that for her too. That fucker doesn't deserve a quick death. Joshua already stabbed Liam in the thigh and got rid of his weapon, but McDermott is sly, and he's going to make a run for it as soon as he gets the chance.

"We'll get him," I mouth, hoping to reassure her.

She offers me a terse nod.

"Everyone in position," Massimo says in a calm tone and I'm glad he pulled his head from his ass. We need our level-headed leader now. I ready myself, pointing my weapon at the Barone's new self-appointed don. That prick gave the order to come after J and me and Rowan and it's only right I'm the one to end him. "On my order," Massimo says, lifting his arm, as he waits for everyone to get into position. He quickly updates the key men on the field through our earpiece communicators, so they are forewarned, and issues instructions to the four dons leading our backup teams.

I inhale deeply, keeping my aim locked on my target and my finger curled around the trigger, pulling it when Massimo says, "Now!"

Multiple pops crack through the nighttime air as we fire en masse at the unsuspecting enemy. In the distance, targets drop like flies, and renewed gunfire breaks out on the ground as our backup *soldati* charge forward from four different directions, circling the enemy.

Checking for Joshua, I breathe a sigh of relief to see him unharmed. Cruz is lying on the ground in front of him, incapacitated but not dead. I'm tempted. So fucking tempted, but I shove my personal need for vengeance aside and concentrate on taking as many of the pricks down as I can.

I zone out, blocking out everything but the moving targets in the distance, popping off shots in quickfire succession. Drones drop grenades from above, managed remotely by Mazzone's tech team. Every loyal man here received an updated tracking chip in the last week with an infrared marker which identifies them as an ally from the air. The team under Capo DiNardo who had switched loyalty to our now-deceased underboss Marino are fair game and I won't lose any sleep if they get taken down.

They were never going to survive anyway.

You don't betray our *famiglia* and live to tell the tale.

It's a virtual bloodbath on the ground, and not for the first time I wish I was in the thick of the action.

Our team works well under Massimo's supervision, and it's obvious within minutes we have the upper hand. Our enemy is outnumbered, and the order is clearly given to retreat. I take potshots at the men as they flee toward the ocean and the waiting submarine. Others flee in all directions, chased by our men on the ground and our snipers.

Within twenty minutes, it's all over.

"Gather your weapons and clean up your area. Don't leave any empty shells or other evidence," Massimo says, frowning as he taps on his earpiece and listens to whomever is on the other end. His eyes dart to Fiero.

I clean up fast, tucking everything into my rifle bag before slinging it over my shoulder. "Don't leave without me," I tell Gia. "I need a word with Massimo." I stalk toward where Don Greco and Don Maltese have their heads bent, deep in conversation.

"What's going on?" I ask, pushing myself in between them.

"Rinascita's on fire," Massimo says in a low tone so no one else hears. "They sent in drones with firebombs." Rinascita is the legit company Massimo and Fiero co-own that operates out of Staten Island and is the front for bringing narcotics into the city.

"Shit." We had suspected they may target other locations and had put extra men at the docks, but there isn't much they could do against drones except shoot them from the sky. "How bad is the damage?"

"We don't know until we get there, but fire crews are working to put it out."

"Was anyone in the building?" Hundreds of employees

work out of the place, and I hate to think any innocent got caught up in our *mafioso* shit.

"There were a few people working late, but our men got them out in time."

"They hit the plant in Cali too," Fiero confirms, scrubbing a hand along his prickly jawline. "But the extra reinforcements paid off, and we held them at bay. There is some damage, and we lost a lot of good men, but the plant is still under our control." We had suspected they were planning a hit when Gia found blueprints of the Colombian drug production facility on McDermott's desk. At least our planning paid off, but with the plant hit it's likely to disrupt production which will cause more headaches.

"Thanks to Gia," I say, not realizing she has just materialized at my side.

"What?" Her brow puckers as she looks up at me.

"They tried to take the Cali plant, but they didn't succeed because your intel gave us the heads-up we needed," Massimo replies.

"And your discovery of the chip led us to identifying the traitors. We owe you a lot, Gia," Fiero adds.

"Um, I was just doing my job but thanks."

I poke her rapidly reddening cheeks. "Are you blushing?"

"Shut up." She glares at me, and I chuckle. "Can we go now, please?" She tugs on my arm. "I need to see Joshua and find my family."

"Just give me a second." I return my gaze to our president. "What do you need us to do?"

"Work with the others to clean up the scene. We're heading to Staten Island. We'll reconvene at HQ in a couple hours." He clamps a hand on my shoulder. "Don't plan on getting any sleep tonight."

Everyone is waiting downstairs when the four of us appear.

Men are piling into the truck when a helicopter appears in my peripheral vision.

"That's our ride." Fiero squints as he looks up at the approaching chopper.

"Call if anything happens," Massimo says, and I nod. He pokes his head in through the back of the truck. "Good work tonight. Keep your wits about you down there." He slaps his hand against the side of the truck a few times as I climb up beside Gia in the front. The driver kicks the engine into gear, and we take off.

"Joshua!" Gia races off across the grass, heading for my twin the instant she spots him. Leo jerks his head in my direction, relief evident on his face. Alesso turns to look at me, nodding in acknowledgement even though I know he hates my guts. Beside him, Uncle Ben is barking orders as *soldati* work to clear the site before the authorities show up.

Gia jumps at my brother, wrapping her legs around his waist as he holds her up and kisses her. He's covered in blood but seems unharmed. I give them some privacy to reunite as I hold back and make a call to the Greenwich estate. I'm assuming our stepdad has already checked in, but I want to talk to Mom myself.

"Caleb. Are you okay?" she answers in a panicked voice.

"I'm fine. Joshua is fine, and so are Leo, Alesso, and Ben."

"What about Gia and Rico and the boys?"

"Gia was with me. She's fine, but I haven't seen Rico or his sons. I'm sure they're here somewhere. I'll get Gia to message you when she finds them." As I'm talking, I watch Gia and Joshua walk off hand in hand, and I don't need to know where they are going or who they are looking for.

"How are Leif and Rosa?" I ask.

"Your brother and sister are fine. We built a blanket fort, played games, and ate a ton of junk food. They had a blast and were none the wiser."

"And Lili?"

"She's fine. There were no issues here, and we're all safe, so don't worry about us."

"Good." I consider asking Mom to pass the phone to Elisa, but there's no point. She's still not talking to me, and I have no clue why.

It's bugging me way more than I thought it would.

Truth is, I miss her. Until things turned to shit last year, she regularly sent me texts and messages, and we always talked for hours whenever we were in the same place at the same time.

Now, I'm persona non grata, and she won't even look at me. For the first time in years, I got no special drawing on my birthday, and she refused the delivery of roses I sent to her apartment, just off campus, for Valentine's Day. She really seems to hate me now, and it's killing me inside. Especially when I don't know what I've done to warrant her turning on me like this. I have tried talking to her on several occasions, to find out what I did to deserve the cold shoulder, but she refuses to entertain me at all.

It's seriously pissing me off for a bunch of reasons I don't want to explore. "I've got to go, and I'm sure you do too."

"I'm just waiting for the chopper to arrive to take me to the city," Mom replies. "Leo said there are plenty of injured men."

"Unfortunately." I scan the ground watching men cart dead bodies to one pickup point and helping to move the injured to a different collection point. All casualties will be moved to the new *mafioso* hospital. I knew it would be all-hands-on-deck and Mom would most likely be called in to help tonight.

"Be safe, my love, and message me when you're both home. I don't care what time it is."

A chuckle escapes my lips. "Mom. We're not kids anymore, and you need to stop worrying. You know the score."

"That is an impossibility, Caleb. You're my sons. I will always worry, especially on days like today. Just be a good boy and text your mother. Please?"

"Of course." I struggle to deny Mom anything. I was a little rebellious shit during my teenage years, and I put her through hell on more than one occasion. These days, I go out of my way to make it up to her.

"Love you."

"Love you too." I hang up first because Mom will keep me on the line for ages if I don't.

When I find Gia and Joshua, I'm relieved to hear her father and brothers made it out alive. Antonio took a bullet to his shoulder protecting his younger brother, but he'll live. Rico picked up an injury to his leg, but it's strapped up, and it's not impeding him apparently. Both men are en route to the hospital under sufferance.

"Where is fuckface one and two?" My gaze roams the area, but I see no sign of Cruz or McDermott.

"McDermott is unconscious and on his way to the bunker," Joshua confirms. "But that other prick got away."

"How the fuck did that happen?"

"We don't know, but Cristian took off with some men to see if he can locate him," Joshua says.

I'm guessing that's a futile exercise. The prick most likely escaped on the sub.

"I shot out his kneecaps," Gia says, "so he obviously had help. I should have kept him in my sights."

"It's not your fault, honey." My brother looks at his woman

in a familiar adoring manner. It's grossly endearing. "It was crazy and hard to keep tabs on everyone."

"And they had a fucking submarine," Cosimo says. Gia's brother's eyes are out on stalks. "Like that's some insane shit."

"We couldn't stop them from escaping in time, and a lot of men still got away. I'm assuming Cruz was one of them," Joshua says, articulating my previous thought.

"He must be important to their plans," Gia adds.

"At least we took these motherfuckers out." I glance to the side where Primo and Maximo Greco and Don Calabro are lined up on the muddy ground alongside the bodies of our dead *soldati*. "That's got to be one of the shortest homecomings ever." I kick the side of Maximo's wizened head. "Arrogant fucks."

"Can you actually believe that shit? How the hell did they stay hidden for over thirteen years?" Joshua shakes his head.

"I'd like the answer to that question too," Ben says, walking over to us with Leo.

"Was Maximo the Italian big boss or do you think there is someone else pulling the strings?" Gia asks.

"If he's been hiding in Italy all this time, it's possible his ally is the one pulling the strings," I say.

"Meaning it's not over." Gia sighs as she leans her head against Joshua's shoulder.

"We rounded up a few Italians who are alive. We'll interrogate them and hopefully get some answers this time." Leo cracks his knuckles as a cell phone vibrates in Ben's pocket.

A frown puckers Mazzone's brow as he stares at the screen. "It's the commissioner." His gaze bounces between us. "I'll handle him if you can wrap this up fast." Pressing a button on his cell, he accepts the call and stalks off to smooth things over with his police commissioner buddy.

9

"Help me carry these to the car," Leo says, jerking his head at the three men on the grass beside us.

"Why aren't they shark fodder like the rest?" I ask, tipping my head to where our men are tossing dead bodies into the ocean. Enemies and traitors are taking a permanent swim while the bodies of loyal men are being transported to HQ so their families can bury them with dignity.

"Don Greco instructed us to retrieve the bodies," my stepdad says, hefting old man Greco over his shoulder. "If it was up to me, I'd happily toss this prick over the edge." He doesn't need to elaborate on his hatred for the man or why.

"Just do it. Give Massimo some bullshit excuse. It's not like he's going to punish you for it."

"That kind of attitude does you no favors, Caleb." Alesso plants himself in front of me, pinning me with a sharp look.

He has never been my greatest fan. He hates his daughter has feelings for me and hates that his cousin cheats on her husband with me. Anais is the one who is married, and the main instigator, so I find his attitude more than a little hypocritical. Since Elisa cut me out of her life, her stepdad has barely tolerated me, which suits me just fine. I'm not his biggest fan either, even if Lili dotes on him and he's been an amazing father to her.

"You can't ignore a direct instruction from the president," Alesso says.

"Don't tell me you actually agree with this?"

"They are his family, and Calabro was a don."

"They're all treacherous scum, and they don't deserve any respect."

"That may well be the case, but it's not our call to make. It's our job to follow orders." He drills me with another sharp look, irritating the fuck out of me. Who the hell is he to lecture me?

I'm a fucking don, and he's only a *consigliere*. He would do well to remember that.

"Let's get this over with." Joshua throws Primo Greco over his shoulder. "We need to get to the hospital, and we're wasting time."

Chapter Two
Elisa

"Can you take these supplies to Dr. Kerrigan, please." Natalia hands me a box filled with gauzes, surgical tape, hydrogen peroxide, saline solution, and other medical supplies. "And check if they need more water or food."

"Will do."

"Thanks, Elisa. You've been a godsend tonight."

I smile at Caleb's mom. She's my surrogate aunt, and I love her to bits. I give her a quick hug before taking the box and walking off, ignoring my protesting calf muscles. I've been on my feet for hours, dashing all over the emergency room, doing whatever is needed of me. I have zero medical expertise, but I wanted to help, and Natalia accepted my offer without hesitation. Mom and Sierra stayed behind to mind the kids while I traveled with Natalia by helicopter to the new private hospital.

We have been inundated with patients. All with gunshot wounds, and some with additional knife wounds. As much as Mom and Dad have tried to shelter me and my siblings, there is no escaping the world we live in. I'm not naïve. I know the things that go down, but it's still been a shock. I spent the hours we were holed up in the panic room worrying about everyone we love. Now I see the devastation wrought by the big battle, I'm more acutely aware of the danger they were in. I'm so grateful they all made it out alive.

Reaching the section under Dr. Kerrigan's command, I pull back the first curtain and hand over the box, purposely not looking at the semi-naked man lying on the table. Bloody bandages litter the floor and he's groaning as the medical team attend to his injuries. "I have the supplies you requested," I confirm, handing the box to a male nurse. "Do you need anything else, Ken? More water?"

"We're fine. Thanks, Elisa." He shoots me a quick smile before rummaging in the box.

I turn around, to see where else I'm needed, almost face-planting into a toned chest and broad shoulders I would know anywhere. "Excuse me," I say, not looking up at him. It's hard to hold on to my resolve when I see his gorgeous face or peer into his stunning blue eyes.

Remember what he did, an inner voice whispers in my ear, and suddenly it's not so hard. "Move, Caleb," I say, glaring at him when he doesn't budge.

"You look dead on your feet. You should take a break." Concern splays across his face, but it's as fake as the promise he made me.

"It's busy and I don't need a break." Lowering my eyes, I move sideways, to walk around him, but he follows my movement, blocking me.

"Caleb," I grit out. "Quit this shit. Look around? I'm needed, and you're interfering."

"You can't avoid me forever, Lili." He grips my chin gently, forcing my face up so I'm looking at him. Tingles dart across my skin, and my heart gallops like a racehorse just let out of the gate. I hate how much he still affects me. Why can't my body just get with the program?

Gia has been right all along.

Caleb is bad news, and I'm a gullible fool for thinking he would ever develop feelings for me. He truly doesn't care if he hurts me, and I'm done being his punching bag.

"Watch me." I drill him with a resolute look as I fold my arms over my chest.

"Leave her alone." Gia shoots daggers at Caleb with her eyes as she loops her arm through mine.

"Just tell me." There was a time I would have fallen for his pleading tone, but that time has passed. "Please, Lili. Tell me what I did so I can fix it."

"Fuck off, Caleb." Gia shoves past him, knocking into his arm. "Lise has told you she doesn't want to speak to you anymore, and if you care for her at all, you'll respect her wishes."

A muscle clenches in his jaw as he levels a lethal look at my best friend. "Butt the fuck out, Gia, or you and I will have problems."

Gia flips him the bird. "Do I look concerned?"

I shift uncomfortably on my feet. I love how readily Gia rises to my defense, but Caleb will be her brother-in-law someday, and I don't want to be the reason they don't get along.

"This isn't the time." I fix both of them with a warning look. "Drop it. Please."

"I'll get it out of you." Caleb pins me with a look that ordinarily weakens my knees, but I'm resisting these days and...hell.

I cling to Gia's arm harder as I feel my knees buckle.

Who am I kidding?

I'm still hopelessly fixated on Caleb Accardi. The only difference now is I don't want to be. I want to be cured of my addiction, and I'm prepared to do whatever it takes to detox him from my system. "Let it go, Caleb. Just let it go."

He stares at me, and whatever he sees in my eyes is enough for him to back off. For now. I watch him walk off with a pain in my chest and knots in my stomach.

"He's not going to give up," Gia says. "He's a stubborn motherfucker, and he won't stop until he knows the truth."

"I don't understand how he hasn't figured it out yet." I shuck out of her hold as we walk across the busy space. "He's smart, and it doesn't take a rocket scientist to realize how badly he messed up."

"Let's grab a quick coffee break. I told Antonio I'd get him one. They're keeping him overnight because they can't operate tonight. There are more urgent cases who take precedent."

"What about your dad? Is he still here?" I ask as we walk off.

She shakes her head. "He went home with Mom and Marco. His injury wasn't serious. He got a couple of stitches and some pain meds, and they sent him on his merry way. Cosimo insisted on staying with me. He feels guilty Antonio took a bullet for him."

"I can imagine."

My cell pings in my jeans pocket just as we step into the elevator. Gia pushes the button for the cafeteria as I extract my phone and swipe my finger across the screen. My best friend leans over my shoulder as I open the text from Seb. "He's so smitten."

"I know." The elevator moves as I tap a quick reply telling him I'm still with my family, which isn't a full lie though it's not the truth either. It's hard dating someone outside *la famiglia* because they can't know anything about the *mafioso*. It means I have to lie to him sometimes, which I hate. He's a nice guy, and he doesn't deserve it.

"Wow, enthusiastic much?" Gia arches a brow as the doors ping open on the cafeteria level.

"I like him," I protest. "And I'm giving it a shot, Gigi, which is a really big deal for me." He is the first guy I have ever dated. All the others who asked me out were instantly rejected because I could never see past Caleb. I have been pathetically clinging to hope for years, and I feel like the biggest fool.

"I know it is." She links her arm in mine as we make our way to the counter. It's after four a.m., but the cafeteria is still moderately busy with loved ones anxiously awaiting news. "I'm proud of you for sticking to your guns."

"It's not easy. He's not making it easy."

"I think Caleb took you for granted for far too long. This is good for him. Let him see what he's missing."

"He doesn't care," I mumble. "Not really. His ego is bruised 'cause no one says no to him ever. This is a novelty, and it'll wear off."

"Hmm. I'm not so sure."

We pause our conversation to order coffees, taking a seat at a nearby table while we wait for our order.

"What do you mean?" I knot my hands on my lap under the table.

"Joshua said he's really down over it. He was upset you sent back the flowers."

"I can't accept roses from a man who isn't my boyfriend, and I want nothing from Caleb anymore." He always sends me flowers on Valentine's Day, and this is the first time I've refused them. "He's hurt me for the last time." My choked tone conveys how much further I have to go with my rehabilitation.

"I'm glad to hear it. He has never deserved your love and attention."

Tears prick the backs of my eyes. "Why was I never good

enough, Gigi? I know I'm not beautiful like most of his conquests but I'm not ugly either."

"Babe." Gia reaches across the table to hold my hand. "You're drop-dead gorgeous, and don't let anyone tell you otherwise. You have that whole willowy model look going for you. I would kill for your figure."

"We should swap," I joke. "Then you wouldn't need to have surgery."

"I can't wait to reduce these puppies." She casts a glance at her large chest.

"And I'd love to increase mine." I peer at my modest B-cup chest.

"You're perfect, Lise. It's Caleb's loss, and you are worth a million of the skanks he usually hooks up with."

"He has hooked up with supermodels and actresses and other celebrities," I remind her. "Most are not skanks."

"None of them mean anything, Lise. He flits from one woman to the next like they're a dying breed."

"Except for *her*." I pout, like always when I think of that horrible woman. I don't know how Caleb has put up with Anais for years. Gia told me it's revenge because Cruz stole Bettina from Joshua, but that was years ago, and Caleb still sleeps with her, so I'm not sure I buy it.

"He can't stand Anais," Gia reminds me before getting up to grab the two trays with our takeout coffees.

"It hasn't stopped him having sex with her. If she's the kind of woman he's into, I never stood a chance. I just wish I'd realized it earlier and not wasted so many years pining for him." I take one of the trays, and we walk back toward the elevator, waving at a couple of people we recognize on the way.

"Are you going to give it up to Seb?" Gia keeps her voice low so no one overhears.

"I don't know." I was saving myself for Caleb, but that

dream died a death last year. "After waiting this long, I don't want to just give my virginity to anyone, and this thing with Seb is still new."

"How does he feel about that?"

"He's been decent about it. I explained, and he said he won't pressure me, and he hasn't. We mostly only kiss."

Gia's features soften as we step into the empty elevator. "I'm glad he's letting you set the pace, and you shouldn't feel under pressure to lose your V-card."

"Says the girl who spontaneously gave hers up to Cristian DiPietro." I grin at my bestie. I remember the morning after when she was gushing to me about it. "Maybe I should give him my V-card. I bet that would seriously piss Caleb off."

"It would but we both know you'd never do it. You wouldn't willingly hurt him even if he deserves a dose of his own medicine."

"I couldn't do that," I readily agree as the doors ping at the lower level. "I wish I could be as heartless as Caleb, but I refuse to lower myself to his level. I'm not going to compromise who I am just to get even no matter how tempting it sometimes seems."

"And that is why you are one of the sweetest, most authentic people I know." Gia smiles at me. "The best revenge is cutting him out of your life and moving forward. Seb might not be the one, but at least he's helping you to heal, and in time, you'll forget all about Caleb Accardi." She presses a kiss to my cheek. "I bet you'll find your Prince Charming when you least expect it. Just like how it happened for me."

I don't have the heart to tell her I've given up on ever finding true love because, if this is what it feels like when it all goes wrong, I want no part of it anymore.

Chapter Three
Caleb

"How bad is the damage to Rinascita?" I ask as soon as we are all settled around the conference table in Commission Central. We came directly from the hospital after checking on our injured men, making a pitstop at the penthouse to drop Gia off. Outside, traffic is already building in Manhattan though it won't be sunrise for another forty minutes. None of us have slept, and everyone looks exhausted even after showers and a change of clothes.

"There is significant damage to the roof and the top floor, but the lower levels are intact, and the structure seems solid," Massimo explains.

"We called the various management teams, and everyone will work remotely for a few days until the engineering team inspects the building and ensures it's safe," Fiero adds before shooting Massimo a knowing look.

Our president clears his throat. "There was another casualty." His gaze dances between my brother and me. "The Accardi cruise liner docked at the port was also targeted. They couldn't save it."

Joshua and I exchange troubled glances. "We had security staff on board. Did they get out safely?" my twin asks.

"You lost two men. They were on the top deck when the first bomb dropped. They died instantly according to the *capo* on duty. Several others have minor injuries or suffered smoke inhalation. We sent them to the hospital before we left to come here."

"Why are we only hearing about this now?" I stifle a yawn as I swing my gaze from Massimo to Fiero.

"Your *capo* called Marino, and when he didn't pick up, he called Joshua."

What am I, chopped liver?

"I lost my phone during the fight," my twin explains as I try to rein in my frustration.

I haven't forgotten we need to cleanse our *famiglia* of every scumbag traitor and rebuild loyalty. By the time we're through with them, no one will ever dare to disrespect us again.

We plan to deal with McDermott first before handling the traitors we left stewing in crowded cells in the bunker. It's timely because after my encounter with Lili in the hospital I'm itching to murder a few pricks.

"There wasn't anything you could've done. We were already on-site, so we handled it."

"I will contact the insurance company later," Joshua says as I quietly seethe.

"I'll call the commissioner and have him send someone to your office to take a statement. You'll need an official police report to submit a claim," Ben says. "He can weigh in if we need to take the heat off you. A cruise liner being bombed is not something we'll be able to conceal."

"It'll be a shitshow, and we'll have to lay low for a while," I say.

"This complicates an already complicated situation." Fiero

looks grumpy as fuck, and I don't blame him. The street trade is already on shaky ground, and this doesn't help.

"Thank fuck we offloaded the shipment earlier." Joshua leans back in his chair, dragging a hand through his damp hair.

"How badly will this affect the supply chain?" Cristian asks, loosening his tie and opening the top button of his shirt.

"It will undoubtedly cause major issues," Joshua says, "but I'll call our new airline contact and see if we can put a regular schedule in motion to cover the gap."

"The bigger issue is production." Fiero scrubs a hand down his face. "The authorities have temporarily shut the plant down. Juan Pablo will pay the bribes and get it reopened fast, but a few warehouses were damaged and require repairs, and a lot of the product in the storage warehouse was destroyed during the battle. It will be at least three weeks before full production restarts."

"We need to negotiate a deal with another producer, and possibly we should keep this contact as a backup resource, given all the recent issues. We haven't helped the situation by having no Plan B," I say.

"I don't think we have any choice," Massimo agrees. "Set up a meeting with O'Hara," he instructs Joshua. "He mentioned a possible contact in Sinaloa."

"I don't think we should get mixed up with the cartel." Cristian shifts in his chair, the leather squelching with the movement.

"I don't like the idea either," Ben says, "but we don't have many options. We need someone powerful with established production and distribution channels. They've had their sights set on New York for some time, and they won't reject the opportunity."

We cease talking when there's a knock on the door. A hot brunette in a tight pencil skirt deposits a tray with coffee, doughnuts, and pastries on the table, asking if we need anything else. She flashes me a flirty look as she passes, and I struggle to place her. I suspect I screwed her a couple of years ago, but I can't be sure. After a while, all the names, faces, and bodies blend together. None are ever memorable, and it's starting to get old.

We resume our conversation after the door is firmly closed.

"Partnering with the biggest Mexican cartel is a recipe for disaster," Cristian says. "I really think we should consider other options."

"I'm not a big fan of the idea either," Fiero agrees. "Their product quality is often inconsistent, and we could be inviting bigger trouble by opening our doors to them. But we don't have time to waste, and we know they can dig us out of this hole right now," Fiero says, in between chewing mouthfuls of an almond croissant. "I think we have to take the risk. We have only just driven the other operators out of the city. If they discover we're incapable of meeting demand, they'll be back, and it'll be harder to permanently push the various entities out."

Joshua pours me a coffee and slides it over.

"What are we doing with Vegas?" I ask before taking a sip of the hot bitter liquid.

"We've sent Mantegna and Agessi to Vegas to restore order," Massimo says.

Dominic Mantegna is the Chicago don, and Dario Agessi is the Philly boss. Both have history with some of the men in this room. They are trustworthy, loyal as fuck, and solid additions to The Commission. Volpe, from Pittsburgh, and Pagano, from Detroit, are wild cards because we haven't had many personal dealings with them, but both seem dependable.

"When are we announcing the four new board appointments?" I ask.

Although the men were sworn in a couple of months back, they haven't attended meetings because the decision was made to keep it all hush-hush until after we dealt with the threat. I'm assuming that will imminently change.

"We'll do it this week," Massimo says. "Right now, the priority is supply chain, dealing with the traitors, and reasserting control without our *famiglie*, settling Vegas, locating DiPietro, and finding out who the fuck in Sicily or the mainland was bankrolling my father and brother and orchestrating a takeover."

"How are you dealing with all that?" Ben asks, eyeballing Massimo.

"I'm not." Massimo sighs heavily. "It's a complete mindfuck. How could they have been alive all this time and I didn't know?"

"None of us knew," Ben reminds him. "It shocked the hell out of me too."

"They would have killed me in order to regain control." Massimo stares idly out the window, but it belies the transparent tension written all over his face. "I always knew I didn't matter, but this has totally driven it home."

Fiero sits up straighter, staring directly at his best friend. "You have always been the better man, and you got the upper hand. You killed them first. That's the ultimate punishment for always underestimating you. Fuck them, Massimo. They got what they deserved."

"What do you plan to do with the bodies?" Joshua asks.

A deep crease lines Massimo's brows. "I need to speak to my mother. It will be her decision."

"Is she capable of making it?" I ask what everyone is thinking.

Joshua scowls at me, but I ignore him. Sometimes he takes the older twin routine to extremes, and it pisses me off. He's not

25

my parent or my babysitter even though he seems to take both those roles on when he considers the need arises.

"I don't know." Tiredness resonates from Massimo's tone. "But I want to at least give her the option of burying her son and husband. If she can't or won't make the decision, I'll burn their bodies and toss their ashes in the trash."

"And Calabro?" Ben asks, clenching his jaw.

"We will afford him respect as a don."

"We wiped the Barone out. Who the fuck cares about showing that prick respect?" I eyeball the boss. "It should be Don Mazzone's call. It was his son they came after. We don't need proof to know it was Calabro who gave the command."

Massimo rubs at his mouth. "The decisions we make now will affect what Lorenzo Rizzo does in the future. Do we really want to make an enemy of the Barone for a third time?"

"It might already be too late. Leave that problem for future generations to handle. We've got enough shit on our plate and they're small fry."

This is bullshit and Massimo knows it. It's clear his head isn't where it should be. Under normal circumstance, he wouldn't hesitate to make the right call.

"I'm with Caleb," Ben says. "That prick doesn't deserve to die with honor."

"We should vote," Fiero says, silently communicating with his buddy.

"Fine," Massimo concedes.

The vote is unanimous. Calabro is going swimming with the fishes.

———

"How do you want to play this?" I ask the following night as Joshua, Gia, and I make our way down the stairs that lead to the underground interrogation bunker on Staten Island. Howls of pain comingle with cussing and the whirring sound of chain saws and other torture instruments as we pass by cells on either side of the narrow passageway, heading for the last one at the end that houses McDermott.

The bunker is heavily guarded, and there is barely room to move past all the *soldati* on duty outside individual cell doors. We are taking no chances because we have no clue where that sub went, where Cruz is, or whether the big Italian boss is here or calling the shots from Sicily or the mainland. Massimo sent Volpe and Pagana back to Florida in case Don D'Onofrio is sheltering his buddy Cruz. While we haven't found any evidence of treachery, none of us trust the new Florida don.

Massimo and Ben are currently interrogating the Italian *soldati* we captured for intel, Cristian is dealing with the traitors within the DiPietro *famiglia*, and I left Giulio and Vittus— our new *consigliere* and underboss—to continue pushing the Accardi spies and Marino supporters for answers. Most of them appear to have been completely in the dark, blindly following their underboss out of stupid, misguided loyalty.

"Gia is taking the lead. We're just here to support her." Joshua tightens his grip on the duffel bag slung over his shoulder, nodding at his girl as they walk side by side in front of me.

"Please say we're dragging this out and I can have some fun." My hands flex at my sides in anticipation of inflicting more pain.

Gia glances over her shoulder, her nose scrunching at the blood drying on my face, coating my hair, and clinging to my clothes. "Didn't you have enough fun earlier?"

I've been here for hours, interrogating the ninety-nine rats we locked up before the battle along with those who switched allegiance from Marino to us at the last minute. Not that there are many of them left. Most were taken out in A.C.

By this time tomorrow, no one who supported our dead underboss will be alive. The only way to be sure we regain full control is to end every last one of them. It will send out a clear message to the rest of our *famiglia* and ensure no one attempts to mutiny in the future. "Not really," I truthfully reply, cracking my shredded knuckles. I waggle my brows and flash her a dark grin. "There is no torture sufficient enough to repay those traitorous pricks for their betrayal, but I'm enjoying trying. The fifteen I've killed already haven't come close to sating my thirst for revenge." Bloodlust surges through my veins, and I can't wait to get my hands on McDermott.

"You seriously scare the shit out of me sometimes, Caleb." Gia pokes her finger in my face when we stop at the end door. "Please stay away from my best friend."

"Fuck off, Gigi," I bark, earning a warning look from my twin as he talks in hushed tones with the *soldato* on guard outside McDermott's cell.

I know Gia is whispering in Elisa's ear, encouraging her to cut all ties with me. I'm still wired after our hospital run-in, and I got fuck all sleep last night when I finally crawled into bed. I can't lose Lili. No matter what she thinks, she's important to me, and I'm not giving her up without a fight.

"You fuck off," she snaps. "You have no idea how badly you've hurt her, and it's not the first time."

"Park this shit," Joshua commands as I open my mouth to spew venom at my future sister-in-law. "Unless we go in there as a team, you're not coming in, Caleb."

"I want that shithead to suffer as much as you do, but if you don't want me there as backup, that's your call." I take a few steps back. "Plenty more Accardi traitors to flay alive."

Agonized shouting emits from behind some of the cell doors, ramping up my bloodlust.

"I'd like you there," Gia quietly says, staring at me while

clutching Joshua's hand. "We should agree Elisa is an off-limits subject."

I nod.

"Are you sure about this, honey?" Joshua brushes his fingers across Gia's cheek. "No one will think less of you if you want to bow out."

It's easy to forget Gia is only twenty-two because she handles herself like someone much older. But her vulnerability is showing right now, and I regret my outburst. Liam put her through hell, and this is a big deal for her. I already know what she's going to say before she says it, as does her boyfriend.

"I'm not walking away." Gia visibly pulls herself together, stretching her spine, thrusting her shoulders back, and lifting her head. "I refuse to give him any power over me. I'm doing this."

As much as her interference with Lili annoys me, I'll admit she's an impressive woman. A woman definitely worthy of my brother.

"If you change your mind or you need to walk away at any time, do it." Joshua cups one cheek. "Caleb and I can finish him off if needed."

It's why I'm here. I want to support them and be there as a backup if needed.

"Okay, but I really want to do this myself." Steely determination races across her face.

"You promised me his fingers," Joshua reminds her.

Gia smiles. "His dick and his ass are mine."

"And she has the nerve to call me scary," I murmur, fighting a grin.

Chapter Four
Caleb

"Take the gag from his mouth," Gia instructs as the three of us stand in front of the prick tied to the chair.

We left Liam McDermott to stew in his cell for the past thirty-eight hours, happy to let him wallow in his own filth. Blood continues to trickle from the wound in his thigh, pooling under his feet. Dried blood clings to his hands, congealing around the slash marks my twin inflicted. Someone went to town on his face and his torso, and my money is on my brother. Though it could have been Ben or Massimo. They were interrogating him earlier. One of McDermott's eyes is swollen shut, his left cheekbone is clearly broken, he's missing three teeth, and bruises and gashes cover most of his face and bare upper body.

Joshua's instructions were crystal clear. No food. No drink. No bucket to shit and piss in. Consequently, the smell in this small stone-walled cell is enough to level a three-hundred-pound man with minimal effort.

Joshua grips the prick's chin and pries the dirty rag from his mouth before tossing it on the floor. Not like fuckface will need it much longer. Dead men don't breathe.

"I'm going to kill you," Gia says in a calm voice walking closer to the man who hurt her. "But we can do this the hard way or the easy way," she lies, flipping a knife over in her hand as she stalls before him. "Tell us who the Italian boss is, and we'll give you a quick death."

None of us expects him to offer the dude up. Liam is not a lowly soldier we can bend to our will. He's been brought up in this world, like we have, and he's been trained to withstand interrogation. Massimo and Ben already took a crack at him earlier, but he didn't give them anything, and we're done wasting our time trying.

"Fuck you, whore," he pants.

Joshua drives his fingers into the bloody wound in McDermott's thigh, and he yells out in pain. "Speak to her like that again, and I will never let you die. I'll bring you to the brink over and over and prolong your hell for *years*."

He'd do it too, only Gia needs closure. McDermott *will* die tonight, which is a shame. I like the idea of leaving him here to rot and letting him reach the edge of death before building him back up only to starve and torture him all over again.

It'd be a great way to let off steam.

I wonder if I can find someone else to do it with, I ponder while my brother continues to poke inside Liam's leg, and the man shouts and bucks as tears stream down his battered face.

"We asked your brother if he wanted to see you one final time, and he declined." Gia drags the tip of her knife up his bare arm, drawing fresh blood. "He hates you, and he's already celebrating your death." She trails her knife down his other arm as Joshua walks to the side table where he left the duffel bag. He begins removing items from the bag and setting them on the table.

I lean against the side wall and smirk. This is about to get interesting.

"All your men are shark fodder, and your allies have abandoned you to your fate. No one gives a shit about you," she continues. "No one will care when you die, and you won't be remembered. You'll be a cautionary tale men laugh about over beers and cards. Diarmuid is the legacy. He's the one everyone will remember. You'll be forgotten." She crouches down and puts her face all up in his. "You're nothing. A nobody. And you will die without honor."

Although he's considerably weakened, the Irish prick lifts his head and smirks. "I should have fucked your ass too," he rasps, struggling to get the words out. "I should have let my men screw you until you bled." He casts a glance at where my brother has gone rigidly still at the table. "I fucked your whore, and she loved it, Accardi. Her pussy hugged my cock so tight, and she came all over my dick screaming my name like the slut she is."

Joshua calmly picks up a machete and walks over with murder raging in his eyes. "Liar." His gaze darts to mine, and I stride across the room and grip McDermott's right hand holding it steady under the restraints. My brother swings the machete with the careful precision he brings to every aspect of his life. McDermott screams in pain as his pinkie is cleaved from his hand. I maintain a firm hold of his upper hand as Joshua removes each finger on both hands, one at a time.

Gia is silent, watching her boyfriend with a look of twisted satisfaction on her face. "That was so hot." Striding over to Joshua, she wipes blood off his lips before kissing him.

Out of nowhere, my mind conjures up an image of me and my Lili. I imagine I'm the one weaving magic with the machete and she's the one kissing me with passion for defending her honor.

I snap out of the fantasy as quickly as it arrived.

That will never happen.

Lili is too good, too kind, too pure, to ever get messed up in shit like this.

And she's not my girl.

She never will be because she's far too good for me, and she deserves someone who doesn't have a black soul and empty space where his heart should be.

Why am I even thinking like this? She's *my friend*, and I have never entertained ideas of us being anything more, and it's never changing.

"I love you," Joshua tells her when their lips break apart.

Something rattles in this empty chest of mine every time I hear him freely say those words to Gia. I had almost given up hope of getting my brother back, but Gia bulldozed her way into his life, and she coaxed him back to his true self.

"My turn." Gia's gleeful smile turns downright vicious as she grips the handle of her knife firmly and spins on her heel. Wasting no time, she begins carving McDermott's chest. More pained howls rip from his lips as she writes her name on his skin. Standing back, she inspects her handiwork with a grim smile before getting to the real work.

I stand beside my brother as his girl rips the remaining clothes off the prisoner until he's stark naked. I can't help wincing as she gleefully attacks his ball sac before digging her knife into his cock, stabbing him over and over. Despite his draining strength, McDermott bucks and writhes as she destroys his manhood, slicing his cock from his body with one final flourish of her knife.

I'm betting every man in this bunker can hear his tortured shouts and cries.

Gia is sweating and panting heavily as she stands. She nods at Joshua, and I help him to remove the bindings from McDermott's wrists and feet, and we carry his limp body from the chair, throwing him on the hard ground on his back.

He's moaning and whimpering like a pussy. It's just as well O'Hara isn't here to bear witness to this pathetic display. Liam's arms are shaking, and blood gushes from his crotch as he sobs like a baby, irritating the fuck out of me. I stand on his chest, jumping up and down until I feel his ribs crack, while Gia and Joshua grab supplies from the table. "This is fun," I say, flashing Gia a wide grin as I continue bouncing on his bones.

Anguished cries fill the small cell, and he's sobbing and pleading for death now.

"Don't accidentally kill him before the big finale," Gia says, yanking me off his body as the telltale crack of another broken rib greets our ears.

"He doesn't have long, darling." Joshua lowers the zipper on his pants and pins me with a knowing look.

I bark out a laugh as I sink to my knees, guessing what he wants. My grin expands as I hold McDermott's mouth open while my brother pisses into it. Gia looks horrified for a few seconds, stopping mid-tie to watch. Then she shrugs and continues trussing him up.

After Joshua is finished, I urinate all over Liam's face, and I wish we had thought to film this. I could use it when training new soldiers. Call it Creative Killing one-oh-one. I have a long list of ingenious ways to murder cocksuckers I would happily teach others. I chuckle to myself as the thought pops into my head.

"Give me the bat." Gia holds out her hand, standing over McDermott and surveying her rope-typing skills with a critical lens. They trained her well in Nepal, and she should be proud. She has his ankles tied to his stumpy arms, exposing the space where his dick used to be and his shit-smeared asshole.

"Oh, I'm liking where this is going." I waggle my brows and laugh. "I'm recording this."

"No." Gia levels me with a look. "This is just for me."

"Spoilsport," I mumble, but it's in jest.

"Make it hurt, honey," Joshua says, handing her the bat.

"That is guaranteed." Gia kneels between McDermott's legs, her face contorting in a grimace at the state of his dirty ass. Steely determination races across her pretty face, and she slowly starts forcing the wide end of the bat into his puckered hole. When it's in as far as it will go, she pushes on it with her full body strength, and McDermott howls with renewed pain. She twists it inside him in a continuous circle, and the sounds coming from the Irish prick don't even sound human anymore.

"Damn," I whisper to my brother. "She isn't holding back."

"I fucking love her." J stares at her with love and admiration glistening in his eyes.

"When are you planning to propose?" I ask in a low tone as we watch Gia shove the bat in and out of McDermott's ass with growing intensity. The man is crying pitifully, and she is asking him again who the Italian boss is, but he's still not giving up the name. If he even knows it. McDermott may have been way down the pecking order.

"Soon. I was hoping you'd come to Cartier with me this weekend."

"Text me the time, and I'm there." I'd be pissed if my brother bought a ring without me. We have been there for each other through every significant moment in our lives, and I don't want that to stop even if he has Gia to share things with now.

"I can't wait to call her my wife."

I know my brother. Once he has set his mind to something, he's all in. I wouldn't be surprised if they were married by summer.

"How does it feel, asshole, to be violated in front of an audience?" Gia slams the bat in deep and glowers at a rapidly fading McDermott. "How does it feel to have no control over your own body? To be helpless when someone is trying to strip you of your identity and your existence?" Grabbing her knife, she makes a succession of gashes across his stomach. "You thought you had control of me, but you were wrong. You didn't destroy me." She moves, holding her knife poised over his chest. "You remade me, and I'm stronger than ever." Slowly, she drives the knife into his chest. "Burn in the fiery pits of hell where you belong, Liam McDermott."

A couple more frantic gasps leave his lips, and then there is silence.

Joshua walks to Gia and pulls her up and into his arms. She hugs my twin as she stares at the dead mutilated man on the ground.

"You did good, Gia." I squeeze her arm as I walk past her to grab the canister, silently handing it over. She doesn't speak as she drips gasoline over his body. Joshua takes the can and packs it back in the bag with the remaining supplies. Slinging the bag over his shoulder, he takes her hand, and we pull back to the door.

"Fuck you, McDermott. My woman got the last laugh in the end." He flips his lighter open and presses down, igniting the small stream of fire. The lighter sails through the air and hits its target. McDermott's body is engulfed in flames, and we watch as it eats his flesh and melts his bones, waiting until he is an unrecognizable pile of charred remains before we leave.

Chapter Five
Caleb

"How's my favorite cousin?" Vittus asks, meeting us out in the hallway after we exit McDermott's cell.

Gia rolls her eyes. "You think I don't know you say that to all your female cousins?"

"With them, I'm lying."

She shakes her head, but she's smiling as she embraces him. "Congrats on your promotion. Your pops must be really proud."

Vittus shakes it off because he's too laid-back to care about shit like that. He was genuinely shocked when Joshua and I asked him to be our new underboss. We had only promoted him to *capo* last year, so he wasn't expecting a second promotion, and certainly not so soon.

Loyalty is of paramount importance to us, and promoting two of our closest friends to the most critical roles in our team was a no-brainer. We need men we can trust, and that was more important than experience. Giulio and Vittus are both intelligent and fast learners and they won't take any shit from us. They will give it to us straight, and that's what we need.

"Thanks, G. I think Pops is proud, but it's hard to tell with him sometimes. He's a man of few words, as you know."

"How are Tosca and Geneva? I haven't seen them in so long."

"Tosca is busy with her family, and Geneva moved to Paris a month ago. She got a transfer with the bank."

"Oh, my mom mentioned that to me briefly. That's fantastic. We need to organize a night out to catch up."

"Organize something with Tosca and I'm there."

"How is the interrogation going?" I ask, purposely redirecting the conversation.

"It's a waste of time. The lower levels knew jack shit. Marino deliberately kept them in the dark."

"Let's finish this then." I crack my knuckles and grin. Watching Gia butcher McDermott has supercharged my bloodlust.

"I'm taking Gia home," my twin says.

More men for me. Yay.

"We've got this, J." I reassure him with my eyes.

"Thanks for being here, Caleb." Gia surprises me with a hug. "I couldn't have done that without Joshua and you."

"No problem, sis. I'm always down to watch you obliterate made men. I especially liked the bat-in-the-ass move." I bring my fingers to my lips. "Chef's kiss."

"You're a disturbed individual."

I bark out a laugh. "You're not in any position to throw shade after what I just witnessed in there."

Her lips kick up at the corners. "Yeah, I guess not."

Gia waves at her cousin and me before looping her arm through Joshua's. We watch them walk down the hallway and up the stairs.

"Is she okay?" Concern is splayed across Vittus's face.

"Mom told me what happened." Vittus's mom is Gia's dad's sister, and both families are close.

"I think she's more than okay. Gia is tough as nails."

"Giulio said wedding bells are in the works."

"J would frog-march her to city hall right now if he thought she'd let him."

"Good for him. I'm happy he's happy." He thumps me in the arm and smirks. "That shit ain't for us, but Joshua was always destined to settle down."

Six months ago, I would have wholeheartedly agreed.

But now?

Now I don't know where the fuck my head is at except this sense of futility I've felt recently hasn't settled even after I've given up an active management role in our legit businesses and taken over the running of our *mafioso* responsibilities. Something is still lacking, and I'm terrified to acknowledge what I sense is behind the sentiment.

I'm not nearly ready to face up to that truth.

———

Four hours later, I pull into the quiet parking lot of our building and kill the engine. Hours of cold-blooded murder have finally sated my bloodlust, and I'm physically drained and emotionally exhausted. Hopefully it means I'll get a good night's sleep as that has been sorely lacking recently. Not that it's unusual. I can't remember a time when I ever got more than five or six hours of fractured sleep. Mom said I've had trouble sleeping since I was a little kid, but it's all I know, and I'm used to functioning on fumes at this point.

My bed is calling me tonight, so I climb out of my SUV and head for the elevator that will take me directly to the top floor where my penthouse adjoins my brother's.

I'm waiting for the private elevator when a broad-shouldered man dips out of the small security office. "Don Accardi." He nods respectfully. "You're wanted in the main lobby."

"What the hell for?"

"You have a visitor. She's been waiting two hours for you."

"Fuck." I have a strong suspicion I know who it is. "I do not have the patience to deal with her at this hour," I grumble, scrubbing my hands down my tired face.

"I can tell her you're not coming home," he offers, but I wave him off.

"It's fine. I might as well deal with it now. She'll only come back." I can't shirk my responsibilities even if I need this like a hole in the head.

I step into the elevator and press the button for the main reception area.

Anais accosts me the instant I emerge from the elevator. Her heels click off the polished marble floor as she races toward me. Throwing herself at me, she is sobbing and shrieking and clutching my shirt like I'm not dripping in blood, sweat, and other bodily fluids.

"I didn't know where else to come," she says over a sob as if she doesn't have other viable options. Like her sister or her uncle. "I'm scared, Caleb. Cruz will know I was feeding you information, and he's going to come for me." Her voice elevates a few notches, grating on my ears. "He's going to kill me!" she screeches. She's borderline hysterical as she grips my shirt more tightly. Sharp-tipped nails dig into my chest through my shirt, and I'm counting to ten in my head for patience that is in limited supply. Anais peers up at me, sporting wide doe eyes that are blatantly pleading. "You need to protect me. You're the only one I feel safe with." Sniffing, she takes hold of my hand as my eyes wander to the mountain of luggage stacked against the wall by the front desk. "Please let me stay with you. You're the only one I trust."

Elisa

"I copied my notes for you," I say, handing Shea the envelope with lecture notes from the past three days. She couldn't attend classes because her space cadet Mom did a vanishing act again, leaving her to care for her baby brother.

"I would totally flunk without you." She leans in to hug me. "You're the bestest friend I've ever had. I'd go insane if I didn't have you."

"Ditto. I might have flung myself off the bridge last year if you hadn't been there for me." Back then, Gia helped too, but she was in the thick of a dangerous mission, and it wasn't safe for us to meet. Dad ripped me a new one when he discovered Gia had broken protocol to meet me in Chelsea Market that one time. I promised him and Caleb I wouldn't risk my safety like that again, and I stuck to it.

For Dad.

Not Caleb.

Pain lances across my chest like always when I think of him, but I purposely force it aside.

"Please don't say that or ever mean it," she says, stuffing the envelope into her book bag, as I stand and stretch my back. I won't miss the seats in the auditoriums after I graduate in a few months. "Those cunts aren't worth it. And *he's* definitely not worth it."

"I know, and I wasn't serious. Even though I was devastated, I'd never do that." I shuffle along the row behind the best friend I have at NYU. For multiple reasons, I need to keep my friends list small and tight-knit. It's not easy to let people in when you have to hide a huge chunk of your life from them. Shea knows more than most because she has proven herself trustworthy over the past three and a half years. But I have kept most of my secrets from her, because they could get her killed, and I haven't divulged details to any of our other friends, and that's the way it'll stay.

"You have Seb now, and he's totally head over heels for you." She loops her arm through mine and smiles as we make our way out of the lecture hall.

"He's sweet and very attentive." I chew on my lip as we exit through the doorway.

"Spit it out, babe."

Heat warms my cheeks. "He told me he loves me last night."

She examines my face. "Isn't that a good thing?"

I shrug. "I don't know." We part to sidestep a dude charging through the exiting crowd like a gun-toting madman is hot on his heels. "I wish I returned his feelings, but I'm hoping in time I will. Mom says there are many different kinds of love and some relationships are quick to develop while other love takes longer to grow. Perhaps Seb and I are a slow-burn romance, like some of the romances I read. Mom and Alesso took their time being together, even though they had strong feelings for one another from the start. Now, they are so in love and ridiculously happy, and I really want that someday."

"I thought you didn't believe in love anymore?" she asks, steering me out through the main doors.

"I still believe in love. I just don't know if I believe in it *for me* anymore."

"Well, don't look to me for a pep talk. You already know my thoughts on the subject."

Shea's bio dad skipped out when she was two, and she

hasn't seen him since. Her mom went through a succession of boyfriends, enduring three canceled engagements before marrying Pedro. He lasted long enough to knock her up before he ran off with his assistant. On his way out of town, he cleaned out their bank account, sold Shea's mom's car for cash, and they only discovered he hadn't been making the mortgage payments when a dude showed up at their door a month later with a repossession order.

After Shea's little brother was born, her mom fell off the rails, drowning herself in the bottom of a bottle. Then she started stripping and hooking to afford her newfound alcohol and drug addiction, leaving her daughter to pick up the pieces time and time again.

Shea is on a scholarship, and she has come close to losing it a few times, thanks to her deadbeat Mom. So, yeah, I get why Shea doesn't believe in love and why she has sworn off dating. She fucks guys when it suits her but never accepts any of their offers to date. Can't say I wouldn't do the same in her shoes.

"Maybe I should be more like you." I grip the straps of my backpack. "Perhaps I should give up on dating and just find some fuck buddies to screw my way through the last few months of college."

Shea's face scrunches up. "I'm a bad example. Don't emulate me."

"You don't have it in you, *Lili*," someone says in a sneering voice from behind, and my stomach plummets to my toes.

"Fuck off, skank." Shea immediately has my back, keeping close to me as we turn to face my archnemesis.

"You're pathetic, and it's only a matter of time before Seb grows tired of you." Gwyneth rakes a derisory gaze up and down my body. "How the fuck you convinced him to date you is beyond belief, but he'll wise up soon."

I don't disagree, not that I'm voicing that sentiment. Seb is one of the most popular guys on campus, and he's been asking me out all year before I caved and said yes. I still don't fully understand it or why I'm not more into it because he's hot, charming, smart, and funny. Perfect boyfriend material, and I'm the envy of lots of girls at NYU.

Gwyneth pushes her face all up in mine. "Just like Caleb did."

I grind my teeth to the molars and glare at her. "You think you know it all, but you know nothing."

"I know I rocked his world and you never will." She flashes me a smug grin. "You're always destined to be a loser, and losers never get the guy."

Chapter Six
Elisa

"**A**re you sure this is a good idea?" Shea asks me for the umpteenth time as I wait outside the NYU bookstore for my Uber to show up.

"No, but I'm still doing it." I level a resolute look at my best friend. "I need him to look me in the eye and tell me why he broke his promise. It's the only thing I have ever asked of him, and I need to know why. And why *her*? I don't get it."

"Maybe you'll get full closure if you have all the answers," she muses. "You sure you don't want me to come with for moral support?"

"I'm sure." I can't bring Shea with me to the Caltimore Holdings building where Caleb and Joshua live. It's one of the designated *mafioso* apartment buildings and chock-full of dangerous made men. Shea is going nowhere near that place. "I need to do this alone."

"Give him hell, Elisa," she says when my car pulls up to the curb. "And call me later," she hollers as she backs away.

"Here you go, Miss Salerno." The hot security guard holds the private elevator doors open for me, smiling politely as he tries to pretend like he's not checking me out. Not gonna lie. It does wonders for my ego which I sorely need in this moment.

Nerves fire at me from all angles as the doors close and the elevator starts ascending.

I have only been to this building a handful of times, and every time, it's been to visit Gigi. I have never actually stepped foot in Caleb's place. Gia says it's a pigsty and she avoids going over there.

Smoothing my sweaty palms down the front of my tight jeans, I watch the numbers climb on the wall panel with trepidation. Perhaps this is a mistake. And maybe I should have gone to my apartment and gotten changed first. I'm only wearing jeans, an off-the-shoulder sweater over a tank top, and my trusty ballet flats. I have minimal makeup on because I can't be bothered applying it most days when I'm stuck indoors attending lectures. If I was wearing something that projected more confidence, maybe I'd be feeling it instead of this jittery sensation that is twisting my stomach into knots.

Oh god. This *is* a bad idea. I'm not sure I'm strong enough to hear his truth. It's going to hurt again, and I've only just started healing. I could pretend I'm here to visit Gia, but I know she and Joshua are out tonight at dinner with her folks.

Air whooshes from my slightly parted lips as I hold my head up high and give myself a silent pep talk. I'm here now. I'll just suck it up and stick to my guns. I came here to have the conversation I should've had months ago, and I'm not backing down until I have answers. Caleb owes me an explanation, and I'm not leaving until I get one.

Maybe then I can finally cut him from my life.

The thought of it sends slivers of pain shooting through the flawed organ in my chest. I wish I wasn't still so invested in him. I hate how pathetic I am. How much I still love him even after he has decimated my heart and shattered my self-esteem. If I could sign up for a heart transplant, to replace my malfunctioning one, I'd do it without hesitation. Anything to be free of years of anguish, pain, heartbreak and the unrequited feelings that were never returned.

The elevator pings, and the doors open. Drawing a brave breath, I step out into the dark, decadent private lobby and walk toward Caleb's door. Before I can talk myself out of it, I lift my hand and press the bell.

The door swings open a few seconds later, and all the blood drains from my face in a split second.

"If it isn't the little virgin princess." Anais scoffs as her gaze rakes over me from head to toe.

It's nothing new. It's how she always looks at me. It doesn't matter that we are cousins by marriage, she has never liked me, and she is always a complete bitch. Dad doesn't know the half of it, and he'd be mad if he ever found out. I stopped telling him and Mom the bitchy things she says to me years ago after Dad continued to tackle her on it each and every time. It didn't stop Anais. It just made her more determined, so I ceased giving her extra ammunition. Even Caleb isn't aware of how she treats me. I didn't want to go running to him like a little kid every time she made me cry.

"What are you doing here?" she asks, leaning against the doorway and smirking. The side of her almost transparent knee-length robe falls off one shoulder, exposing the top of her naked breast. Those ridiculous melons on her chest are obvious in the extreme. She really should fire her cosmetic surgeon. First, he messed up her boobs. Then her swollen lips. She's more than a little fond of Botox too, judging by her perpetual frozen forehead and unnaturally arched eyebrows.

What does Caleb see in her? And why is *she* here? I'm

aware of what went down with her husband, and Dad said two of the new don hires to The Commission had gone to Vegas to question her and their men.

"I could ask you the same thing," I say. "You're supposed to be in Vegas."

"I'm exactly where I'm supposed to be." Her bee-stung lips curl at the corners. "You don't belong here, Elisa. Run away home and play with your dolls."

"You really need some new lines, Anais."

"And you need to know when you're not wanted. Caleb is with me. I'm living permanently here now, and I satisfy all of his needs." She lets the robe fall farther down her arm, exposing more of her breast and a nipple. She truly has no shame. My cheeks heat, and bile swims up my throat. "He doesn't need you or want you, so fuck off and leave us alone." Her eyes darken in a familiar way, and I brace myself for whatever hateful words are about to spew from her hideous mouth. "In case your innocent mind hasn't figured it out, you interrupted our fuckfest, and my man is waiting for me. We've been screwing nonstop since I arrived, but my Caleb is insatiable. He just can't get enough of me."

I can't hide the hurt from my face, and she laughs. "You're not his type, and you never will be. Now fuck off, and don't come here again." She fakes a sweet smile as she slams the door in my face.

I stand outside seething, clenching and unclenching my hands, seriously contemplating murder, before anger is replaced with deep-seated pain.

Fuck him and fuck her.

They deserve one another.

I am officially done with Caleb Accardi.

"Hi, sweetheart. This is a pleasant surprise." Dad's smile is tinged with concern as he exits his office and walks toward me. "Is everything okay?"

Swallowing the lump in my throat, I nod because I'm afraid I'll burst into tears if I attempt to speak.

"Come here." Dropping his briefcase, he envelops me in his arms, and I sink into his embrace, inhaling the comforting scent of his favorite cologne. I close my eyes and hug him tighter. "Are you sure everything is all right?" he inquires again, rubbing a soothing hand up and down my back.

"Yes," I croak. "I just decided to come home a day early." I spend one weekend a month at home in Greenwich so I can hang out with my parents and my brothers and little sister. I wasn't planning on traveling until tomorrow, but I've been upset since my encounter with Anais earlier, and I want to go home. I only have two classes tomorrow, so skipping one day won't make much of a difference. I am well prepared for my finals in May anyway.

Dad tips my chin up, studying my eyes. "You know you can always talk to me, right?"

"I know, Dad." My features soften as I stare at Alesso's handsome face. Mom definitely won the husband lottery. One of the happiest days of my life was the day Mom married my stepdad. I already loved him so much by then, and I count my blessings every day that he came into our lives. He is my father in every way that counts, and I rarely give my bio dad a second thought. He was a monster, and I'm glad he died. He deserved it for the things he did to Mom. "I love you," I add as a sudden rush of emotion swirls in my veins. "I'm so happy you're my dad."

His Adam's apple jumps in his throat. "Thank you for bringing so much joy to my life, Elisa." He kisses my brow. "I love you more than I can say." He presses a second soft kiss to my brow before letting me go. "We better hurry, or the chopper will take off without us." He grabs his briefcase in one hand and me in the other, and then we make our way to the roof to meet Uncle Ben and Uncle Leo for the helicopter trip home.

Once on board, I close my eyes and rest my head against the window, letting the three men talk business through the intercommunication headsets. I turn music on and try to empty my mind of all thoughts of Caleb, but it's futile. I wish I could find a way to scrub my brain with bleach and erase every memory and thought of him because I am sick of feeling like this.

"Elisa!" Mom rushes out the door toward me with the biggest smile on her face, and I lose control over my tenuous emotions. My lip starts wobbling, and my vision blurs as moisture gathers in my eyes. Her face dissolves with concern as she notices my expression, and by the time she's reached me, I've dumped my weekend bag on the ground and silent tears are streaming down my face that I'm powerless to stop.

Chapter Seven
Elisa

om and Dad exchange a worrying look as I collapse against Mom and quietly sob. "I hadn't started dinner yet," Mom tells him over my shoulder. "Let's order pizza."

"I'll call it in." Dad kisses Mom on the lips before pressing a tender kiss on the top of my head. "Whatever it is, know we are here for you." They talk in hushed tones for a bit while I try to pull myself together. Gravel crunches underfoot as Dad walks off into the house.

"Do you want to go for a walk?" Mom asks, easing back and holding my arms so she can look at me. "Or we could talk over a glass of wine in the sunroom?"

"Wine sounds good," I say, pulling a tissue from my jeans pocket and dabbing at my eyes. "Sorry, Mom. I didn't mean to break down like that."

"Better out than in." She smiles lovingly at me, brushing strands of hair off my brow. My brown hair is the same color as Mom's, and we share the reddish tints running through it. Although she is only a few years away from fifty, there isn't a gray hair on Mom's head or a single wrinkle on her beautiful face. I hope I grow older as gracefully as she is. "Is this something to do with Caleb?"

I nod because I never lie to Mom, and she knows most everything anyway.

"Oh, Elisa." She kisses my cheek and squeezes my hand. "I hate to see you hurting so much."

"It's my own fault."

"Don't beat yourself up. Your feelings are natural, and it's not like you can flip a switch and turn them off."

"Wouldn't that be a handy trick?"

Her features soften as she gives me another hug. Warmth surges through my icy veins, and I'm so glad I came home. Mom always makes things better, and I really need her tonight. Shea offered to come to my apartment, but I turned her down because my place is with my family. A weekend at home, surrounded by their love, will go a long way toward gluing back the new cracks in my heart.

She circles her arm around my shoulders and leads me toward the house. Glancing around, I notice my bag is gone. Dad must have taken it inside. "I know everything seems insurmountable right now, but you will heal, and you will move forward with your life. At some point, you will look back and see it differently. During my worst days with Alfredo, clinging to the hope of a brighter future was all that kept me going. Hope, you, and Romeo."

We step inside the house, and I'm instantly bathed in warmth and the scent of lavender and lilies. Mom loves lilies, and Dad buys them every week for her. Auntie Sierra sells aromatherapy oils at her clinic, and Mom is always burning different oils on the various diffusers she has around the house.

"And then you had Dad."

Her face instantly lights up as we walk toward the kitchen,

where the sound of chatter filters into the hallway. "Alesso saved me in all the ways I needed saving. His love lifted me up when I struggled to stand by myself, and when I had healed, he gave me the freedom to soar." She sweeps her finger across my cheek. "Someday, you will have a love like that."

I bite my tongue to smother my negative retort. No point in raining on Mom's parade. She is a true believer in love because she found it after years of enduring sheer hell. I wish I had even a tenth of my mother's inner strength. Compared to what she went through, my heartbreak is nothing but the whimsical yearnings of a foolish girl who still hasn't grown up.

I tell myself this all the time since I discovered Caleb slept with Gwyneth and her despicable friends, but I have yet to drill the point home.

"Lisa!" Aria barrels toward me as we enter the kitchen, throwing her arms around me with gusto.

"Hey, cupcake. Missed you." I crouch down to her level and hug her properly.

"I missed you more," she says. "It's boring being at home all the time. I can't even see my friends," she pouts.

"It's important to keep you safe." I tell her something she's already been told a lot, but when you're eight it's hard to wrap your head around the fact your father is a powerful man with dangerous enemies who wouldn't think twice about hurting you to get to him.

"And it won't be forever," Mom adds, messing the top of her hair. It's darker than Mom's but lighter than Alesso's. "I'll talk to Daddy and see if we can arrange a playdate for next week."

I doubt Dad will agree. Not while the big Italian boss is in the wind. All the kids are still being homeschooled because the threat is far from over, and the memory of Rowan's attempted assassination is still way too fresh in everyone's mind. There is no point in taking risks.

"Where is Will?" I ask, straightening up and approaching the counter where Dad is talking with Romeo.

"Where do you think?" Romeo snorts out a laugh. "We should hook him up with an IV to the PlayStation and just be done with it."

"You weren't much different at his age," Mom reminds him as Romeo reaches for me.

My brother bundles me into his arms, whispering in my ear. "He's not worthy of you, and he doesn't deserve your tears."

Everyone instantly knows the cause of my heartache because I'm just that obvious. Gawd, it's so humiliating.

"How come you're back early?" I ask, shucking out of his embrace.

"I don't have much going on tomorrow, and I wanted to come home early and check up on everyone." We were all worried this week after the big battle, and Romeo is a total Mommy's boy, so I'm not surprised he came home from college a day earlier too. My eldest brother is a nerdy genius, and he graduated high school early last year. Now, he's a freshman at Yale studying accounting, and I couldn't be prouder of him.

"Dad's ordering pizza," Mom confirms as she grabs a bottle of chilled wine from the refrigerator.

Aria jumps up and down and claps her hands. A wide smile graces my lips as I watch my little sister whoop and holler. You'd swear she never got takeout, but I love she's excited and she doesn't take it for granted. Our parents are extremely wealthy, but they are careful not to spoil us too much. Dad came from humble beginnings, and he was even homeless for a short period while he was a teenager. It's important to him that he instils the right values in us, and it only makes me love him more for it.

"Rowan is coming over in a bit. Better order an extra pizza," Romeo says. There is only a year between the cousins, and they are as close as brothers. Have been since they were little even though they are so different.

"Better make it two," I quip, remembering how bulked up Rowan has gotten lately. Now he has initiated, he is embracing it fully, and he's training and working out a lot in between study.

"Come on." Mom jerks her head to the side, holding two wineglasses. "Let's sit down and have a talk."

I trail Mom out to the sunroom, shutting the sliding doors behind me to keep prying ears out. Settling on the comfy couch, I accept a glass of wine and kick off my ballet flats, tucking my legs up. Outside, the perfectly manicured gardens are lit up under the dark night sky by a multitude of pretty outdoor lights.

Mom is best friends with Natalia—Caleb and Joshua's mom—and she got Mom hooked on gardening. We have a rose garden and a small vegetable patch though we mostly get our produce from the large garden Natalia planted over on the far side of the estate. There are copious apple trees, and we enjoy homegrown pears, peaches, strawberries, and blueberries too at different times of the year. Sometimes I go out to the orchard for a walk because the scent in the air is heavenly and I find it soothing.

"Do you want to tell me what happened?" Mom asks, quietly sipping her wine.

Although I haven't mentioned Anais to Mom in years, I'm too hurt and too angry to hide it from her, so I tell her what happened when I dropped by Caleb's place.

Mom shakes her head and sighs heavily. "That woman."

She takes a big gulp of her wine. "I know she's your dad's cousin, but I regularly wish I could throttle her." She pats my thigh. "I wouldn't be surprised if there is a very different side to the story she told you. Anais can't be trusted, and I sincerely doubt Caleb has let her move in."

"It doesn't matter anyway."

"It matters if it upsets you." Her eyes probe mine. "How long has she been treating you like that?"

I gulp back a giant mouthful of wine, feeling Mom's eyes on me. I turn to face her. "Don't ask me to lie to you."

"She never stopped, did she? Not even after your dad asked her to be kind to you."

"That only made things worse. You know she doesn't listen to a word Dad says. I know why he keeps trying with her, but it's painful to watch."

"Your dad has the patience of a saint. I'd have lobbed her and her fake boobs off a cliff a long time ago."

"Mom!" I snort out a giggle. "I swear she's had them done again." My face contorts. "Unfortunately, I got an up close and personal look at them. She was virtually naked at the front door."

"She has no shame and no morals." Mom turns on the couch, angling her back and kicking off her shoes. "When she was a child, I had sympathy for Anais. Growing up without a mom and having Saverio Salerno as a father could not have been easy. But any sympathy I felt ended when she tried to mess things up between Ben and Sierra. Anais has been playing the same game for years. A man is only truly attractive to her if being with him hurts another woman. I'm disgusted she has been treating you like this for years. All because you care for Caleb and he cares for you."

"He doesn't care for me. Not really. He wouldn't have done what he did if that were true."

"I won't interfere or tell you what to do, love, but Caleb gets a lot of bad press that isn't justified. Don't get me wrong, some of it is, but he's not completely heartless, and I refuse to believe he would deliberately hurt you. He has always been so protective of you and considerate of your feelings. You need to talk to him. I don't see how you will move forward unless you get answers."

"I know it happened, and it's not like I can erase those images from my brain. At this point, I'm not sure answers will even help. Look what happened this evening? I thought it was the right thing to do but seeing her there has only made things worse. I don't know how he can bear to be with her. She's awful."

"You're preaching to the converted." Mom clinks her glass against mine. "Nat despises her. She knows why Caleb started it but wishes he would just let it go now."

"Revenge for Bettina." Gia confirmed it a few months ago. "It explains how it started between them. But why is it still going on all these years later? He must like her."

"It's a complicated situation."

Throwing my head back, I let out a long sigh. "I wish I had crushed on anyone but him."

"Don't regret it. You were so adorable, and he was always so good to you. Even when he was putting Leo and Nat through the wringer during his rebellious phase, he always made time for you, and he never complained when you followed him around everywhere like a lovesick puppy."

"Gee, thanks, Mom."

"It was super cute."

"If you say so."

"You're special to him, Elisa. I know you are. He just struggles to articulate it. There was a time you received his only smiles, and when he got older, he never forgot your birthday or

Christmas or Valentine's Day. It might not be the relationship you wanted with him, but he does care about you, honey."

"Why don't you hate him like Dad does?"

"I'm not happy he's hurt you, and if you discover it was intentional, I will be having words with him, but Caleb is not a bad guy. He's just misunderstood." She peers off into space for a while. "There was a time when Nat and I wished you two would get together. It has always seemed like it was written in the stars to me."

"Go easy there on the wine, Mom."

"I want the world for you, Elisa. Your dad does too, and he doesn't hate Caleb. He just doesn't want him for you."

"Well, he doesn't need to worry about that. It's never going to happen." I knock back the rest of my wine. "Even if Caleb came crawling on his hands and knees begging me to be with him." I take Mom's empty glass and stand. "I'm going to give my all to Seb and put Caleb out of mind. Seb loves me and wants me, and he'd never make a promise and then break it and trample all over my heart."

Chapter Eight
Caleb

The shower door opens, and I stall the hand wrapped around my dick cursing the bitch for interrupting the fantasy playing out in my head while I was jerking off. My straining cock leaks precum, screaming for release, as Anais drapes her naked body around me from behind. "I can help with that," she purrs in what she thinks is a seductive voice, but it has always sounded like she has a hairball stuck in her throat.

I snag her wrist as she moves her hand around my body, heading for my cock, stopping her progress. "I've got it covered, and you weren't invited to shower with me."

"Why are you being like this?" I hear the pout in her tone as I pry her arms off me and step back, creating distance between us. Overhead, water flows from my rainforest shower cascading over my shoulders and streaming down my back. "You haven't fucked me once since I got here."

"I'm busy," I lie, switching off the water and grabbing a towel. I wrap it around my waist, ignoring my protesting cock as I brush past her scowling face and exit the shower.

"You're not busy now." She yanks the towel from behind, and it falls to the floor.

I'm struggling to rein in my anger. Truth is, I should just fuck her to shut her up, but I can't. Her touch makes my skin crawl, and I've reached my breaking point. Years of tolerating her bitchy, whiny ass have taken a toll, and I'm done. Except I must continue playing the game while her dickhead husband is MIA. Anais is our best hope of finding Cruz, so I need to keep her on our side. President's orders.

"Don't." I glower at her, grinding my teeth, as I grab a fresh towel and tuck it around my waist, covering my rapidly deflating erection.

"This is about *her*, isn't it?"

"I don't know what you're talking about," I say, striding out of my bathroom.

"Don't walk away from me when I'm talking to you, Caleb!" she screeches, trailing after me into my large closet.

"I'm not doing this with you now." Or ever. I pick a black shirt, boxers, socks, and ripped jeans from my closet. I should have just showered at J's place, but I needed clean clothes. I've been staying with my twin and his girl ever since Anais showed up on my doorstep, much to her chagrin. I've used work as the excuse, but that won't wash for long. Case in point.

"Is *she* the reason you've been avoiding me?" she accuses, jabbing her finger in my face. Her red nails are long and sharp and can inflict pain, as I've learned in the past. Anais is a spoiled bitch who lashes out and throws temper tantrums whenever she doesn't get attention or get her own way. As much as I fucking loathe Cruz DiPietro, I can't say I blame him for cheating on the bitch. She would drive any man to the point of insanity.

I drop the towel, swatting her hand away when she reaches

for me again. Rage flares from her eyes before a more calculated look washes over her face. I watch her warily as I pull on my socks, boxers, and jeans. Leaning her naked body back against the wall, she spreads her legs and pulls her pussy lips apart, fully exposing herself to me. "I know you want it," she pants, sliding one finger inside her cunt. "I know what you like, and I'll give it to you." Spinning around, she thrusts her ass up and out and parts her cheeks, looking over her shoulder at me and licking her lips. "Take my ass, sexy. Fuck me hard, just how you like it."

Pulling up the zipper on my jeans, I tuck my completely flaccid cock away. I feel nothing as I look at her naked body, offered to me on a silver platter for the taking. Years ago, this would have turned me on. The knowledge Cruz's wife let me do whatever I wanted to her body always aroused me more than the sex itself, but not now. Now, I feel nothing but contempt for her. My cock will never touch any part of her body ever again.

"I'm going out. I'll check when your apartment will be ready," I add, shoving my arms into the sleeves of my shirt and grabbing my wallet, gun, keys, and watch.

"Caleb, please."

I glance back at her as I strap my watch to my wrist, noting the fake hurt plastered on her face as she switches gear. She's so predictable. If she can't seduce me, she'll turn on the waterworks.

There is so much I want to say to her, but I bite back the words, remembering my duty. Shoving my feet into black sneakers, I force my features to soften before walking over to her, trying not to flinch as I hold her face in my hands. "Anais, I explained how precarious the situation is now. I don't have time for distractions. I promised I would protect you from Cruz, but that is all I can offer."

Her eyes narrow. "Have you screwed her? Is this why you're acting so fucking weird?"

I know who she's referring to because Anais has always felt threatened by Elisa. She's always been jealous of our close bond even though I have never laid a finger on Lili in a sexual way. My cock jerks behind my boxers, and I frown. "Not that it's any of your business, but no, I have not screwed her. For the last time, we are friends."

Smug pleasure glistens in her eyes, and I instantly drop my hands from her face. I need to get her out of my personal space and fast. Buttoning my shirt, I walk out of the bedroom and back into the bathroom. I apply some gel to tame my hair, brush my teeth, and slap on some cologne while the she-devil pouts from the doorway.

"I need you, Caleb. I'm so scared all the time, and you're never here." She doesn't know when to quit, and it's exhausting dealing with her.

"You're safe here, Anais. No one is getting through security. Your new apartment is being fitted with a hi-tech alarm system and panic buttons in every room"—along with hidden cameras with audio recording ability, but I'm not mentioning that—"for your peace of mind. Cruz can't get near you while you are living in this building."

"I don't understand why I can't just live here with you." She walks toward me, still completely naked, dragging one finger down the front of my shirt-covered chest. "Think of all the perks."

She attempts to waggle her brows, but they are frozen stiff from all the shit she injects in her face. Anais used to be pretty, but she has ruined herself with multiple cosmetic procedures she doesn't need. If she keeps it up, she'll rival The Bride of Wildenstein for her crown.

"I don't do roommates. I like living alone, and I have zero desire to live with any woman, including you."

"You're such a prick," she snaps, stumbling over an errant shoe lying under a pile of dirty clothes on the floor. "And a messy pig to boot! This place is disgusting!"

I shove my face all up in hers. "So, clean it! Let's call it rent." I doubt Anais has ever lifted a single finger to clean up after herself or anyone else.

"I'm not your fucking housemaid!" she screeches, her face awash with indignation.

"And I'm not your punching bag. I'm sick of listening to your shit. If you don't want to be here, you know where the door is."

"I don't care about the mess!" she says, completely contradicting herself. "I love you!" she cries, clinging to my arm, turning the tables again. "I know you love me too. If you'd just give us a chance. Please, baby. I know we can be so good together, and there is nothing standing in our way now. We can make things official."

"You're fucking delusional." I pin her with a hateful look. "I don't love you, and I never will. You were a hole to fuck when I was bored, or I wanted to fuck with your husband. Now he's gone, I've realized I don't need to put up with your mood swings and manipulations. I have never cared for you. I barely tolerated you, and I'm all out of patience." I remove her hands from my body, leaving her jaw trailing the ground as I walk out of my bedroom.

Fuck this shit.

I'm telling The Commission I'm out. I can't do this anymore. We should be able to get the intel we need from the cameras in her new place and the tracking device I implanted in her phone. She doesn't have a tracking chip, but the *soldato* I have assigned to shadow her will follow her whenever she leaves the building, and that will have to be enough because I am so done.

My cell pings in my pocket as I stride along the hallway, aiming for the stairs.

"What?" I snap as I pick up.

"Sorry to interrupt you, Don Accardi," the new security guard downstairs says. I've already forgotten his name. "I, um..."

"Stop acting like a pussy and spit it out," I bark, grabbing my jacket from the back of a kitchen stool. I must talk to Ben about staff hires at this building. I seriously have my doubts about this new guy.

Anais is shrieking demands as she stalks me to the front door, but I tune her out.

"I'm not sure what you said to her," the man says in my ear, "but Miss Salerno was very upset leaving." There is fire behind his words I didn't think him capable of. "I thought you'd like to know."

I slam to a halt with my hand curled around the door handle. Anais slams into my back with a piercing fake cry. "What are you talking about?"

There's a momentary pause. "Miss Salerno." Confusion threads through his tone. "She dropped by to see you. I escorted her into the private elevator myself."

I hang up on him as it instantly clicks into place. Spinning around, I grab Anais and roughly push her against the wall, gripping her chin tight.

"Ow, Caleb. You're hurting me," she whines.

"What. Did. You. Do?" I clip out, through gritted teeth, glaring at her.

"I didn't do anything!" She forces a tear from her eye.

I squeeze her chin harder, purposely digging my nails into

her flesh. "What did you say to Elisa, and don't lie because I will ask her."

"I told her you weren't here and to fuck off."

"Anais," I hiss, moving my hand to her throat and squeezing. "What. Else?"

A defiant look crosses her face, and I squeeze her throat tighter. Panic flares in her eyes as I push my face all up in hers and tighten my grip again. She bucks against me, trying to bring her leg up to knee me in the balls, but I flatten her legs against the wall with my free arm, restraining her.

"Caleb," she croaks, grabbing my wrist. "Stop."

I loosen my grip, only so she can speak.

"I'll tell you," she rasps, struggling to breathe.

I release her and step back before I accidentally kill her. She bends over, gasping while sucking air into her lungs. When she straightens up, she glares at me like she might hate me. Good. That I can work with.

"You have three seconds before I riddle your lying cunt with bullets," I say, removing my gun and prodding her brow with it. "What did you say to Elisa?"

"I gave it to her straight," she snaps, rubbing her neck and shooting daggers at me. "She's such a pathetic little bitch, pining over you with her schoolgirl crush. I did her a favor. You too. I told her we were together and I was living with you now." A smirk ghosts over her surgically enhanced lips. "She won't bother you again." Her grin expands. "You're welcome."

I curl my finger around the trigger, so fucking tempted to pull it.

"You won't shoot me." Her cool tone and demeanor aggravate me to no end.

"Don't be too confident, Anais." I drag the gun down her face, over her chin and her collarbone, poking the muzzle into the silicone encased behind her skin. "Elisa is off-limits to you.

Pull a stunt like that again, and I'll fill your body so full of bullets there will be nothing but a bloody mess left."

Shock mixed with disbelief and anger fills her eyes. "You don't mean that."

"I suggest you don't test me." With one final glare, I walk out the door, slamming it behind me before I prove it right then and there.

I call the building manager from the elevator. "I need that apartment ready ASAP."

"We're working as fast as we can, Don Accardi, but—"

"I don't want excuses. Just get it done. Mrs. DiPietro will be moving her stuff in tomorrow." I hang up before he can protest further. I need to get Anais into her own space where I can keep tabs on her without having to fuck her for intel.

I place a call to Elisa as I step out of the elevator on the lower-level parking lot and head toward my Lamborghini. Predictably, she doesn't answer, and I throw my cell on the passenger seat as I climb behind the wheel, grinding my teeth.

Why did she come here? She has never visited my place before, and she's been avoiding me for months. Is she finally ready to talk to me? Or did something happen to her? Panic swells in my chest as I start the engine and reverse out of my spot. Whatever the reason, I'm guessing she's hurting right now, and pain stabs me through the heart knowing I am inadvertently the cause.

When I'm out on the street, I make a left and head in the direction of Lili's apartment near NYU.

She might not want to ever speak to me again, but I'm not taking no for an answer.

We are thrashing this out tonight, and I'm going to do everything in my power to set things right.

Chapter Nine
Caleb

I hammer on Elisa's front door, impatient to speak with her. The door swings open a few seconds later. "Where's the fucking fi—" Beatrice's face pales as she cuts off mid-sentence when she sees me.

"Where is Elisa?" I ask, barging my way into the modern apartment the two girls share. Beatrice is from a good *famiglia*, and Alesso deemed her suitable to room with his daughter even if the girls aren't overly friendly. They seem to cohabit easily, so it works. I know Serena didn't want Elisa living alone in the city.

"She's not here, Don Accardi," she calls after me as I leave the open-plan living space for the hallway that leads to the bedrooms.

"I can fucking see that," I holler after checking both rooms and the adjoining bathrooms and finding them empty. I storm back out to where she is still standing by the open doorway. "I need to find her. Immediately."

"I don't know what you want me to say." She waves her

hands around. "She wasn't here when I got home from classes. She left a note saying she'd be back Sunday night."

She must have gone home. Unless she is staying with friends, but it's unlikely. Elisa is careful about her safety, not wanting to worry her parents. I should have called Serena or Lili's bodyguard in the first place. "Never mind. I'll find her myself."

I am almost to the door when a guy with slicked-back jet-black hair steps into the apartment with a frown on his face.

"Who the fuck are you?" I ask, instantly reaching for my gun.

"I'm Sebastien," he says as if it should mean something to me. "Elisa's boyfriend," he adds.

I blink profusely, staring at him as I consider the words. Lili has a boyfriend? "Since fucking when?" Removing my gun, I point it at his face willing him to give me a reason to use it.

His eyes pop wide as he holds up his hands. "Woah. There's no need for that. I have no beef with you."

"Answer the fucking question, asshole." I stride right up and prod him in the chest with my gun. He is tall, but I'm taller by at least a couple of inches, and I'm definitely packing more muscle. A clean-shaven jaw, clear olive skin, and perfect hair point to immaculate grooming. He has Mediterranean looks, but he's not Italian American, and he's not *mafioso*. Raking my gaze over the rest of him, I note the preppy loafers, designer jeans, fitted sweater, and tan woolen coat with a modicum of disgust. An expensive watch is strapped to his wrist, and he's carrying a black Berluti leather bag. He exudes money and arrogance and I instantly hate him.

"I go to NYU, and I met Elisa at the start of our senior year. I've been asking her out for months, but she finally said yes just before Christmas. We've been dating ever since."

"Is that true?" I ask Beatrice while keeping my gun and my

eyes trained on the preppy douche. Never trust a man who wears loafers and a tan coat.

"Yes, and I don't think Elisa would appreciate you holding a gun on him."

A muscle ticks in my jaw as I stare at the guy, and he stares back. He's got balls, but he's still not good enough for her.

Is this the kind of guy she wants? Because he is nothing like me.

Perhaps that's the appeal.

Reluctantly, I lower my weapon and tuck it back in the waistband of my jeans.

The asshole has the nerve to glare at me. "Who are you?" he asks after a few beats of silent staring.

"None of your business." I square up to him. "Hurt Elisa, and I'll end you. That's a promise, not a threat."

His jaw tightens as he tersely nods.

I'm halfway to the door when he calls out after me. "You're him, aren't you? You're the one who broke her heart."

I flip him the bird as I stalk toward the door and exit the apartment thoroughly enraged.

Back in my car, I slam my hands down repeatedly on the wheel as frustration powers through me. "Fuck, fuck, fuck!" Images of that douche touching my Lili flit through my head to

torture me, and I don't like it. I'm close to racing back up there to pump his body full of bullets when an incoming call waylays me.

"What's up?" I growl when I answer my stepdad's call.

"I think I should be asking you that," Leo says. "Who has your panties in a bunch?"

"Elisa's boyfriend," I grumble as I power up my car.

"I heard something about her dating."

"Thanks for fucking telling me."

"I didn't think you two were talking."

"We're not, but that's all on her. Is Mom there?" I ask, backing out of the parking space and speeding off. Tires screech on asphalt as I round the corner and drive up the ramp leading outside.

"She's at the hospital, but she'll be home later."

"Ask her to find out the guy's full name. I want to run a check on him."

Leo chuckles. "Do you honestly think Alesso hasn't already done one?"

"I want to get another check. I don't trust him. Douche was wearing loafers, for fuck's sake."

Leo's booming laugh trickles down the line. "If I didn't know better, I'd say you have a touch of the green-eyed monster."

"Don't be stupid. I'm watching out for her is all."

"Sure, son."

I exhale heavily. "Come on. Drop that shit. You know my stance."

"Was Elisa's sad face today anything to do with you?" he asks in a more serious tone.

"You've seen her recently?"

"She traveled with us this evening. Came home early for the weekend."

I pull a sharp left to reroute my direction, already deciding to head to Greenwich.

It's after eight by the time I reach the Greenwich estate. Mom beat me home, and she drags me inside to share a late dinner with her. She's exhausted because she's been pulling long shifts every day since the battle, and I don't protest when she hits the sack early because it gives me time to hunt down Lili. It's almost ten as I set out on foot toward the Salerno home.

I am passing the side of their garden when voices tickle my eardrums. It's coming from the gazebo area at the back, which is a familiar hangout of Romeo's and Rowan's. Especially if they want to smoke dope or drink a few beers. I set out in that direction, my ears perking up at the sound of girlish laughter.

Elisa is with them.

I'm not sure why I do it, but I crouch down and duck between shrubs and trees as I creep up on the cozy structure. Cushioned benches rim the perimeter of the circular wooden structure on all sides, and a large circular coffee table resides in the center space. Patio heaters glow warmly, flickering shadows across three familiar faces. Overhead, string lights are hung haphazardly, and decorative wall art is affixed to the side panels. A couple of candles fight for space alongside copious bottles of beer and wine on the table as I crawl up alongside the gazebo, concealing myself behind a large shrub.

"You should do it, sis," Romeo says, stretching his long legs out on his side of the seated area. "It's time." He passes a blunt to his sister, and I'm shocked when she drags on it with expertise. This isn't the first time she's smoked, and that is news to me.

"I feel like I've waited this long I shouldn't rush to make the decision now."

"Don't overthink it, Lise," Rowan says, rolling onto his stomach. Elisa's head is on her brother's lap, and her feet are at Rowan's head. He tickles the soles of her feet, and she giggles as she reaches for the wine bottle. "You get too up in your head sometimes, cuz. Just go with the flow when you're next making out with Seb and see where it leads."

I stuff a fist in my mouth as I contemplate intervening. But I've more to glean from eavesdropping, so I stay quiet.

"I want to, but every time it's getting close, I can't stop thinking about...he who shall not be named, and it ruins the mood."

"I should have punched his lights out years ago," Romeo says in an angry tone.

"Caleb is cool," Rowan says, taking the blunt from Elisa.

"Hey!" Lili sits up and glares at him. "No saying his name out loud. You agreed!"

Wow, things have really sunk to new lows. I rub at the tightness spreading across my chest.

Elisa is slurring her words a little, and I wonder how much she's had to drink.

"He's not cool," Romeo hisses. "He's a fucking prick and an idiot. What sane man would pick whores and skanks over my beautiful sister?"

A man who knows he's not worthy of said beautiful sister.

I'm aware Romeo is wary of me, but he's usually not so vocal. He's a sensitive soul and fiercely loyal to his sister. Something I admire—when he's not throwing shade my way.

"I love you, Romeo." Elisa turns around to hug her brother. "You're the best brother ever."

"He doesn't choose them over Lise," Rowan says, leaning on his side. He takes another pull on the blunt before passing it back to Romeo. Elisa swigs greedily from the bottle of wine, and I frown. This isn't like her at all. "He uses them to distract himself from her."

What the fuck? Is Rowan Mazzone psychoanalyzing me? And could he be fucking right?

No.

He's wrong.

I'm not interested in relationships, but sex is important. I'm a horny fucker with a healthy libido, and I regularly quench my thirst.

Who I fuck and why I fuck them has nothing to do with Lili.

"Do you really think that?" Lili asks in between mouthfuls of wine. She's going to have some hangover tomorrow.

"Yes, I do. The thing is Caleb doesn't even realize it. He's hellbent on avoiding relationships because his feelings scare him. It's why he won't confront his feelings for you."

I'm getting schooled by an eighteen-year-old.

Awesome.

"It doesn't matter anyway," Elisa says. "I am officially done with him, and you're right. It's stupid to continue holding on to my virginity. Even if he begged me to have sex, I wouldn't give it up to him. It was a stupid fantasy I've been clinging to for far too long. It's time to let that dream go."

Chapter Ten
Caleb

O kay, hold up. Is she saying she is still a virgin because she was waiting to give that honor to *me*? The arrogant part of me might have considered that on occasion, but mostly I thought she was holding back until she met the right guy. Not gonna lie, my chest puffs with pride, and my dick swells behind my zipper, more than down with the idea, which is insane. I don't screw virgins. They have zero experience, and you have to go slow and be careful, which is the antithesis of how I like to fuck.

Resolve is etched upon Elisa's gorgeous face as she says, "I'm going to do it." She swigs from the almost empty wine bottle as Rowan grins at her and Romeo grins at his phone while typing out a message. "I'm going to have sex with Seb," she proclaims, and I instantly see red.

"Over my dead fucking body are you screwing that preppy douche," I snarl, stepping out from behind the bush.

Elisa screams and drops the wine bottle. Romeo jerks his head up, the smile instantly fading from his face. Rowan quirks a brow and smirks, finishing the blunt and reaching for a beer.

"What the...what the hell are you doing here, and were you eavesdropping on our private conversation?" Elisa asks, swaying a little as she climbs to her feet.

"I came looking for you after Anais told me you showed up at my place, and yes I was eavesdropping." I step up into the gazebo and glower at her. "You are not giving your V-card to that prick."

Her cheeks stain red, and the vein in her neck visibly throbs. "You don't get a say, and he's not a prick! He's my boyfriend, and he's a decent guy."

"He's a dead guy if his cock goes anywhere near your pussy, your mouth, or your ass."

Her cheeks are fire-engine red now.

"If you're blushing hearing those words, you are not ready for sex anyway." I smirk as her blush deepens further.

"Fuck you, Caleb."

"I might if you ask me nicely," I blurt without engaging my brain.

"What?" all three ask in unison, their voices incredulous.

"I didn't mean it. You know we're not like that."

"No, of course not." Elisa attempts to storm past me, but her feet crunch on broken glass, and she shrieks as her arms and legs flay, and she almost loses her balance.

"I've got you." Grabbing her by her slim waist, I lift her over the mess on the floor. She is light as a feather, and she fits perfectly in my hands.

"Let me go," she says, attempting to wriggle out of my arms, but I'm taller, stronger, and broader, and I'm not letting her go until I'm ready to.

"No. Not until you talk to me."

She snorts. "Get lost and go back to that bitch. I hope you two make one another miserable."

"Anais lied."

"Shocker," Rowan says, sarcasm underscoring his words.

"I don't care." Elisa tries to wriggle again. "Let me go."

"No." I smirk. "What're you gonna do, Lili, huh?"

In an unexpected move I didn't consider him capable of, Romeo grabs my gun and points it at my temple.

"Dude!" Rowan hops up, his eyes almost bugging out of his head. "What are you doing?"

"Something I should have done a long time ago." Romeo prods the gun into the side of my head. "I should have protected you better, Elisa. I'm sorry."

"Romeo, put the gun down," Lili says.

"Not until he lets you go."

I turn and grin at him. "About time you found your balls."

"I hate you," he says in a deceptively calm voice. "My sister is far too good for you."

"I agree," I honestly admit.

"I'm done doing nothing while you shit all over her feelings and hurt her over and over again."

"I have never intentionally set out to hurt Lili. I could never do that."

"It doesn't matter if it's intentional or not!" Romeo yells. "You see she is hurting, and you never change your ways!"

"You need to put the gun down," Elisa says, sounding way more sober now. "This is between Caleb and me, and I don't want you to get involved."

"We're all involved! We've all had to watch this shit from the sidelines for years." He digs the gun into my temple, and he's so wound up he might actually shoot me. "He knows how you feel about him, and he just continues screwing anything in a skirt, uncaring how much it hurts you."

I release Lili from my grip, trying to reassure her with my eyes. "Romeo, I—"

"Shut. Up," he snaps at me.

79

Out of the corner of my eye I see Rowan furiously typing on his phone. Calling in reinforcements, I'm guessing.

"Romeo, I appreciate your loyalty, but this isn't Caleb's fault." Elisa flashes me a look. "Yes, he broke a promise to me, but I have no claim on him. He's free to sleep with whoever he likes, and he's not responsible for my feelings. I can't force him to return them, and I should have gotten over him years ago. That's on me, not him." She moves forward and bravely puts her hand on her brother's arm. "This isn't you. You don't want to do this."

"I will do it for you. So you can move forward."

"Do you honestly think I could ever move forward if you killed him because of me?"

"Romeo, no!" Alesso yells, racing toward us from the direction of the house with Serena hot on his heels.

"Please, Romeo." Lili's soft tone pleads with her brother. "Put the gun down. This has gone far enough."

"I'm only doing this for my sister," he says, lowering the gun and handing it to me.

"I know, and I respect you for it." I tuck the gun away.

"I don't want your respect, and I still hate you."

"That's your right. I would feel the same way if it was Rosa."

"What is going on here?" Alesso asks when he reaches us, his gaze bouncing around all of us.

"I'm defending my sister." Romeo folds his arms as his phone vibrates in his jeans pocket. "And I'm not sorry."

"You can't pull a gun on a don," Alesso says.

"I don't fucking care," he yells.

"Romeo!" Shock splays across Serena's face. "What has gotten into you?"

"I'd say weed and alcohol by the look of it." Alesso's face is grim. "Apologize to Don Accardi and then go inside, immediately."

"I'm not apologizing to him."

"Romeo." Alesso's stern tone brokers no argument.

"It's fine," I say, letting him off the hook. "It's not necessary."

Alesso drills me with a lethal look. "No son of mine will disrespect any don." *Even if it is you* is left unspoken.

"There are right ways to defend your sister," Serena says. "But this isn't one of them. We raised you better than this, Romeo. Apologize to Caleb now."

Romeo looks like he's swallowed a bucket of lemons when he turns to me and hisses, "Sorry, Don Accardi," in his most scornful, unapologetic tone.

I work hard to smother a laugh. Who would have thought Romeo Salerno had it in him? He has only gone up in my estimation. "Apology accepted though next time you're threatening a man with a gun you might want to turn the safety off."

Romeo flips me the bird behind his back as his mother steers him into the house, and a chuckle escapes my lips.

"Go into the house, Elisa," Alesso says before swinging his gaze on Rowan. "Home. Now."

Rowan holds up his hands. "I'm going. I'm going." He leans into me as he passes. "Thanks for dropping by, man. This was the most entertainment I've had in weeks." He waggles his brows and grins before walking off.

The sad thing is it's probably true. Sierra has wrapped him in cotton wool since the assassination attempt.

Alesso sighs, rubbing the back of his neck as we face one another. I'm preparing myself for some kind of lecture, so his words surprise me. "I know I bust your balls, Caleb, but it's not because I dislike you."

"Could have fooled me."

"I have nothing against you personally. I just don't want you with Elisa. She deserves someone who will burn the world down for her. Someone who will love and cherish her because she is inherently good and kind and compassionate with the biggest heart. Elisa deserves to find true love with someone who reciprocates it, a man who can shower her with affection and remain loyal to her. We both know that man isn't you."

"Thanks for the glowing recommendation."

"Why do you do this?" His tone carries an edge. "Grow up and quit with the attitude and all the fucking around, Caleb. You wonder how Marino could so easily turn loyalty? It's not just because he was the one close to the men on the ground. They had respect for him."

My jaw tightens as I grind my teeth and clench my hands at my side. I wish I could dispute his sentiment, but I can't. It's obvious there is a faction within our *famiglia* who doesn't respect Joshua or me. If they did, they never would have sided with our deceased underboss and signed up to annihilate us.

Alesso's features soften. "To gain respect, you need to earn it first. Be the leader the men need you to be, Caleb. There is a reason why family is so revered in our world. A wife and kids ground a man. I was like you once. I thought I would never marry, and then I met Serena. She was married to that monster, and I still believed I would never marry. If I couldn't have her, I didn't want anyone."

"Is there a point to this?"

Alesso stares me in the eyes. "I get it. You're in your prime, and women are throwing themselves at you, but if you want to be taken seriously as a made man at your level, you need to find a woman and settle down. And maybe then Elisa can properly put her feelings for you to bed and find a man worthy of her."

He might as well have bitch-slapped me in the face.

"What if that man *is* me?"

"We both know it isn't."

"So, what you're saying is you want me to deliberately hurt her? Is that it? I need to be sure I've got this right."

"You may not have meant to, but you have strung her along for years, Caleb, and it's not right." He steps back, combing a hand through his hair. "Do the right thing, Don Accardi. Cut the strings and set her free."

Chapter Eleven
Elisa

"I am never drinking again," I grumble to my reflection when I finally surface the following morning. My mouth feels like dusty mothballs are hibernating inside, and my stomach is queasy. After brushing my teeth and sloshing half a bottle of mouthwash, I take the longest shower in history, only getting out when my skin wrinkles to the point of no return.

I blow-dry my hair, apply some lip gloss and mascara, and get dressed, choosing my favorite black skirt with the yellow daisy pattern and a tight-fitting, white, long-sleeved top. I slide my feet into my trusty ballet flats, catching a glimpse of myself in the full-length mirror as I leave my childhood bedroom. At least I look decent on the outside, even if I feel like shit on the inside.

"You look like you need this," Mom says, handing me a mug of steaming coffee a few seconds after I step foot in the kitchen.

"I so do. Thanks." Sliding onto a stool at the island unit, I watch Mom spooning mixture into the paper liners lining a muffin pan.

"Please tell me they're your oatmeal muffins?" I ask as my nostrils twitch. Mom is the muffin queen, and this recipe is my favorite. They're full of yummy goodness because Mom adds dates, cranberries, and pecans and it's the perfect combo.

"One and the same." She lifts her head, locking eyes with me. "I thought they might put a smile back on your face."

"Thanks, Mom." Stretching across the marble top, I kiss her on the cheek. "I'm going to work on your new logo today. I'll send you some options to review in a few hours."

"That would be great. I can't wait to see what you design."

Mom has a thriving human resource management consultancy business, but she hasn't rebranded in years. Graphic design began as a hobby for me when I first started at NYU. I was hand-drawing my favorite scenes from romance books before digitally completing them, and I posted them on Insta for fun. I very quickly built a large following, which was exciting and cool, and then authors began reaching out asking if I was available for commissions, which was even more exciting and cool. It all snowballed from there, and now I have several loyal clients who give me tons of repeat business. My artwork is still super popular, but I also design book covers, interior illustrations, graphics, and I recently branched out into logo design.

It seemed natural to offer to help Mom when she mentioned she wanted to rebrand, but I've been so busy lately with paid work, classes, and studying that I haven't had the time to finish the rough draft I started a couple of weeks ago. I might as well take advantage of my free Friday and get it done now.

"Have you given any more thought to what you want to do after you graduate?" she asks, sliding the two muffin pans into the oven.

"Yeah. I've been thinking about what we spoke about before." I nibble on my lip before taking a sip of my coffee. "I think I'm going to do it. I'm going to officially set up a graphic design company and look to expand my clientele."

Mom beams. "That is wonderful news."

"You're not sad I didn't go the artist or art gallery route?" When I graduated high school, I chose to study art at NYU because those had been my dreams.

But my dreams have changed—in my career and my love life.

"We just want you to be happy, Elisa, and your passion for graphic design is obvious. You love it, and you're too talented not to pursue it."

"It's a little scary though."

"The best things usually are." She reaches across the island unit to squeeze my hand. "I'm betting it'll be a huge success, and we'll be proud of you no matter what."

"Thanks, Mom." Tears prick my eyes. "You set the best example."

"I remember feeling scared when I walked away from my job at Caltimore Holdings to go it alone. I was afraid of failing, but it was also exhilarating. Owning your own business is as enthralling and rewarding as it is challenging and scary. I'm here to help. Sierra will help too, and your grandma is a great person to speak to. She took back control of Lawson Pharma and completely transformed the organization. You have lots of people to lean on for support."

"Lots of strong, independent, smart women. You are all so inspirational."

"I couldn't agree more," a man with a deep voice says from behind, and all the tiny hairs lift on the back of my neck.

Mom glances at me briefly before fixing a smile on her face. "Caleb. It's lovely to see you."

"Sorry for barging in like this, Serena, but I need to speak to Lili."

My heart jumps hearing my nickname spill from his lips. It has always made me feel so special, but now it's hard to believe it was real.

"What if I don't want to speak to you?" I swivel on my chair to face him.

He's wearing the same clothes as last night, and in the bright light of day, he looks even more gorgeous. Like he just stepped off the catwalk or one of his notorious photoshoots. Why does he have to be so drop-dead gorgeous? Why do his big blue eyes ensnare me like I'm the most precious thing in his world? I even hate how his hair flicks over his brow in messy gloriousness like he styled it that way, when I know he most likely just ran his fingers through it this morning.

"You wouldn't have shown up at my place if you didn't want to talk." He produces a bouquet of flowers from behind his back, holding them out to me. I recognize the sticker on the front. They're from my favorite florist in town, and he's chosen a pastel pink, peach, and white bouquet with roses, tulips, peonies, and a few lilies.

"Those are beautiful." Mom smiles sadly as her gaze bounces between us, and I imagine she's visualizing all the lost moments we might have shared if we'd ever become a couple.

"They are, but why are you giving me flowers?" I inquire, eyeballing him.

"Do I need a reason?"

"Yes. I'm not your girlfriend, and you don't buy me random flowers, so why now?" I quirk a brow.

His Adam's apple bobs in his throat as he peers deep into my eyes. "You were upset yesterday. It's partly my fault, and I wanted to do something nice for you." He shrugs. "There's no big ulterior motive, Lili. It's just a bunch of flowers."

Mom is watching our interaction with avid interest, and I can almost hear her whispering in my ear how it's a sweet gesture and to stop busting his balls. I'm still mad at him, but it *is* sweet. "Thank you. I appreciate the thought." I bury my nose in the petals, inhaling the glorious scents.

"Could we go somewhere to talk in private?" His earnest eyes pin mine in place, and I stop breathing for a second.

"Sure."

"I'll put these in water," Mom says, taking the bouquet from me.

"Let's talk in the sunroom," I suggest. "Would you like a coffee?"

"I can get my own." He strides toward the large coffee machine and opens the overhead cupboard to remove a mug.

Mom smiles as we watch him make himself at home.

A few minutes later, we walk silently toward the sunroom at the rear of our house both nursing coffees and an abundance of unsaid words.

A sleepy-eyed Romeo emerges from the playroom, in sweats and a plain white tee, as we approach the sunroom. His scowl is instant when he sees Caleb. "Douche," he mutters under his breath as we walk past, and I'm more than a little shocked. Romeo gallantly rose to my defense last night, and I assumed some of that bravery stemmed from the weed and alcohol in his system, but it seems I was wrong.

"Nice to see you too, Romeo," Caleb says over a chuckle, holding the door to the sunroom open for me.

"Thank you for not making a big deal of last night," I say, ducking into the room.

"I wouldn't want anyone to get in trouble for protecting you. Romeo is a good brother."

"He's the best," I agree, flopping down on one end of the couch. A surge of butterflies swoops into my chest and nerves fire at me from all directions. I guess we're doing this, and I'm apprehensive now the moment is here.

Caleb sits at the other end, quietly watching me as he drinks his coffee. "I am sorry for whatever Anais said to upset you yesterday."

I shrug, not wanting to regurgitate it.

He twists to the side so he's facing me head on. "None of it was true. She's concerned Cruz will discover she was spying on him and passing me intel. It's a legit concern and being his wife won't protect her. She needs someplace safe to hide out. That and The Commission would prefer to keep tabs on her. She's our best chance at finding Cruz."

"I get it." I've had time to think about it since fleeing the penthouse. There has always been an ulterior motive behind Caleb being with her, so I figured there was a reason now.

"She's not living with me, and we're not together. I have been staying at Joshua and Gia's place the past few days while Anais stayed at mine. She's moving into an apartment on the floor below today."

His words help, but only a little. "Why have you stayed with her all these years, Caleb? I understand she was revenge for Bettina, but it can't be that after all this time."

Air expels from his mouth, and his gaze is pensive as he eyeballs me while considering his reply. "It's hard to explain. Even to myself. At first, I got a kick out of screwing Cruz over, and then it was convenient. I had an itch; she scratched it."

I don't know what expression he sees on my face, but it's enough for his features to soften. He scoots down a little closer. "I have never cared about her the way I care about you, Lili. She's toxic. *We're* toxic together, and she brings out a streak in me I liked indulging for a while. It was only when she moved to Vegas that I realized how much of a destructive force she was in my life. I have only been with her a handful of times in these intervening years and only recently because The Commission needed me to use her."

"I should probably feel bad for her because it's not nice to be used. But there's no part of me that could ever feel bad for Anais DiPietro. She's poison, and she's loved rubbing my nose in it any chance she gets."

His brow puckers. "What do you mean?"

"It doesn't matter now. It's water under the bridge." I gulp a mouthful of my drink.

Caleb is still frowning. "It matters to me."

I bark out a bitter laugh. "Why?"

"What do you mean *why*?"

"You've made it clear I don't matter, so who cares if she's been giving me shit for years?"

"Of course, you matter!" He slams his mug down on the coffee table. "I know we don't have the relationship you hoped we'd have, but it doesn't mean I don't care for you deeply, Lili, because I do. I truly do." Sincerity bleeds from his eyes, but I'm not sure I believe it.

"If you really meant that, you wouldn't have broken your promise to me."

"I didn't. I haven't." He exhales heavily, clawing a hand through his messy dark-blond hair. "You need to tell me why you believe I have."

A shaky breath flees my lips, and my fingers tremble around my mug. I briefly close my eyes.

"Lili, please." Caleb takes my free hand in his, and my eyes pop open.

Fiery tingles skate over my hand and up my arm, and I yank it back. He doesn't get to touch me at will. He lost that privilege when he broke my heart. And why don't I feel all tingly when Seb holds my hand? It would solve all my problems if I did. Draining the last of my coffee, I place the mug on the table and draw a brave breath. "You know what you did, Caleb."

He vigorously shakes his head. "I don't. It's been killing me for months, and I've wracked my brain trying to find the reason, but I have not slept with any NYU students. I promised you I wouldn't do that, and I *have* kept my promise."

Tears flood my eyes as that horrible video resurfaces in my mind's eye. I squeeze my eyes shut, attempting to erase the image, but it refuses to disappear.

"But you didn't, Caleb. You didn't." Sadness shrouds me as I open my eyes and finally confront the issue. I knot my hands in my lap as bile swims up my throat. "You had a foursome with three girls from my college. One of the girls has spent years tormenting me, and she loved showing me the proof she'd had sex with you."

Chapter Twelve
Caleb

"No." I shake my head. "There must be some mix-up. I always ask women how old they are and where they work, and I never frequent college bars or clubs." I did that for her after she asked it of me. It was just before she left for NYU. I can still recall the conversation and the longing in her eyes and pain lingering behind her words. I remember feeling like a piece of shit and wishing I could be enough for her.

"There's no mix-up!" she yells, clenching and unclenching her hands. "She sent me a video." She lowers her eyes to her lap. "I saw you very clearly." Her voice turns meek, her words laced with hurt. "Gwyneth was riding you while Susie was... she was sitting on your face and your...your fingers were inside Cara."

"Lili." I move right down next to her. "Please look at me."

"I can't," she whispers.

Gently, I tilt her face up with two fingers under her chin. Tears glisten in her eyes and her cheeks are flushed. "Gwyneth is the girl you mentioned to me last year, right? The one you said was a bitch? I wanted to handle her, but you made me swear not to intervene. I haven't forgotten her name, and I would never fuck anyone named Gwyneth on the off chance it was the same girl." I press my free hand to my heart. "I swear it. There must be some other explanation."

"There isn't, Caleb. I know what I saw."

"Show me the video."

A tear rolls down her face as she cranks out a bitter laugh. "Why on earth would you think I'd keep something like that?" More tears flow down her face, and pressure sits on my chest. "It hurt so much." Pain is etched upon her beautiful face as she looks out the window. "She cornered me and gave me a blow-by-blow account of their night with you, even explaining how Joshua showed up and Susie called him your clone and wanted him to join in."

Horror crawls over me as that triggers a memory. "Show me what she looks like."

"Give me your phone." She quickly wipes the tears streaming down her face with her fingers before holding out her palm.

I unlock my cell and hand it over. Tension bleeds into the air as she types away. Hair curtains her face in soft waves, and my fingers twitch with an urge to touch the silky strands—a completely alien urge for me. The only time I touch a woman's hair is when I'm fisting it as I'm plowing into her from behind.

"There." Her face contorts into an angry grimace as she thrusts the cell at me.

All the blood drains from my face as I stare at the pixie-haired woman on the screen.

"That's Gwyn." She swipes her finger to the left. "That's Susie, and this bitch is Cara." She swipes again, showing a picture of the redhead.

I remember them, but it's a little fuzzy. Delving into the

depths of my memory, I try to recall the exact circumstances. The pixie slut was the one to approach me after the fashion show. Of that, I'm sure. I also remember the IDs all three were wearing confirming they were a buyer, a stylist, and a publicist from a leading global store chain. Pretty sure those names weren't their real names. It's not like I'd ever forget the name Gwyneth. Clearly, they stole the IDs or manufactured them, and it's not like I was going to verify their references. My twin is the one who used to make his fuck buddies sign contracts and provide documentation. That's never been my style, and now it's coming back to bite me in the ass in a major way.

I'm opening my mouth to proclaim my innocence and conduct damage control when I falter. Alesso's words return to haunt me. I swallow thickly over the lump in my throat as acid churns in my gut.

This is the perfect opportunity to make her hate me forever.

Am I selfless enough to set her free?

Pain obliterates me on the inside as a startling realization dawns on me.

I think I love her.

I think I have for years.

"Well?" Her cutting tone drags me back to the moment. "Do you remember the skank now?" She glares at me while trying to hide her hurt.

If I do this, there will be no coming back from it.

She will hate me for eternity.

But I don't see how I have any other choice. I could never be good enough for a woman like Elisa Salerno. She wants rainbows and unicorns, and I'm darkness personified. She craves a committed relationship, and I move from one casual encounter to the next without looking back. Even if I wanted to try with

Siobhan Davis

her, I have no clue how to do it, and I'd probably only end up hurting her and disappointing myself.

No. This is the only way.

I force a smirk on my face, already hating myself for what I'm about to do. "Damn straight." My smirk grows wider, and I die a little inside as abject pain shimmers in her glassy eyes. "That was a wild night," I lie. It was actually some of the worst sex I've ever had. "I wasn't aware she was a college student, and I'm not sure I even got her name. But yeah. My bad." I hold up my hands and grin like it's not a big deal and I'm not just crushing her heart all over again. "I did fuck her. I fucked all of them. Multiple times. In multiple positions. I even—"

"Shut up!" she roars, covering my mouth with her hand as more tears course down her face.

Bile crawls up my throat, and I'm disgusted with myself. It doesn't even feel like the right thing to do, but it's done now. There is no coming back from it.

"Get out," she sobs, removing her hand. "Get out of my house and out of my life." She climbs to her feet and her lower lip wobbles. "You are dead to me, Caleb. I never want to see you again."

I hang my head in shame as she races out of the sunroom crying and try to convince myself I haven't just made a terrible mistake.

"Hey, sexy." The stool beside me screeches as someone hops up onto it, sliding their warm body against mine.

"Not interested," I snap, pouring more Macallan into my glass. After my first few whiskies, I told the bartender to give me the bottle, and I've lost count of how much I've drank by now. Enough to make me drunk, but I'm still way too conscious

96

for my liking. I want to blot it all out. Those three lying sluts and my Lili. My sweet, adorable Lili. The woman who wants to shove my balls in a meatgrinder and pulverize them. Can't say I'd blame her.

"I've been watching you," the woman purrs, placing her hand on my arm. "Whatever you're drinking to forget isn't working. I can help. I bet fucking it out of your system will do the trick."

I snort out a laugh. Why does she think I came to Club H in the first place? That had been my initial plan. To fuck my way through the memory of Lili's face when I hurt her so cruelly. Until I showed up here and the thought of touching any woman sickened me. I was propositioned plenty of times, but I turned them all down. Even watching the kinky shit going down in the orgy room didn't get my juices flowing. My dick is like a lump of Jell-O, flopping from side to side with nothing stirring. Which is why this bitch needs to fuck the hell off. I couldn't fuck her even if I wanted to, which I don't. "Don't pretend like you know me or know what I need or want because you don't," I drawl.

"You don't remember me, do you?"

That statement has me whipping my head to face her. Relief shuttles through me. For a second there, I was terrified it was one of those lying bitches. In my current mood, if I see any of them, I'm likely to shoot them on the spot. They used me to hurt Lili, and I am going to make them pay.

"Caleb?" The dark-haired woman touches my face. "Do you remember me?"

"Nope." I slap her hand away, only for her to drive it between my legs. She wastes no time stroking me through my jeans.

"Remember me now?" She wets her lips in what I'm sure she thinks is a provocative manner, but it does nothing for me.

Same with her ministrations between my legs. My dick is limp with zero interest in anything sex related.

I might need a doctor.

"I was visiting the city last year on business, and I came here with a couple of friends. You fucked all of us, but tonight, I'm hoping for a solo special." She waggles her brows and thrusts her enlarged fake chest forward as if that will change my mind.

Removing her hand from my groin, I thrust it back at her and snarl, "Fuck off. My dick is allergic to your touch."

"You weren't allergic the last time."

"My dick obviously wised up," I say before ignoring her and going back to my drink.

"You can't just ignore me! I have come here every night this week hoping to see you."

"Not my problem." I wave a dismissive hand in her direction, already done with this convo.

"You're a complete prick, and I'm making a formal complaint to the owner," she snaps, the legs of the stool screeching across the floor as she climbs down.

"Funny, I don't remember any rule that states assholery is grounds for being written up."

"Club rules are to be respectful to other members, and you've totally disrespected me!" she shrieks.

"You're not even a member," I say without looking at her. I swirl the amber-colored liquid in my glass, wishing it would take effect and numb all thoughts in my brain. I turn and smirk. "And I rejected you, sweetheart. It's not the same thing. Perhaps you should spend your nights reading the dictionary instead of frequenting sex clubs."

Her nostrils flare. "You are *such* a jerk."

"Never pretended to be anything else."

"I'm going to report you right now."

I chuckle. "You do that, babe. I'm sure my uncle will get a kick out of it."

Her brow puckers. "Your uncle?"

"I'm related to Bennett Mazzone, but be my guest. Write me up. I don't give a shit."

She finally storms off, muttering expletives under her breath.

"Making new friends?" Cristian jokes, sliding onto the stool the woman just vacated.

"What are you doing here?" Cristian is currently in a committed relationship, and he hasn't darkened the doors of Club H in months.

"Rafael called me."

I turn and glare at the bartender. He shrugs and raises his palms. He's lucky we have to leave weapons at the front door.

"Is there a reason you're trying to drown yourself in scotch?" my friend and fellow don asks.

"My dick is broken," I blurt before draining my drink and reaching for the bottle.

"What?" Cristian grins.

"It's not funny. I haven't had sex in weeks, and my dick has shown zero interest tonight in anything or anyone."

"If you've drunk this much," he says, eyeing the half-empty bottle. "I'm not surprised."

"I think I screwed up," I mumble, resting my head on the counter as sudden exhaustion washes over me.

"Let's get you home, buddy, and you can tell me all about it."

Chapter Thirteen
Caleb

I wake the next morning with a thumping headache, and my tongue is flattened to the roof of my mouth. I'm lying on my stomach on my bed, still in my clothes from last night. Lifting my head off the pillow, I groan as splinters of pain stab me in the skull. I roll over onto my back and lift up a little, pleased to see I at least had the sense to take off my socks and shoes.

Or maybe not. I rectify my thought as I spy the glass of water and pain pills on my bedside table. Pulling myself up against the headboard, I knock back the pills, grimacing at the note Cristian left me.

Tell her the truth.

Fuck. I rub at my sore head as I glance at my watch. It's still way too early to contemplate any of this. I have no clue what crap I spewed last night. I was more inebriated than I realized. I'm unsure how I got home, but I'm guessing my buddy is responsible. Love that dude like a brother.

I'm trying to make myself get up and into the shower when my twin appears in the doorway of my bedroom like a ghostly apparition. "Jesus Christ, Caleb. It smells like a fucking brewery in here."

I casually flip him the bird as I begin unbuttoning my shirt.

Joshua scowls at the piles of clothes on my floor as he picks his way across the room. "I'm going to schedule the cleaning crew to come here on the daily," he says, shaking his head and grimacing. "How can you live like this?" He perches on the edge off my bed, surveying my messy room with obvious disgust.

"It's not all my doing this time. Anais didn't lift a finger while she was here." Thank fuck, she moved into her new apartment yesterday.

"You let her sleep in your room?" He jumps up, glaring at my bed like it's infested.

Hell, it probably is.

"Of course not. I put her things in the guest room, but she did what the fuck she wanted while I wasn't here."

"I hope you kept tabs on her."

"I'm not a moron." I send him daggered eyes. "I had a couple of guys watch the camera feeds twenty-four-seven while she was here. Apart from trashing my place, eating all my junk food, and binging on reality TV, she didn't do jack."

"I still don't trust her."

"Same," I agree, tossing my shirt onto the nearest mound of clothes on the floor.

Joshua rolls his eyes. "Cristian called."

Now it's my turn to eye roll. "He's worse than any pussy."

"He said you told him you love Elisa and you've fucked it all up."

My mouth hangs open. "I did *not* say that."

Joshua grins. "You so did. It's about time you admitted the truth."

I flip him the bird again—'cause I'm mature like that. "I'm not admitting anything."

"You confronted me when I was in denial about my feelings for Gia, and now it's my turn." My twin tips dirty clothes off the chair by my window and sits down. "I'm a judgment-free zone, brother. Talk to me."

I pull off my jeans and flip them onto the floor, sitting on the side of my bed in my boxers. I rest my head in my hands as my stomach churns violently. The nasty taste in my mouth reminds me I consumed half a bottle of Macallan last night. "We have to be at Cartier soon," I say, remembering the appointment and why my brother has shown up at the crack of dawn on a Saturday morning.

"Nice try, but it won't work. We have plenty of time." He crosses one ankle over his knee as he smiles. "Spit it out."

I heave a sigh. Joshua is a stubborn prick when he gets something into his head. Might as well do this now. "Did you know she has a boyfriend?"

"Gia mentioned something about him, yeah."

I glower at my twin. "And you didn't fucking say anything to me?"

He shrugs. "What was the point when you were still in denial?"

"I hate this shit." I flop down on my back. "I don't know what I feel. I don't believe in love. You know this. I have feelings for her, but I don't know if it's love. Lately, it's getting harder to be around her and not want to hold her and kiss her. When I'm jerking off, it's always to images of her. She is consuming my thoughts, and my head is a bigger fucked-up mess than usual." I sit back up. "I fucking hate the thought of that preppy prick putting his hands anywhere near my Lili." My hands ball up of their own volition. "See?" I hold them out. "I want to pummel the douche into next year."

"I don't think it's serious with him."

"*Yet.*" I stand and pace the floor. "As soon as he realizes how amazing she is, he'll try to put a ring on it."

"What are you going to do about it?"

"I don't know. I think it might be too late." I rub at my stomach. "I did something stupid."

"Wow, shocker right there."

"J," I grit out. "Not fucking helpful."

His expression sobers as he lowers his foot to the floor. "Cristian told me about those girls and what you said to Elisa. I also know Alesso put the thought in your head, and I'm pissed at him for interfering even if I understand why he did."

"I thought it was the right call, but it felt all wrong."

"You need to tell her how it really went down."

"She won't believe me." A messy ball of emotion clogs the back of my throat. "I was deliberately cruel. I really hurt her." I slump to the ground and cradle my aching head in my hands. "You should have seen her face. She was hurting bad, and this isn't the first time I've caused her pain." I wet my dry lips and look up at my brother. "I have made so many mistakes when it comes to Elisa. I have hurt her so much even though it was never intentional. I was a selfish prick who didn't give a second thought about anyone else. I deserve to lose her, and let's face it, I have never been good enough for her. I could never be good enough for her. I—"

"Are you done with the pity party?" J says, cutting across me.

"Fuck you."

"Quit this pussy shit. This isn't who you are. Yes, you've made mistakes, but you don't have a time machine to go back and change it. All you can do is try to make it up to her and commit to doing better from now on. Starting with being brutally honest. Make yourself vulnerable. Lay it all on the line.

Lili has loved you from the time she was a little kid. She'll forgive you."

"What if she doesn't?"

"You won't know if you don't try."

"What if I'm no good at it? Relationships," I add when I see the confusion in his gaze. "I don't have a clue how to be in a relationship. That was always your forte."

"When it's the right person, it'll come naturally. Now quit being a whiny bitch and get your ass in the shower." He offers his hand, and I take it, letting him pull me to my feet. "What about those girls?"

"They did it deliberately." I grind my jaw as tension fills every nook and cranny of my body. "It's the only explanation. They purposely sought me out and planned it to hurt Lili."

"They need to pay."

"My sentiments exactly."

"Do you have a plan?"

"I'm going to ruin them, starting with getting them thrown out of NYU. I should've done it last year when Elisa mentioned that girl was harassing her. I wanted to step in, but she made me promise I wouldn't interfere. I should have followed my gut and put those bitches in their place, then none of this would've happened."

"Let me know how I can help," J says, glancing at his watch.

"I need their full names to run a background check. Ask Gia."

He shakes his head. "Don't involve her. Things could easily get messy, and Elisa is her best friend."

This is fucking priceless. He just asked how he could help, and now he's saying no. Screw that. Gia will do it when I explain. "Fine. I'll ask her myself."

"Ask me what?" Gia says, materializing in the doorway.

"Darling, what are you doing here?" Joshua flings a pair of dirty sweats at me. "Cover up."

You'd swear Gia had never seen a man in boxers. My brother is totally overreacting, but what's new. He's like a Neanderthal on steroids when it comes to Gia Bianchi. I pull on my sweats as Gia crosses the room, smiling sweetly at her boyfriend.

Cold steel presses against my temple as she pulls a gun on me.

"Gia! What the hell?" Joshua stares at his girlfriend in disbelief.

"What the fuck is up with everyone pulling a gun on me?" I grumble, sighing as I shove my hands in the pockets of my sweats.

"It's called karma, asshole." Gia digs the muzzle in deeper. "I had to console my friend for two hours on the phone yesterday. I had hoped there was some logical explanation, but I gave you too much credit. Tell me one good reason why I shouldn't pull this trigger."

"I lied." I turn my head so I'm looking at her, uncaring she has a gun pressed to my skull. She won't pull it. In her own funny way, she likes me. You'd just have to inject her with alcohol to get her to admit it. "I lied to her because I thought it'd help if she really hated me, but I instantly regretted it. I should have told her the truth."

"Which is?" Gia eyeballs me with healthy skepticism.

"Those girls targeted me. They faked their IDs and used different names. I had no idea they went to NYU or that they even knew Lili. If I'd known who they were, I would have drop-kicked them into the ocean with concrete-covered feet."

"Honey, put the gun down before you accidentally kill my twin."

"He'd deserve it for being such a fucking dumbass and the

biggest slut." Reluctantly, she lowers the weapon, flipping the safety and tucking it into the back of her jeans. Her evil grin is the only warning I get before she lifts her leg and knees me in the balls.

"Fuck," I hiss through gritted teeth, crouching over and cupping my groin as pain flares between my legs. Black spots flash behind my retinas as my eyes water. Crippling pain grips me, and I'm panting as I struggle to push through it. After a few beats, the excruciating pain settles, and I straighten up, glowering at my future sister-in-law. "That wasn't fucking necessary. I don't disagree, and for the record, I haven't fucked anyone in weeks. I'm turning a new page."

She arches a brow. "I'll believe it when I see it." Sarcasm laces through her tone.

"Those girls need to learn a valuable life lesson, and I'm going to be the one to deliver it."

Her eyes glisten with interest. "I want in."

I pin my brother with a smug grin. "I thought you might."

"What do you have in mind?"

"I'm going to make them regret every single hurtful thing they've said to Lili. By the time I'm done with them, they'll wish they were dead."

Chapter Fourteen
Elisa

"They're arguing again," Aria whispers, her pretty brow scrunched in concern.

"It'll blow over," I say even though I have no idea why Mom and Dad have been fighting almost nonstop since yesterday. They rarely raise voices to one another, so I understand why my little sister is scared. This is not normal for them.

I'm old enough to remember screaming matches between Mom and my prick of a bio dad. Though mostly it was him shouting at her and her screaming when he hurt her. I haven't forgotten how terrified it used to make me feel, but I always downplayed it for my brother.

Romeo used to cry, shake, and sometimes pee his pants whenever that monster went off the rails. He was always berating Romeo. Mostly for being too soft. But he was only a little kid, and there was no justification for the awful things our dead father said to him. Thankfully, my brother doesn't remember much. Even if he sometimes has nightmares when his subconscious attempts to remind him of how that bastard taunted and scared him.

"Don't worry." I reach over and hug her, inhaling the scent of peaches that always clings to Aria's hair. "They still love one another, and they'll resolve whatever it is."

"I hate when they shout," she admits, coloring her picture as she sits at the desk beside me. She is so careful with the lines, wanting it to be perfect. From the time she was three, Aria has drawn pictures for her papa every year for his birthday. I still draw for him too, and I love that my little sister is following the tradition. "Mariah says her mommy and daddy are always shouting at one another. It's something to do with the maid."

Yikes. That doesn't sound good.

"That's sad for Mariah, and I hope everything is okay. Every couple has disagreements, and at least our parents don't argue that often." Or if they do, they usually do it behind closed doors.

"I'm never going to argue with my husband." Her tongue peeks out as she focuses on coloring neatly within the lines. "I'm just going to kiss him any time he tries to shout at me."

My lips twitch at the corners. "Sounds like a good plan."

She lifts her head and stares at me. "Do you have to go back to college tomorrow? I love it when you're home."

My heart melts into a puddle at my feet. "Me too, cupcake." I mess up her hair as an idea comes to me. "How about a slumber party tonight? Just you and me? We can build a blanket fort in the playroom, and we'll do our nails and put on face masks, and then we can play Monopoly and Candy Land and watch *The Princess Bride*." We've already watched it a billion times, but I'll watch it a billion more times if it makes my sister happy and helps to distract her from whatever is going on with our parents.

"Yay!" She hops up and spins around, sporting a wide

smile. She flings her little arms around my neck. "I love you, Elisa. You're the bestest sister in the whole entire world."

"I could say the same of you." I kiss her soft cheek. Her excitement has helped to take the edge off my hurt.

"I'm going to get blankets," she says before racing off.

I'm smiling as my phone vibrates across the desk. It's probably Sebastien again. I've been ignoring his calls since I left the city, which is unfair, but I've got a lot on my plate, and I don't want to explain. I'll call him in the morning and arrange to meet him tomorrow night.

But it's not Seb. It's my bestie. "Hey, Gigi," I answer. "I'm okay," I reassure her, assuming my meltdown on the phone with her yesterday is the reason why she's calling me again. I laid into her for not telling me Anais was at Caleb's place, but she explained how she didn't want to upset me and if she'd known I was going to drop by on Thursday she would have forewarned me. "I haven't jumped off a bridge or overdosed on sleeping pills."

"Don't even joke about something like that."

"You're right. It's not something trivial I should joke about. I just don't want you to worry. I'm hurt and I'm angry, but I'd never kill myself over a man or anything else. Caleb did me a favor. It's easy to hate him now."

A pregnant pause ensues, followed by a tired sigh. "I'm calling to give you a heads-up. Caleb is en route to Greenwich, determined to tell you the truth. I only just found out, so it's possible he's already there."

My brow puckers. "I already got the truth, and I have zero desire to hear him repeat that sordid shit."

"He lied, Elisa."

"That's a likely excuse." I harrumph as I kick my legs up on the footstool under the desk. "More like he couldn't think of a plausible lie on the spot."

"He's an idiot, but I think you should hear him out."

"I am doing no such thing. I have drawn my line in the sand, and I'm not regressing. Caleb is dead to me. He is in the past, and that's where I'm leaving him."

"You know I don't—"

I tune her out as Mom pokes her head in the door, wearing a bright smile. "Caleb is here. He says he needs to speak to you urgently."

"He's here. I need to go," I say into the phone. "I'll call you when I get back to the city tomorrow." I hang up on my bestie and stand, thrusting my shoulders back and leveling Mom with a serious expression. "Tell him to leave. I don't care what he wants to say. I don't want to hear it."

Her face pales. "Are you sure, sweetie? He seems desperate to talk to you."

"What is with you and Gia suddenly taking his side?" I plant my hands on my hip and steady my resolve.

"We are always on your side. I'll do whatever you want, but he seems frantic and eager to make amends."

"Mom, I told you what he did. I can't look at him anymore. It doesn't matter what he has to say. There is nothing he can do to take it back." Hurt stabs me in the chest, and I avert my eyes, blinking back tears. I promised myself this morning I was done crying over Caleb, and I meant it. "Tell him to go, please. I don't want to see him or speak to him."

Silently, she envelops me in her arms, hugging me close. "If that's what you want."

"It is."

She kisses the top of my head. "Okay, I'll make him leave."

After she's gone, I lean my head back against the wall and bolster the steel walls I've erected around my heart. I don't believe he lied to me. Caleb is trying to cover his tracks, so I don't cut him completely from my life, but it's too late.

He has hurt me for the last time.

I'm done with him.

"Lili!" His deep voice hollers dangerously close to this room, and I quietly and quickly shut the door.

What the hell, Mom? I thought you were throwing him out? My entire body tenses at his voice, and I want him to leave me alone.

"Lili, please, just give me five minutes!" he shouts. "I'll get on my knees. I'll beg. Please just let me explain."

I hear Dad's voice, talking in muffled tones, and I can't pick up what's being said. Sounds of a commotion in the hallway outside the room have me widening my eyes. *What on earth is going on?*

"I'm not giving up, Elisa!" Caleb shouts, his voice beginning to fade. "I'm going to make it up to you, Lili. I swear."

It's quiet then, for a few minutes, until the sound of tires kicking up gravel outside. Slowly, the tension eases from my rigid limbs. Until Mom and Dad start arguing again. They're too far away to hear what's being said, but they appear to be really going for it.

The door flies open, and Aria bursts into the room, weighted down with blankets and the saddest eyes. "They're doing it again."

I take the blankets from her and pull her into an embrace. "It's going to be okay." Smoothing a hand down her hair, I hope I haven't just lied to her.

"What is going on with you and Dad?" I ask Mom the following morning when I enter the kitchen to find her alone.

"Ask your father," she says, her lips pulling into a grim line.

I gulp over the ball of nerves clogging my throat. Romeo

said Mom spent all last night with Sierra and Natalia and she slept in one of the guest bedrooms. Despite my reassurances to Aria, I'm growing concerned. "Are you getting divorced?" I ask, hating to even contemplate that scenario. It's not something I have ever had to worry about with Mom and Alesso, but they have been fighting like cats and dogs for two days, and I'm sufficiently worried.

Her eyes startle. "What? No." She vigorously shakes her head. "Of course not. This isn't about our relationship. It's just a disagreement."

"But you hardly ever fight, and this seems bad."

"You don't have to worry about divorce, Elisa." She walks forward and wraps her arms around me. "I promise it's not that. I still love your father, and he loves me. I'm just angry with him over something he meddled in."

"What did he do?" I ask, easing back to examine her face.

"He needs to be the one to tell you." She shucks out of our embrace. "He's in his study. Go talk to him."

"Okay." This is so weird. "I'm getting coffee first. I have a feeling I might need it."

"Let me get it." Mom hurries to the coffee machine. "Thanks for looking after Aria last night."

"We had fun, but you might want to talk to her. Your arguing has scared her."

Mom's face drops. "That is the last thing I ever want to do." Guilt splays across her features, and I can guess where her head is gone.

"It's not the same," I rush to reassure her. "It's only concerning because you two are usually all lovey-dovey and grabby hands and smushy kisses."

She thrusts the mug in my hands. "Talk to your father, and I'll talk to Aria and Will. I don't want to worry them."

My hands are warming against my mug of coffee as I walk

toward Dad's home office. Mom didn't drop any clues, so I really don't know what this is about. I knock on his door, waiting for him to call me in before opening it.

"Hey, honey." He greets me with a slightly off smile as I step into his study and close the thick door behind me.

My lips curl up, like always when I step foot in here. The wall behind his desk and half the wall on the right are covered in framed drawings. Most are mine with a few of Aria's. He started a separate section to proudly display my sister's birthday drawings. It never fails to raise a smile. If I ever doubted my stepfather's love for me, I only need to enter this room to be reminded of it.

"I'm guessing your mom sent you," he says, getting up and walking around the desk to me.

I nod. "I don't know what it's about though."

He rubs the back of his neck, the strain evident on his face. "I fucked up, honey."

My brows knit together at his words. He circles his arm around my shoulders and steers me toward the long, cushioned window seat. I sit at one end, pulling my knees up to my chest. Dad sits at the other end with his legs firmly planted on the ground.

"With Mom?" I inquire before sipping my coffee.

He claws a hand through his thick dark hair. "With your mom and with you."

"I don't know what you mean."

"I thought I was doing the right thing. I just wanted to protect you."

"What did you do?" Prickles of anxiety lift the fine hairs on the back of my neck as I suddenly have an inkling of what this might be about.

"I told Caleb if he cared for you to set you free."

I blink repeatedly as my mouth hangs open. I open and

115

close it several times before I can form a sentence. "You told him to lie to me?"

Pain flashes across his face as he winces. "Not directly, but I implied he should do whatever was necessary to let you go."

"Why would you do that, Dad?" I can barely get the words out over the lump in my throat.

"I overstepped, and it was a bad call, but I had your best interests at heart. I have watched you loving him most of your life and dealing with the fallout every time he hurts you. I know he hasn't done it intentionally, but I couldn't stand back and say nothing. I have bitten my tongue for years." He reaches out and touches my leg. "I shouldn't have interfered, and I'm very sorry for it, but I will never apologize for trying to protect you. That is what I was trying to do."

This is about protecting me?

Anger mushrooms inside me as I swing my legs onto the floor and stand. "You say that, yet you didn't see what was right under your nose because you always make excuses for Anais."

He frowns. "What are you talking about?" I guess Mom kept her promise and didn't tell him what we discussed on Thursday, but she wasn't happy I asked her to keep it a secret.

"Anais has been spiteful and nasty to me for years," I admit, slapping my mug down on the side table. Lukewarm coffee splashes over the rim of the mug, trickling down the sides and onto the marble tabletop. "She has been spiteful and nasty to *you* for years, yet you put up with it. I'm having a hard time not finding this hypocritical."

He has the decency to look ashamed. Dad stands and reaches for me, but I shake my head, take a step back, and fold my arms across my chest. "You're right that Caleb has never purposely set out to hurt me, not that it changes the outcome. But Anais has deliberately spewed venom at me for years, doing it slyly when you weren't looking, and you didn't protect me from her!" It's unfair to throw that at him when I stopped telling him about the things she was saying, but I'm hopping mad he interfered even if it was coming from a place of love.

Gia was telling the truth. Caleb lied to me because he was attempting to push me away. Not sure why or how he changed his mind, but he clearly did.

"Even if you didn't know she was being mean, you have continued to inflict her on all of us knowing none of us like her and we can barely tolerate her!" I'm really on a roll now as I release years of pent-up stress. "Mom, Auntie Sierra, and Auntie Natalia all feel the same way. We have put up with her annoying ass for years for *you*." The words leave my mouth in fast succession. "If you're trying to protect me, protect me from her instead of interfering in something you had no right to interfere in!"

"I'm your father, and I have every right to step in and try to stop you from hurting. I won't say sorry for that either." Agony splays across his face. "But I was wrong to force his hand, and I apologize." His Adam's apple bobs in his throat. "I have failed you," he softly adds. "I have failed to put my family first by allowing Anais to continue treating me, treating all of us, like shit."

"Why did you?" I ask, losing some of the ire from my tone.

"She is the last link to the Salerno bloodline, and I promised her father I would always look out for her."

"I think you're oversimplifying it. I think your childhood trauma has made you hold on much more than a person with a normal upbringing would have. I understand that better than most."

"I hate that you do."

I shrug because we can't change the past. "Maybe it's why I held on to Caleb for far too long. Maybe the damage from my trauma is the reason I saw hope for us even when there was none."

"I'm not a therapist, so I don't know if you are right." He reaches his hand for me, and I meet him halfway, placing my palm in his. "But I'm done keeping promises to dead men." Gently reeling me into his arms, he kisses my brow. "Why didn't you tell me? I thought she'd stopped after the last time I talked to her about it."

"That never helped," I truthfully admit even though it will probably hurt him to hear this. "She was always worse after you spoke to her. It's why I stopped telling you. I knew you'd keep trying to get her to behave and she'd antagonize me in worse ways." I shuck out of his embrace. "It seemed less stressful to just let it go."

"My cousin has hurt this family for the last time. I'm going to visit and tell her I'm done. She's cut off now. You won't have to face her anymore. I promise."

I'm sitting in the back of our family SUV as Dad's driver drives me back to the city, contemplating everything that went down this morning. Mom and Dad are good again now he's fessed up, and my little sister is no longer worried.

My initial anger has faded. Dad was only trying to safe-guard my heart, and I couldn't ever stay mad at him for that. I wish he hadn't interfered, but it's not like it's going to change the outcome. It doesn't matter what Caleb has to tell me. He can't undo the damage. He still had sex with those girls, and I don't think I can forgive him for it. It's one thing to know he's sleeping his way through every girl in Manhattan and quite another to have an actual visual image of him doing it imprinted in my brain.

My cell pings in the pocket of my skirt, and I take it out, biting the inside of my cheek when I see it's Seb calling again. I have kept him at arm's length for long enough. If I'm serious about making a go of things with him, I need to act like it. "Hi, Seb," I say, smiling as I answer his call.

But the smile doesn't last long when he tells me what happened at my apartment Thursday night and how some "lunatic" pulled a gun on him.

I am going to fucking murder Caleb.

After ending the call, I lean forward and stick my face in between the two front seats. "Change of plan. Please take me to Don Accardi's penthouse."

Chapter Fifteen
Caleb

I hang up on security and review the state of my living area with mounting panic. "Shit!" It's a complete mess, and I don't want Lili seeing it like this. Racing to the kitchen, I grab a trash bag from under the sink and run around my kitchen and living room, scooping all the empty bottles and takeout cartons into it. I should have implemented Joshua's suggestion and asked the cleaning company to come by every day. I make a mental note to call them later.

The bell chimes as I stash the bag in the hall closet, cringing at how messy the place still is. But there isn't anything I can do about it now. I'm not leaving Elisa at the door to change her mind.

Striding down the hallway, I grin to myself. I knew she wouldn't stay mad at me for long. She never does. Lili is just too sweet and kind. Ignoring the strange sensation whirling in my chest, I swing the door open sporting a wide smile. I stumble back as her small fist lands squarely in my nose, shocking the shit out of me. Pain radiates from my nose and across my cheeks. There was nothing feeble about that punch, and I'm feeling the consequences now. "Ow." I dab at the tiny trickle of blood seeping from my nose. "Who taught you to throw a punch?"

"Alesso," she says, storming past me into my apartment.

I don't know whether to thank him or kill him.

"I know you're angry I lied to you, but—"

She twirls around, fixing me with a poisonous look I've never been on the receiving end of before with her. She looks fucking gorgeous in a flower-patterned, knee-length skirt and a fitted black top under a black leather jacket. Her hair is down, just how I like it, with wavy strands tumbling over her shoulders and down her back. Her stunning hazel eyes are ablaze with indignation, matching the pink flush on her high cheekbones and the pouty jut of her full lips.

Lili is exquisite.

Prettiest girl I have ever seen.

I have always known this but refused to admit it because then I'd have to confront the feelings I've pushed away and shoved deep down inside for years.

But the lid is off, and I'm denying nothing anymore.

Even though I'm most likely all wrong for her, I want her too badly to do the right thing and walk away.

I'm going to be selfish to my core and fight like hell to reclaim her heart.

"You, you—" She jabs one slim finger in my chest. "How dare you pull a gun on my boyfriend!" she screams, glaring at me like she'd love to chop my head off my neck. "You had no right to show up at my place and threaten him." She throws her hands in the air. "What the hell is wrong with you?" She shakes her head, briefly looking around, and her face contorts in a grimace. "Seb doesn't know anything about *la famiglia*, and I want to keep it that way. You showing up and shoving a gun in his face isn't fucking helpful."

"Damn, your cursing really gets my juices flowing." I waggle my brows and move in closer. My gaze drops to her tempting lips as my dick stirs to life. "Angry Lili turns me on like you wouldn't believe."

Her eyes pop wide. "What?" she splutters.

I risk moving a step closer until there's only scant distance between us. "I like this side of you." I reach up and thread my fingers through her hair before leaning into her ear. "I like every side of you. You're perfect, Lili."

"What are you doing? What even is this?"

"I like you, Lili. I like you a lot." She stares at me with confusion etched all over her face. I need to do better. Swallowing a sudden bout of nerves, I force the words from my mouth. "I think I love you."

She blinks rapidly, shock written all over her face. I spot the moment she snaps out of it. "You *think* you love me?"

I nod, clasping the back of her head and drawing her face closer until our mouths are only a hair's breadth apart.

"What...what are you doing?" she whispers, watching me devour her lips with my eyes.

"I'm going to kiss you."

She shoves me so hard I stumble over my feet.

"Like hell you are!" She steps around the kitchen counter, placing a solid barrier between us.

"I'm putting the cart before the horse, I know, but this doesn't have to be complicated. You like me. I like you."

She snorts out a laugh, muttering under her breath. "Are you seriously for real right now, Caleb?"

I frown. "Why wouldn't I be?"

She throws her hands in the air as anger replaces the dazed look on her face. "Oh, I don't know. What about how you've ignored me for years while you screwed your way across the city? Or how you're suddenly interested in me now I have a boyfriend." She leans her palms on the counter and glares at me. "Or how about the fact you only *think* you love me?" Fire dances in her eyes, and I'm seriously aroused. I adjust my dick behind my jeans, purposely not disguising the motion.

Elisa glances briefly at my crotch before lifting rage-filled eyes to meet mine. "And let's not forget the biggest reason of all. You had sex with the girl who's made my life a living hell at NYU, or did you forget you let her take a ride on your dick?" she shouts.

"I didn't know she was *that* girl, or I never would've fucked her."

"The reason how it came to be really doesn't matter. It doesn't change the facts."

"She set it up to cause you pain, and I am going to make her pay."

"If that's true, it only worked because you fell for it. If you weren't such a fucking manwhore, she never would've been able to hurt me like that. So who is really at fault, Caleb?"

Shock flitters through me at her words and the venom laced behind them. Worry creeps up my spine. "I wish I could take it all back."

"But you can't, and it's irrelevant now anyway. I have moved on. I'm over you," she says, emerging from behind the protection of my island unit. "I am sooooo over you." She looks at me like she means it.

Panic jumps up and slaps me. "I lied about how it went down. I didn't know who she was, who they were. They tricked me."

"And you lied because my dad told you to cut me loose. I know, and I don't care anymore." Resignation threads through her tone, and my panic accelerates a few notches.

"I want to take you on a date," I blurt like a thirteen-year-old geek with his first crush.

Sadness shrouds her beautiful face. "There was a time that would've made me ecstatically happy, but that time has passed."

Remembering what my brother said in the car on the way to Cartier yesterday, about making myself vulnerable and showing her the real me, I prepare to admit some truths. "I've never been on a date. Never asked anyone out. You're the first. Deep down, I was saving this for you. I don't know the first thing about being in a relationship, but I'm willing to try for you because you mean everything to me, Lili." Raw sincerity bleeds from my eyes and my voice as I open myself up in a way I have never opened myself up to any other woman. "I'm sorry it took me so long to get on the same page, but I'm there now."

Her jaw momentarily trails the floor before she picks it back up. "I wish I could believe it, but I don't believe a word that comes from your mouth anymore, Caleb."

"Please, Lili." I tentatively step toward her. "I know I have fucked up real bad when it comes to you, but let me make it up to you. At least let me try."

"You can't undo the fact you had sex with my enemy. And you're too late, Caleb. It's just too late. I'm worn out from the effort involved in loving you. It took too much from me, and now it's time I put myself first." She steps right up to me with defiance in her eyes. "You're not good for me, and I don't want to be an experiment. I want to be with someone who loves me for me. Someone who doesn't deny the truth for years while screwing around with anything in a skirt. I want someone who would never hurt me like that. Someone who puts me first, and I will never come first in your life. Someone like me could never satisfy someone like you, and vice versa."

"That isn't true." I snatch her hand as she moves to walk away from me. "You are all I need and want. My past, the way I've behaved, it was never about you. It was always about me. I never believed I was worthy of you. Of love. Of having the things my brother craved, but I was wrong. About a lot of things."

"If you're having some kind of epiphany, I'm glad for you because you deserve to be happy, Caleb." She yanks her hand out of mine. "It just won't be with me."

Pain infiltrates every nook and cranny as I watch her walk down the hallway and out of my life. She stops with her hand curled around the handle, casting a glance back at me. "I like Seb, and I'm committing to my relationship with him. If you *think* you love me, you won't mess this up for me. Leave him alone, Caleb. Let me be, and maybe in time, we might be friends again, but that's all we will ever be." Steely determination resonates in the look she gives me. "You had your chance, and you blew it. Now you get to watch from the sidelines while I'm with someone else. Let's see how you like it."

Chapter Sixteen
Caleb

"How do I woo her? Tell me. You're good at this shit," I say to my buddy a week later when we're out for a drink.

Cristian chuckles. "If I have to tell you, you're going about this all wrong."

"She won't talk to me," I grumble, knocking back more of my beer and avoiding looking at the woman across the way eye fucking me every time her boyfriend gets up from the table. "It's been a week, and she's dating that douche and avoiding me. How do I fix this? How do I get her attention and get her to agree to give us a try? How do I woo her?"

"You know who she is, Caleb. You already know how to claim her attention." He taps my temple. "You have that knowledge up here. You just need to unlock it."

"What if I don't have the key?"

He chuckles. "Man, I never thought I'd see the unconquerable Caleb Accardi tied into knots over a woman. Elisa really has you in a tailspin."

"I've lost my appetite, and my sleep is shot to shit. She has consumed my brain, and she's all I think about. Even all this *mafioso* crap isn't distracting me from my Lili. I need to be with her, but she has completely shut me out. I think she blocked my number too as my text bounced back last night."

"I know you're hurting, but I'm proud of Elisa," he says, earning him an elbow in the ribs.

"You're supposed to be on my side."

"I am on your side, but you've got to admit it's poetic justice at its finest. Elisa was your little puppy dog for years, and you gave her scraps, Caleb. Fucking *scraps*."

"I know all the ways I've fucked up. I don't need you to rehash it."

"Think about how you'd feel if the shoe was on the other foot." He arches a brow as he pulls his bottle to his lips. "Imagine her out there screwing her way through the city."

"Do you actually want me to put a bullet through your skull?"

"The truth hurts, bruh." He clamps a hand on my shoulder, fighting a grin. "You pushed her to her breaking point. You forced her to move on. If you want to prove you are serious, you have to show her. No matter how long it takes, you go the distance, Caleb. You prove you can be loyal and patient. Just like she's been." He eyeballs me with a solemn look. "Are you committed enough that you'd wait years for her like she did for you?"

"Yes," I reply without hesitation.

He shakes his head. "You haven't dived deep enough to answer that with complete commitment. Until you do, don't chase after her. Give her space, and when you're sure you are completely committed to her, and only her, when you're prepared to wait for her, no matter how long that is, then and only then should you pursue her." He finishes his beer and stands. "You'll only get one shot at it. Don't blow it."

"What's this about?" I ask Joshua the next day as we meet bright and early at Commission Central for an emergency meeting.

"I don't know. Must be an update on Vegas or Florida or maybe Cruz."

"Thanks for meeting on such short notice," Massimo says, opening the meeting when we are all seated around the table. It's the first time the four new dons are here. The official announcement was made recently, and now all made men in the US are aware The Commission is a ten-man fully representative board.

"I have some intel to share, but first I'd like an update on the situation in Vegas." Massimo hands the floor to Mantegna and Agessi.

"The territory is a mess," Mantegna confirms, placing his palms on the table in front of him.

"Some things never change," Ben says, smoothing a hand down his tie.

"There are legacy issues, no doubt." Agessi sits upright in his chair. "Loyalty hasn't always been forthcoming. Saverio was a lazy asshole who never recovered from his underboss's betrayal. Catarina kept his house in order," he adds, eyeballing Massimo. Massimo's wife and Dario Agessi's wife are best friends, and Dario was her *consigliere* until he took over running the operation in Philly.

"Maybe she should step in now," Joshua says.

"No." Massimo instantly dismisses the suggestion. "My wife is not getting dragged into Vegas's shit again. We keep Cat out of this."

"How loyal are the men to Cruz and Anais?" I ask, drumming my fingers on my knee.

"There is little love lost or loyalty for those two," Mantegna replies, and it's not really a surprise. "Some of the older men are loyal to Anais because of her father, but most intensely dislike her. Cruz hasn't won many fans either. Those who were loyal to him were with him in A.C., and none of them have returned to the fold."

"We wiped a lot of them out," Cristian reminds everyone.

"He still got away with fifteen or twenty men," Volpe says.

"And he has allies," Joshua adds.

"Vegas needs to be on high alert. We can't let it fall back into Cruz's hands," Massimo says. He eyeballs Mantegna and Agessi. "How do you suggest we best protect it?"

The two men exchange a knowing look. "Neither of us can afford to be away from our territories for an extended period of time. We propose to alternate shifts. One week at a time so one of us is always there to oversee a restructure," Mantegna says.

"That seems like a workable solution," Fiero says, tossing his tie on the table. "The rest of us can take it in turns coming down for a day or two to help out."

"That would be good," Agessi says. "Morale is low, and seeing we have the support and full backing of The Commission will go a long way toward repairing the damage."

"We need to strengthen forces in the city and watch the airports and ports for any sign of Cruz. We need to devise a plan of attack that we can implement immediately should Cruz resurface in Nevada." Massimo looks directly at me. "I'd like you to go to Vegas this week to work out a strategy with Dario and Dom."

"I can't go this week. We are still rebuilding things at the grassroots level, and I'm making inroads with our men." Being on the ground every day, talking with the men and getting to know them, is already paying dividends. I'm confident in time we will have completely rebuilt loyalty, but we're still on shaky ground. I can't fuck off now without ruining all my progress. "If I take off for Vegas, it'll send the wrong message."

"I'll go," Fiero says, and Massimo nods.

"What about Florida?" Massimo eyeballs the older man with the salt-and-pepper hair and sharp gaze.

"There has been no sign of Cruz," Volpe confirms. "He hasn't shown up there."

"And he hasn't been in touch with Don D'Onofrio either," Pagano adds. "We have bugged his home, his cars, his cell phone, and his computers. We have drones and cameras watching his every move. They aren't in contact with one another."

"What were they involved in?" Cristian asks. "We know from Anais that Cruz was making weekly trips to Florida."

"He has a woman there," Volpe supplies.

"Cruz has women everywhere. That isn't the draw," I interject. "There is another reason those two became friends, and we need to discover what it is."

"Take shifts down there," Massimo says, eyeballing Pagano and Volpe. "Use the excuse we expect Cruz to make an appearance and we're concerned about the territory. It will explain the additional men I'm assigning to travel with you. I want our people all over this. Get them to befriend the Florida *soldati*. Someone knows something. If we can't get it from D'Onofrio, we'll get it from his men."

Volpe and Pagano nod their agreement.

"We learned some valuable intel from one of the men in the bunker," Massimo says, staring at Joshua and me. "He was one of the Barone we picked up in A.C. He says they were tasked with breaking into Joshua's office to get to the files in the locked room."

"Why?" J asks, his brow puckering. "What were they looking for?"

"He didn't know exactly what it was just that Maximo

wanted something in those files. Something that was clearly important."

"What's in the files?" Agessi swivels in his chair to look at us.

"They were our father's files," Joshua explains. "When we were clearing out the old apartment to sell it three years ago, we came across them buried under a mountain of crap up in the attic."

"We went through them at the time," I say. "Carefully reviewing everything because it seemed important he'd keep them at the house. They were mostly intelligence reports, details of business deals, and money in and out etcetera. Nothing stood out."

"Yet you still kept them," Pagano says.

"The one thing our father instilled in us was the need for insurance," my twin says. "It seemed remiss to just toss the files. We didn't know when they might come in handy, so I had a small storage room installed in the office and secured the files in there. Only Caleb and I have access via a retinal scanner. It has an alarm system, and we have cameras inside so if anyone breaches the room we'd know immediately."

"We need to find what my father was looking for in those files." Massimo's gaze dances between us.

"I'll go through them with a fine-tooth comb," J says.

"I'll help," Ben adds. "I was around for part of your father's time in charge, and something might stand out to me."

Chapter Seventeen
Elisa

I climb out of the taxi, holding the gift-wrapped parcel under one arm, and smile as Seb approaches, looking handsome in slim-fit designer jeans, a crisp white shirt, and a black blazer. His signature loafers cover his feet.

"Let me take that," he says, snatching the gift from under my arm.

"Thanks."

"You look gorgeous," he adds, his gaze raking appreciatively over my figure-hugging party dress before he leans in to kiss me.

"You look good too." Looping my arm through his, I cling to his side as we walk toward the exclusive club where Joshua is hosting Gia's twenty-third birthday party. I'm on edge, and not just because I'm dressed way more provocatively than normal.

I haven't seen Caleb in five weeks, and I know he's going to try to talk to me tonight.

Initially, in the week following my visit to his apartment, he bombarded me with texts and pleading messages. Then there was radio silence until a week ago when he appears to have upped the ante. Much to my boyfriend's chagrin. Seb is not a fan of Caleb or his recent attempts to woo me. My apartment smells like a flower shop, and our living space is inundated with lilies, roses, orchids, and tons of other flowers, thanks to Caleb's daily deliveries. Beatrice isn't impressed, but I think it's just jealousy talking.

The other reason I'm nervous is because tonight is the first time my parents, Romeo, Rowan, and Gia will be meeting my boyfriend, and I really want them to like him. Although he doesn't set my world on fire, and he's definitely not endgame, I'm enjoying dating Sebastien. We meet for lunch on campus a few days a week and enjoy dates a couple of nights a week. He texts me daily, making his intentions clear without smothering me. He's a decent guy, and I feel cherished, so I'm going to go with the flow for as long as this thing plays out.

We make our way inside the busy club, giving our names to the man standing guard at the door to the VIP section, which Joshua has reserved for the night.

We climb the stairs and enter the plush private space that is already heaving with partygoers. Noisy conversation, raucous laughter, and loud music accost my eardrums from all directions. The clear glass wall on our left overlooks the main club downstairs. A small square dance floor abuts the wall, and it's already filling up with gregarious guests. Beats thump through speakers from the DJ booth at the back of the room. A half-moon-shaped bar is tucked into one corner, and the rest of the place is a mix of velvet-backed circular booths and tall glossy tables and stools.

"Incoming," I murmur, smiling as Rowan walks toward us.

"Woah, sexy. Look at you!" He grabs me into a hug, lifting me off my feet.

"Put me down before I flash my panties to the entire place." I'm not even joking. My lilac bodycon dress is short though not indecent. It hits mid-thigh, and I'm flashing a lot of leg.

The second I spotted this in the store, I knew it was the perfect choice for tonight. The tight minidress is adorned with heart-shaped, iridescent, crystal-encrusted embellishments. Wide lilac-pink straps crisscross over my shoulders and in an X at my back. It dips dangerously low, just about covering my ass. My hair and makeup were professionally done, and I feel like a million dollars. The hairdresser went for a wavy beach style with a neat braided headband to keep hair out of my eyes.

"You must be Seb." Rowan loses the flirty tone and grin as he eyeballs my date.

"This is my cousin Rowan," I explain, warning Rowan with my eyes to back off.

"Nice to meet you." Seb smiles while curling his arm around my back, keeping me tucked into his side.

"Elisa is practically my sister," Rowan says, maintaining eye contact with Seb. "If you hurt her, you'll have me to deal with." He flexes his bulging biceps, ensuring the message is delivered.

"And me." Romeo appears beside Rowan, skimming his gaze up and down Seb's length with obvious wariness.

"Cut it out, you two. You're being rude." I glance up at Seb. "This is my brother Romeo. He's definitely more bark than bite."

"Elisa talks about you all the time." Seb's tone is warm, his expression casual. "You're at Yale, right?"

"Yes, but I have access to a chopper, and I can be in New York within forty minutes." He drills him with a pointed look, and there's no need to articulate the meaning.

"Oh my god, Romeo!" I whisper hiss, feeling my cheeks heat. "You don't need to threaten him."

"Just making sure he understands the score."

"Hurt her, and you hurt me," Seb says, this time forcing a smile. "I got it." He squeezes my waist. "For the record, I care about Elisa, and I have no intention of ever hurting her. You don't need to worry about me."

"And we're the least of *your* worries," Rowan adds, fighting a smirk as he looks at someone over my shoulder.

I don't need to look to guess who it is. "Let's go find Gia." I grab Seb's hand. "I'll be having words with you two later," I add, jabbing my finger between Rowan and Romeo before we walk away.

We stumble upon the oldies on our quest to find the birthday girl. Mom and Dad are seated at a booth with Nat and Leo, Sierra and Ben, and Massimo and Catarina. Dad grills Seb, but he's more polite than my brother and my cousin. The other men eye him warily, and from the way Seb is shifting on his feet, I can tell it's getting to him.

"Wow," he whispers when I finally manage to extricate us from the parents' table. "I'm beginning to understand why you were reluctant to date in the past. Your family is intense."

"I'm so sorry."

"Don't be." He smiles as I spy Gia and Joshua slinking into the room from a side door. "They're protective of you. It's a good thing."

"I know they're a lot, and I appreciate you coming as my plus one."

"It's not a chore spending time with you, Elisa." His eyes probe mine as I watch Gia and Joshua heading this way from the corner of my eye. "You've got to know I'm crazy about you."

My chest swells at his words, but I can't return them.

"You made it!" Gia says, yanking me into a hug, saving me from having to answer.

"It's not like I was going to miss it." I beam at my bestie as she attempts to smooth her hair back into place. "You look beautiful, Gigi." She's wearing a gorgeous red dress that drapes

Cruel King of New York

around her enviable curves, and the diamond pendant resting on her smaller chest is clearly new. I'm guessing it was Joshua's birthday gift. I lightly touch her bare arm. "It's healing well." Three weeks ago, she had surgery to reduce her boobs and a skin graft to repair the damage that Irish asshole inflicted on her arm.

"Yes, thankfully."

Seb's brow furrows, and I quickly change the subject. "I love your dress and your jewelry though you are missing one earring."

Her fingers immediately inspect both ears. "Shit."

"Your fly is undone," Seb says to Joshua with the hint of a grin curving the corners of his lips.

No need to guess what they were up to. Warmth crawls up my neck and onto my cheeks. I wonder if it bothers Seb I am still keeping him at arm's length? We've had oral sex, and we make out a lot, but I don't feel ready to go all the way with him yet. He says he's fine to wait, but he's a hot, virile guy. Don't guys his age have sex on the brain all the time?

Joshua quickly fixes himself. "Thanks, man." Gia's boyfriend wears a familiar mask, shielding his true emotions. The man is a master at hiding in plain sight. "I'll go grab your earring," he says, leaning in to plant a hard, possessive kiss on Gia's lips before walking off.

"You must be Sebastien." Gia thrusts her hand out. "I'm Gia. Elisa's best friend and chief asshole detector."

I barely stifle a groan. "Please, not you too. Poor Seb has already endured interrogations by Rowan, Romeo, Dad, and all the uncles. Cut him some slack."

Seb shakes her hand. "I'm beginning to understand why Elisa hasn't dated before."

"Don't take it personally. She has a lot of people who love her and watch out for her."

"Happy birthday, babe," I say, grabbing the gift from under Seb's arm and handing it to Gia.

It's a shameless ploy to distract her, and it works.

Peeling off the wrapping paper, she gasps when she uncovers the black and gold Valentino purse. "I love it. Thank you." She grabs me into a bear hug. "Don't look now," she whispers in my ear. "But Caleb is coming this way."

I sigh. Of course, he is. He just can't take no for an answer.

Slipping out of Gia's embrace, I thread my fingers in Seb's and squeeze his hand.

"Hey, Lili."

Ignoring how fast my heart is beating, I plaster a sociable smile on my face and turn to face the guy I still love with my entire being. Seb bristles beside me, curving his hand around my shoulder and keeping me close as we face Caleb.

"Hi." I peer deep into his eyes even though every instinct warns me not to look at him.

Fuck. He looks good enough to eat in a black suit jacket with a gold trim. His fitted black shirt is open at the top, revealing a hint of hard, smooth, tan skin. Matching pants and glossy black dress shoes complete his look. His facial hair is trimmed, and his hair is artfully messy.

He steals all the air from my lungs even though I've sworn to forget him. It's hard when I still love him so much. I think I always will. Caleb has this inexplicable power over me, and I hate it. I need to find a way of setting my feelings aside and accepting there will never be an us. I have accepted the latter, but I still need to work on the former.

I cling to Seb's side and draw strength from his body heat. Tension oozes from his every pore. Watching Caleb drag his gaze leisurely up and down my body more than explains it. "You are fucking stunning, Elisa. The most beautiful woman in the room by a mile, present company excluded," he adds, tipping his head toward the birthday girl.

"She's taken," Seb snarls, hooking his arm around me tighter.

"We need to talk," Caleb says, blatantly ignoring my boyfriend.

"I have nothing to say to you."

"I have plenty."

"Tough." Seb grips my hand tight. "We were just leaving for the dance floor." He pulls me away from Caleb. "You'll have to excuse us."

Caleb fixes him with a smug grin, easily stepping back. "Be my guest." He sweeps his arm out in dramatic fashion. "Enjoy it." He loses the grin and sharpens his gaze on Sebastien. "She might be yours for now, but she's always been mine. That will never change." He puts his face all up in Seb's. "Your time is running out, preppy boy."

I glare at Caleb as I drag Seb away, pushing through the busy dance floor until we are hidden in the center of the dancing crowd. A slow number starts, and I wind my hands around Seb's neck feeling the tension cording his muscles. "Do you regret coming?"

"Of course not," he says through clenched teeth. "I just can't stand that guy." His hands press firmly on my lower back, drawing my body into his.

"Ignore him," I say, feeling eyeballs drilling a hole in the back of my head.

"It's hard when he's fucking everywhere." His hard expression pins me in place. "You need to tell him to fuck off, Elisa. He can't keep sending you flowers and cupcakes and making it clear he wants you. It's disrespectful to me. He needs to back off."

"I blocked his number, remember?" Seb was furious when

Caleb kept texting, calling, and leaving messages, so I blocked him to smooth things over. It's just as well he doesn't know Caleb has also been sending me love letters, and yesterday a box full of art supplies was delivered.

Caleb is making it hard to hold on to my resolve. A part of me is reveling in being wooed like this. My teenager self is jumping cartwheels and repeatedly writing his name in love hearts all over my journal.

"You need to get rid of the flowers," Seb adds, moving us back farther. "It makes me sick every time I'm at your place. Imagine it in reverse. How would you feel if my ex was sending me gifts all the time?"

"He isn't my ex." I feel the need to clarify even though Seb already knows this. I might have downplayed my feelings for Caleb, but that was purely self-preservation. What guy wants to date a girl who foolishly spent years pining after a guy who didn't want her? It screams pathetic with a capital P, so I gave Seb the censored version—Caleb and I were friends, but I'd been hoping for more, and now I've moved on.

"He acts like he is." A muscle pops in his jaw as he glowers over my head, and I turn rigid in his arms.

"I'll remove the flowers," I rush to reassure him, willing the murderous glint in his eye to disappear. Perhaps it was a mistake to invite him tonight. All it has done is piss him off and served to highlight all the ways he doesn't fit into my world. "I can't bear to throw them out though. The flowers are innocent. I'll donate them to the hospital," I decide as the idea comes to me.

Caleb appears on our right, dancing with his mother, in what appears to be a deliberate attempt to irritate my boyfriend.

"Hi again," Nat smiles at me and Seb as his grip tightens on my back. His fingers are digging into my bare skin, and it's starting to hurt a little.

"Mind if I cut in?" Caleb fakes a smile as he challenges Seb with a caustic stare.

"Actually, I do." Seb squeezes me flush against his body, pressing even harder on my back in a way that is now definitely painful.

"You're hurting her." Caleb's nostrils flare, and he stares at Seb's hands like he wishes he could incinerate them with his eyes.

"You gonna pull a gun on me again?" Seb asks, loosening his tight grip on my back a little.

A shocked gasp escapes my lips. I can't believe he just said that! Has he no sense of self-preservation?

"Need I remind you it's Gia's birthday?" Natalia says, her warning gaze skating between both men. "Whatever this is, you need to end it now."

"It's fine, Mom. *Sebastien* won't prevent me from dancing with Lili." Caleb drills him with a deadly look. "It wouldn't make a good first impression." Caleb squares up to him. "Now, would it?"

"Stop this," I hiss, aware we are starting to garner looks. I spy Leo making his way toward us wearing a frown.

"Five minutes, Lili. That's all I'm asking for. Just five minutes and I'll leave you alone. I promise."

I look up at Seb's seething face, and I should walk off with him, but I know Caleb. He's stubborn when he wants something, and he'll make this night hell for both of us if I don't let him have his say. I stretch up and press my mouth to Seb's ear. "I'll talk to him and set him straight once and for all."

Seb's anger transforms as he moves his lips to my ear. "You have three minutes and not a second longer. Make it clear, Elisa. He needs to quit this shit."

Three minutes will not be enough, but I'm not splitting hairs. I nod, moving to ease out of his arms when a look of wicked intent passes over his face. Grabbing my ass and pulling me into him, he dips me down low and slams his lips over mine before I can voice my protest.

Chapter Eighteen
Caleb

"Not here," Dad says, pulling me back as I see red.

"He's fucking mauling her in public, in full view of her family," I growl, clenching and unclenching my hands at my sides as I watch that fucking preppy dickhead shove his disgusting tongue in Lili's mouth and squeeze her ass.

"It's not fun being on the other side, is it?" Cristian asks, materializing beside me. He must have just arrived. Over his head, I spot his girl making her way toward the bar. She's linking arms with Zumo's girl, but there's no sign of our other buddy.

It's not fun. It's hell on earth, and I want to pump preppy boy full of bullets and bathe in his blood. The dick straightens up, and I make my move. "You've made your point," I snap, yanking Lili out of his arms and into mine—where she belongs. "Make yourself useful. Go buy drinks." I stuff a hundred-dollar bill in the top pocket of his blazer.

Taking the money, he literally throws it back in my face. "I don't need or want your money."

Lili squirms, attempting to wriggle out of my embrace, but I hold her closer, careful not to hurt her like that prick was doing.

The dick jabs his finger in my face. He's got balls. I'll give him that. "Keep your grabby hands to yourself."

"Or what?" I'm tempted to run my hands all over Elisa's body to wind him up, but I won't objectify her like this douche just did.

"Or maybe I'll be the one pulling a gun next time."

Cristian stiffens. Leo narrows his eyes. Mom glares, and I laugh. "I'd pay good money to see you try." I push up into his face, letting my true darkness rise to the surface. "I guarantee one of us would die, and it wouldn't fucking be me."

"Seb, just go to the bar. Please." I can't see Elisa's face, but whatever she's showcasing is enough to have him spinning on his heels and striding away.

"You cannot be serious about this guy," I say as Lili whirls around, shooting daggers at me with her eyes.

"You just can't help yourself, can you, Caleb? You can't let me be happy. You have to try and ruin it before it's even begun."

Leo pulls Mom into his arms, and they move away to dance even though I can tell Mom is dying to say something. I know she'd love me with Elisa, but she's got to butt out. When I reclaim Elisa's heart, I want it to be for all the right reasons. Not because our moms want it and pushed us together.

I glance at Cristian's retreating back before taking Lili's much smaller hand in mind. Steering her off the dance floor, I guide us over to one of the alcoves. I shield Elisa with my body as her spine presses into the wall. "I don't want to talk about him," I say, looking longingly at her tempting lips.

"My eyes are up here, Caleb," she says, timidly placing her hands on my chest and giving me a little shove. "And you need to back up. You're crowding me."

Reluctantly, I push off the wall and take a step back. Her hands drop to her sides. I keep my gaze trained on her eyes instead of the lush lips I really want to taste. I know I won't have long, so there isn't time to mince my words. "I love you, Lili. I love you so fucking much." Her eyes pop wide in shock, and I press on. "I have loved you for years but denied it for a whole heap of reasons. I messed up the last time we spoke, and I didn't explain myself clearly. I was struggling to decipher my feelings, but I'm not struggling anymore."

Taking her hand, I place it on my chest, right over the spot where my heart is pounding. "I know what I feel in here is true. I love you, and I want to be with you. I understand it's not as simple as that. I know I have hurt you, and I wish there was a way to take it all back, but I can't. I'm just asking you to give me a chance. Let me prove to you I'm serious. Let me prove to both of us what *you* have always known—we are meant to be together."

Tears well in her eyes. "You only want me because someone else does."

"That's not true."

"Isn't it?" She ducks out from the alcove. "You need to let this go, Caleb. It's too late, and honestly, I, I...I don't believe you."

"I'm not giving up, Lili." I take her hand and link our fingers. Delicious warmth inches up my arm, and my skin is tingling all over. "Tell me you don't feel that." She gulps, and I move my hands to cup her beautiful, beautiful face. "Tell me he makes you feel the same things I do, and I'll walk away. I'll concede defeat and leave you alone."

Her mouth opens and closes. She wants to lie, but Lili doesn't have it in her. "It doesn't matter." She removes my hands from her face. "I don't want the same things I wanted before."

"You're settling, and he's not good enough for you." No one ever will be, including me.

"It's none of your business, Caleb. You don't get to control my life."

"I wouldn't dream of trying." I reclaim the distance between us. "I want you to be happy. I only ever want the best things for you. We could be so good together. We *are* good together." I thread my fingers through her soft wavy hair, silently berating myself for all the years I wasted when she could have been mine. "You can't deny we've always connected on a deep level just like you can't deny we have epic chemistry."

"I'm not denying anything. I'm saying I don't want it anymore. There is a difference. I'm making a conscious decision to close the door on any idea of us, and you need to respect my wishes. You have to stop sending me flowers and gifts. You need to walk away, Caleb."

"Please, Lili." I cup her cheeks again. "I know I'm not worthy, but if you give me a chance, I swear I'll never let you down again."

"Time's up, dickhead." Preppy boy hauls Lili into his chest, and pain stabs me through the heart when her arms go around his waist.

"Just like yours will be soon." I eyeball him with all the contempt I feel toward him. "You're not good enough for her, and it's only a matter of time before she realizes it." I swing my gaze to Lili. "I meant what I said. I will wait for you for eternity if I have to." My eyes flicker over her gorgeous face. "I'm going nowhere. I'll be patient and watch you work your way through a hundred assholes if that's what it'll take for you to accept you were always right."

"Fuck off," Seb snaps, earning a scowl from Lili.

"I'll be watching you," I warn him as I force myself to walk away. If I stay, I'll only hit the prick, and I won't ruin my brother's plan. Glancing at the time, I quicken my pace.

Ignoring voices that call out and arms that reach for me as I walk across the room, I make a beeline for the bar where my brother awaits.

"Hey." I climb onto a stool beside him.

"How did it go?" he asks.

"About how I expected."

"She'll come around. She loves you too much not to."

"I guess we'll see." I clamp a hand on his shoulder. "Are you ready?"

"As ready as I'll ever be." He slides his hand in his pants pocket and smiles.

"She's coming out of the bathroom now," I advise, spotting Gia's blonde head across the room.

"It's now or never." Joshua stands, letting his nerves show for a fleeting second.

"You've got this. You already know she's going to say yes," I remind him.

"She might not like I'm surprising her in front of everyone."

"She'll love it." I give him a playful shove, and he walks off.

Cristian comes up beside me as Joshua makes his way to the DJ booth to collect the mic.

"First one down," Cristian says as we stand side by side, listening to my brother call his girl onto the now empty dance floor.

"You'll be next," I say, stealing my brother's scotch and finishing it.

A crowd has formed around Joshua and Gia, but we still have a good vantage point from here. Gia's parents stand proudly at the front, looking like they're about to burst with excitement. Joshua did things the traditional way. He visited Rico and Frankie last night and asked her dad for permission to marry his only daughter. A chuckle rips from my lips as I imagine asking Alesso for Elisa's hand. He'd probably shoot me.

"You sure it won't be you?" Cristian arches a brow, attempting to hide his smirk.

"He told you, didn't he?" I ask. Cristian nods, and I shake my head as I watch my twin get on bended knee before Gia.

"Buying a ring is a big deal, Caleb. It shocked the shit out of me when Joshua told me."

"It's the perfect ring for Lili. I couldn't pass up the opportunity even if it's just burning a hole in my safe and it's likely to do so for some time."

Gia has tears in her eyes as Joshua asks her to marry him. Gasps and oohs and aahs spread around the room.

"I'm making a bet," Cristian says, smiling as Gia flings herself at my brother screaming yes repeatedly while peppering his face with kisses. "Before the year is out, we'll be attending a double Accardi wedding." He bobs his head, still smiling. "Yeah, I can see it now." His smile expands. "And yes."

"Yes, what?"

"Yes, I'll be your best man." He waggles his brows and tugs on my arm, pulling me toward the soon-to-be bride and groom. "Time to offer our congratulations."

Chapter Nineteen
Caleb

"**W**as it sore?" Gia asks, pointedly staring at my groin.

"Is this the way it's going to be from now on?" I ask, glaring at my brother as we duck behind the wall of the apartment building the girls live in. "You blabbing my private business to your girl every time I confide something in you?"

"*Fiancée*." Gia thrusts her hand in my face, and her glistening engagement ring almost blinds me. Joshua bought her the biggest diamond even though he knows Gia would have been equally as thrilled with a much smaller ring. The ring I chose for Lili is more subtle but no less stunning.

"I know," I drawl, squinting as the door to the building opens. "You never stop shoving that thing in everyone's faces."

"It's just so pretty," she purrs. Her arms go around my brother's neck, and I roll my eyes. Here we go again. They have been all over one another since they got engaged. "I'm the luckiest girl alive. I love you, Joshua. So, so much." Predictably, his lips claim hers, and I heave a sigh as the three girls who emerge from the building aren't the three girls we're here for.

Panting and moaning ensues as they devour one another, and I've had enough. Slapping the back of Joshua's head, I hiss, "Quit that shit. All the slobbering makes me want to puke."

"Jealous much, Caleb?" Gia preens while draping herself all over my brother, sporting full lips that are now swollen and glossy.

I flip her the bird.

"Did you really do it for Lili?" she asks, all hint of humor gone from her expression in a nanosecond.

"Yes," I say through gritted teeth, sending a fresh glare my brother's way. We need to have a conversation about privacy. Not that I really mind. Gia is already like a sister to me, and we bicker and bitch like real siblings. It's hard not to like her. She's spunky, smart, and brave, and she makes my brother so incredibly happy. She's got a fan for life in me for that reason alone.

"She doesn't even know though, does she?"

I shake my head as the door opens again, illuminating the lone man exiting the building.

"Why did you get a vasectomy in the first place?" she inquires, genuine curiosity splaying across her face.

"I'm not fully sure," I admit. "I thought it was because I never wanted kids, but now I realize that isn't entirely true."

"You didn't want to risk having kids with anyone else," Gia says, proving her observation and analytical skills are not lacking.

"I didn't consciously decide that, but yes, that's what it boils down to."

"And now that you've finally taken your head from your ass and realized Lili is the one for you, you want to have kids with her," she adds.

"You could be a therapist if this new role doesn't work out

for you," I tease, glancing at the time on my watch and wondering if we should call it a night. It's Thursday, and the PI I hired via Ben's security firm to shadow Gwyneth and her friends said they have a regular Thursday night club date, but maybe we picked the one Thursday they have decided to stay home.

"I like my promotion, and I've got zero desire to listen to other people's problems."

"I like it too," J agrees. "I won't worry now you're largely office based."

Gia decided she didn't want any more field roles after the shit that went down last year. But she's a shrewd informant, so Massimo promoted her to team manager, overseeing the intel-gathering division. She will work closely with Philip, Don Mazzone's IT guy, and together the two teams plan to improve the intelligence available to support our work. Presently, she's working with Joshua reviewing all our bio dad's files to identify what old man Greco was looking for.

The door swings open, revealing three women who are unfortunately familiar to me. Finally. It feels like I've been plotting to take these bitches down forever. "Showtime." Rubbing my hands with glee, I summon patience as we wait for the women to walk by our hiding spot.

When they appear, we spring into action grabbing one each and jabbing them in the neck with the diphenhydramine sleeping aid. They go down quickly and quietly with the element of surprise, and Vittus opens the side door of the van, allowing us to toss them inside.

"The others should be here shortly," I tell Vittus and Giulio ninety minutes later when the unconscious girls are each secured to chairs in one of the interrogation cells of the bunker. We dropped Gia and Joshua off at Elisa's place on the way. I want Lili here to witness this, but I'm unsure if she'll appreciate the gesture or not. I had thought of not including her and telling her after the fact, but I won't hide this part of myself from her. If we stand any chance of a future together, she needs to understand what it truly means to love a man like me.

That's a big *if* though. She's still dating *Sebastien*, she still hasn't unblocked my cell, and she is now refusing my flower and gift deliveries, so I'm trying to think outside the box.

Mom told me Elisa is going to form an official graphic design business when she graduates in a few weeks. I'm not surprised. She's so talented, and she's already got a decent side business. It shouldn't take much to expand it into a full-fledged full-time company. Maybe I can help with that. My brain churns ideas as my cell pings with an incoming call.

It's the doofus new guard from our building. "Accardi," I answer, picking at a nonexistent thread on my shirt as I listen to his boring monotone. "I don't want them in my place. Get them to leave it in the lobby. I'll send a few men down to take care of it."

"Problems?" Giulio asks when I hang up.

"Nah." I tap out a message on my cell. "My new bed just arrived."

"What happened?" Vittus grins. "You break the old one?"

"Nope." I repocket my cell after directing a couple of *soldati* who live on the floor below mine to take care of it. "The old one had to go."

Our underboss and *consigliere* stare at me expectantly, waiting for me to elaborate, but I'm offering nothing.

A muffled moan claims all our attention as we watch the redhead slowly come to. With perfect timing, the door creaks open behind us and Gia, Joshua, and a scowling Lili step into the room. I breathe a sigh of relief at the sight of her. I was a little concerned Gia wouldn't be able to convince her to come.

Her eyes widen, and her mouth forms an O when she spots the three women tied to chairs in the dank, dirty cell. Tears are leaking from the redhead's eyes as she frantically looks around the room, panicking behind the tape covering her mouth.

"Oh my god," Elisa whispers before clamping a hand over her chest.

I get up and walk toward her, trying to ignore how my heart is jumping somersaults in my chest. I'm like an addict in need of a fix any time I see Elisa these days. I miss her so fucking much. Not getting to see her or talk to her is akin to missing a limb. I had taken her presence in my life for granted, but never again. If I'm lucky enough to convince her to take a chance on me, I will cherish every second we spend together.

"Thanks for coming." I step right in front of her, blocking her view of the three girls who have made her life hell. From what Gia has said, the pixie-haired bitch was the main instigator, but the other two have joined in on occasion, so they are far from blameless.

I'm going to enjoy ripping their lives to shreds.

Right about now, our guys should be planting the drug evidence in their apartment. It's enough to have them sent down for at least a couple of years once the call goes out to our police and judicial contacts. They'll ensure they are arrested and sent down for the crimes.

"What is this, Caleb?" Lili asks, her expression a confusing mix of conflicting emotions.

"Payback, angel. It's time these girls got what's coming to them, and I wanted you to see this."

Her eyes drift over my shoulder as additional muffled moaning confirms the other two are now awake.

"This is wrong," she whispers, chewing on the corner of her mouth.

"Is it?"

She continues nibbling on her lips. "Two wrongs don't make a right."

"This is about doling out justice, pure and simple." I place my hands on her shoulders, peering deep into her troubled eyes. "They have tormented you for years, and the bitches targeted me to deliberately hurt you. They also recorded me without permission." Not that I'd have ever given it. I'm usually more careful, but I'd been high as a kite that night and clearly not thinking straight.

"They have this coming," I add. "I should kill them, but I'm letting them live. Their punishment will be payment enough." I can't resist brushing my fingers along her soft cheek. Her skin is so smooth under my fingertips, and I wonder if the rest of her feels the same. My dick jerks behind my zipper, and I caution it to calm down because this isn't the time or place.

I haven't been with any woman in months, and my dick is growing tired of my hand. But I'll just have to get used to it because I'm serious about proving to Lili I'm a changed man. I had no shortage of offers at the party on Saturday, and I easily and happily turned every one down.

The only woman I want is the one woman who wants nothing to do with me.

How's that for irony?

"Caleb?" Elisa snaps me out of my head, and I realize I've just been caressing her face and staring at her like a loon.

"I wanted you to be here, but if it's too much, you can leave. I won't force you."

Something indecipherable crosses over her face, but it's gone just as fast. She moves back, out of my reach. "I want to stay. I want to bear witness to whatever you have planned."

"That's my girl."

"Caleb," she grits out a warning. "That's a surefire way to make me leave."

"I'm sorry," I lie, moving my mouth to her ear. "I love you, Lili." I straighten up and turn around, not waiting to see her reaction.

Chapter Twenty
Caleb

"Let's get this show on the road," I murmur to the room, nodding at Vittus as I stride past him and head for the ringleader. Vittus hops up and together we rip the tape off each girl's mouth. The blonde cries, the redhead screams, and the black-haired cunt glares at me without making a sound.

"This is kidnapping," Gwyneth says, continuing to glare until she spots Elisa behind me, and it's like a switch has flipped in her head. Her glare becomes a provocative pout as she licks her lips and rakes her gaze over me from head to toe. "Unless it's round two and we're role-playing. I'm definitely down for that."

"I wouldn't let your treacherous cunt anywhere near my cock, and I hate to burst your bubble, but you suck at sex."

She barks out a laugh while the blonde continues to sob, and the redhead remains mute. "I know this is for *her* benefit, but you can't lie to me. We were hot together." Before I can retaliate, she fixes Elisa with a cunning look and grins. "He fucking loved my pussy wrapped around his cock." Racing footsteps approach, and I glance over my shoulder as Elisa approaches. "He couldn't get enough. He—" Her head snaps back as Lili lands a solid punch on her nose.

I make a mental note to thank Alesso for that.

"Damn," Vittus says, sending Elisa an admiring glance. I narrow my eyes at him, and he chuckles.

"Give it to her, Lise," Gia encourages. Joshua has his arms wrapped around her from behind, and she's leaning her head back against his chest as they watch this go down.

"Shut your hideous mouth." Elisa looms over Gwyneth. "No one wants to hear anything you have to say."

"I beg to differ," she says as blood trickles from her nose, down over her lips, and onto her chin. "You want to live vicariously through us because we got to fuck the guy you love. You know you'll never be good enough to please a man like him, so—"

This time, I land the punch, shoving my fist in her mouth to shut her up. Mom raised us to never lift our voice or raise our fists against a woman in anger.

But she was talking about ladies.

She said nothing about lying cunts, so my conscience is clear.

The sound of teeth cracking is music to my ears, and my grin expands when she emits an agonized cry as her head whips painfully back.

"Let's get one thing straight, bitch." I grab her hair and keep her head suspended at an angle that's got to hurt. "Elisa is the only woman I have ever truly wanted, and she is more than good enough for me. It's I who isn't worthy of her."

"Fuck. You," she says, spitting blood all over my shirt. A sick smirk ghosts over her blood-coated lips. "Oops, I already did."

"Shut up, Gwyn," the redhead says, finally finding her

voice. The blonde is still sobbing and cowering in her chair. "Stop antagonizing him."

"Wake the fuck up, Cara! We're tied to chairs in some godforsaken shithole. We're not getting out of this alive, so we might as well have some fun."

I drop Gwyneth's head and straighten up, sidling closer to Lili. Turning my gaze to her, I silently ask the question. She nods, and warmth floods my chest. "You're wrong," I deadpan, whipping my eyes to the three women tied to chairs. "You will make it home. There's no fun in killing you, though I seriously considered it."

"You're letting us go?" the blonde asks in a timid voice, her words underscored with weak hope.

"Yes, but don't throw a party yet. You won't be getting off scot-free. Crimes deserve punishment."

"Who the fuck made you judge and jury?" Gwyneth scoffs.

"He's the king of New York," Elisa says, her voice projecting confidence and pride. "Caleb can do whatever he wants, and there's no one to stop him."

"You're so pathetic, you—"

Elisa silences her with another punch to the face, and my dick is fucking loving this assertive side of her personality.

"Elisa, please." The blonde turns pleading eyes on my love. "I'm sorry, all right? I never wanted to be mean. When we met in freshman year, I thought you were cool." She narrows her eyes at her dark-haired friend. "It was all Gwyn's idea because she was jealous."

"Gotta love when the claws come out," Giulio says, spearing me with a smirk.

"Shut your face, Susie," Gwyneth snaps.

"No." The blonde develops a backbone, straightening up. "Cara and I are in this mess because of you."

"Everything was her idea," Cara agrees.

"You were more than happy to go along with it!" Gwyneth snaps.

"She's always been really jealous of you, Elisa," Susie says. "You're pretty and super smart and always so nice. Everyone on campus loves you, and she couldn't stand it."

"She saw Caleb on campus with you a few times, and she wanted him," Cara adds.

I fold my arms over my chest and step back, letting them throw their friend to the wolves. "She overheard you talking about him a couple of times to Shea, so she knew you two were close and that you loved him. She's been plotting to go after him for years, but we could never get close enough."

"You gave her the opening she'd been looking for," Susie says.

"Me?" Elisa's eyes pop wide.

"You told Shea about the fashion show. Gwyn's auntie works for House of Fashion, and she got us in and gave us fake IDs."

At least that explains how they got into the show. I make a mental note to find the name of her aunt and have her fired.

"That might all be true," Gwyneth says, "but we didn't fake our way onto his cock. Caleb was more than happy to party with us and take us home. And I don't care what bullshit you spout, no one fucks girls all night long—"

Elisa bitch slaps her across the face, and it's enormously satisfying. My cock is flying at half-mast now, and I discreetly adjust myself so no one notices.

"Hot damn," Vittus says.

"Don't you get it? He does that all the time," Elisa says.

Did, I whisper in my head, but I don't verbalize it.

"You weren't anything special. He didn't even remember you. He never remembers because you're all replaceable."

Isn't that the truth? None of those nameless, faceless

women I screwed ever meant anything to me. Cruel? Yes, but it's no lie.

I spent years trying to deny my feelings for Lili, submerging myself in booze, easy women, and the occasional recreational drug, because I was scared to confront what was in my heart and terrified I'd never be good enough for her. I don't remember the women I've fucked because they were only placeholders. I never cared enough to even go back for seconds. Lili is the only woman, except Mom, who has ever mattered and the only one I truly love.

Deep-seated contentment settles in my bones as I absorb the truth and fully believe it.

Elisa Salerno is it for me. My destiny. My dream woman. The mother of my children. The keeper of my heart.

Now I just have to convince her of it.

"The only one I ever see is you." I peer deep into her eyes as I say it, hoping she at least sees the truth even if she refuses to hear it. I have a lot of regrets, and I wish I could erase my past with women, but I can't. What I've done may be the cross I die on. I can't rewrite my history, but I *can* ensure I don't repeat the same mistakes.

Even if she never forgives me or never gives me a shot, I am done fucking other women. They hold no appeal.

"Yeah, he was really seeing your face the whole time he was fucking me," Gwyneth snarls, sarcasm thick in her tone as she ruins the moment.

I'm reconsidering keeping her alive.

I slam my fist into her stomach, not holding back. I toss a glance over my shoulder at Vittus. "What, no damn for me?"

"It's not hot when you do it."

"I pity you," Elisa says to the bitch, cutting across our conversation. "Have you really invested all this time and expended all this energy just to one-up me?"

"She has," Cara confirms. "She's the pathetic one. Not you."

"No one could ever replace Elisa in my affections," I say.

"You failed." Elisa lets a grin run free as she stares the mean girl down. "You failed, and you're going to pay for it, big-time." She turns to me, taking my hand and smiling softly. "What did you do?"

"You're not going to hurt us, right?" Susie says, flicking her eyes from me to Elisa.

"You might not have instigated it, but you're both far from innocent," I say, clutching Elisa's hand. Her small palm is warm against mine, and the usual fiery tremors zip up and down my arm. No one's touch has ever ignited my blood like my Lili's touch.

"You could have stopped it, stopped her, at any time," Elisa says, "but you let her belittle me, time and time again. Like Caleb said, you're far from innocent."

Susie starts crying again.

"I'm sorry, Elisa. More than you will ever know," Cara says.

"You're only sorry you got caught," Gia says. She eyeballs me with purpose, knowing how this will go down because she helped to set it all up. "Throw the book at them, Caleb. They deserve it."

My phone pings at that exact moment with a video confirming everything is going like clockwork. Playing press on the video, I turn my screen around so the three girls can see. "What the fuck?" Cara's eyes almost bug out of her head. "What's going on at our place?"

"The cops have discovered a large narcotics stash in your apartment, and a warrant for all three of your arrests has just been issued. News reports are flashing pictures of your faces. The dean has been advised, and your expulsion papers are being typed up as we speak."

Shock splays across Cara's face as Susie dissolves into more tears.

"You won't get away with it," Gwyneth barks. "We'll tell them it's a setup."

"The cops work for us."

"Then we'll hire lawyers!"

"With what money? The large amounts deposited into your back accounts are being frozen as evidence of drug dealing, and you'll never get your hands on it. And don't bank on your families to help either." I swipe my finger across the screen, showing how I've drained their families' bank accounts.

"I'll sell my house," Gwyneth retorts.

"You mean the house your grandma left you that's being repossessed in the morning?"

"You can't repossess a house when the mortgage has already been paid, asshole."

"You can if you know a guy who hacked into the bank system and doctored the records to show a mortgage deficit that has slipped through the cracks." She opens her mouth to retaliate again, but I cut across her. "And don't think the paperwork you have on file will help because we hacked into your laptop and destroyed all the evidence, along with the illegal recordings you made of me, and the backups you saved to the cloud. That USB key in the top drawer of your desk in your bedroom met an unfortunate death, along with your car." Her face finally pales as I show her the video of her car engulfed in flames.

"I'll go the press. I'll tell them what you've done." Her lower lip wobbles as it finally dawns on her.

I grab her chin and thrust her head back, digging my nails into her flesh. "I'll put a bullet in your skull before you get the chance." Letting all my darkness shine, I pour it into the look I give her. "In case you need additional incentive, if you breathe a word about me or Elisa or any of this, I will kill every member of your family." I let her chin go to pull up the files I got from the PI. Her face is like a ghost as I flick through photos of every member of her family. "I can have them all taken out in the blink of an eye." I snap my fingers before turning my attention to the other two girls.

"The same goes for you two." I show them photos of their loved ones as well. I'm banking on Cara and Susie making a deal and hanging Gwyneth out to dry. All of them will do time, but with her friends pointing the finger in her direction, Gwyneth will spend the longest time in jail, and it's how I want it to go down. "In case any of you get ideas in jail, know I can get to you there too. Even whisper my fucking name, and you'll pay a heavy price. *Capiche?*"

"Please don't do this," Susie cries. "I don't want to go to prison."

"You should have thought about that before you hurt the woman I love." Out of the corner of my eye, I spot Giulio and Vittus exchanging a shocked look. "You targeted the wrong people. If Gwyn hadn't sent Elisa that video, maybe this wouldn't have happened," I lie, just wanting them to really drive the knife into her back when they make their statements. "You are lucky I'm letting you live."

Silent tears stream down Gwyneth's face as the truth about how screwed she is finally hits home. "Let this be a life lesson. Don't be a cunt. Serve your time, and when you get out, you disappear. Come near Elisa again, and I won't be so lenient next time."

Chapter Twenty-One
Caleb

"**F**uck, at last! I've been calling you nonstop for the past ten minutes," Joshua says when I answer his call after stepping out of the meeting.

Urgency threads through his tone, and I'm instantly on high alert. "I had that meeting with the brand management company this morning." I did tell him, but he's walking around with his head in the clouds this past week since he put a ring on Gia's finger.

"Where are you?" he asks as I exit the building and nod at the two *soldati* who accompanied me to Midtown. Even though the mysterious Italian boss has reached out and a truce is in place until the big meeting next week, Massimo warned everyone not to drop our security detail.

"I'm on Fifth Avenue. Why?"

"Get to Twenty-eighth Street. We've had a sighting of Cruz at a physical therapy clinic."

I instantly take off running with my men hot on my heels. It would take too long to drive the five blocks, and it sounds like time is of the essence. "You should have fucking led with that!"

I shout into my cell. "I'll call you when I get there," I say before hanging up.

Thanks to daily workouts at my home gym and regular jogs through Central Park, I make it to the clinic in six minutes without breaking a sweat even in suit pants and dress shoes. Police tape wraps around the front of the building, and several cops stand guard, holding the inquisitive crowd back. Reporters aren't on the scene yet, but it won't take long before someone shows up.

Spotting a familiar face, I jog over to Captain Hayes, glancing all around me for any sign of Cruz. It's a busy Saturday, and the city is crowded. I'm guessing if Cruz was here he has since slipped away.

"Hey," I greet Captain Hayes. "What happened here?"

He scrubs a hand over his smooth-shaven chin. "Nothing good." He pulls up the tape. "Come on, I'll show you." We duck under the tape, walking toward the covered body lying on the sidewalk just beside the door of the physical therapy clinic. A stroller is pitched on its side, baby toys spilling onto the asphalt. A sense of dread washes over me as the dots quickly connect in my head.

"She had no ID," the captain says, ensuring no one is looking as we hunch over the body, shielding it from prying eyes. He pulls back the top of the covering to reveal the dead woman underneath.

"Shit." It's as I feared. "Her name is Bettina Da Rosa. I'm guessing her baby was taken?"

Captain Hayes re-covers the body, and we stand off to one side, away from the crowd, to talk in hushed tones. "Yes. Tell me what you know."

"Cruz DiPietro is the father. He did this. We had reports of a sighting. Don't suppose any of your guys got a look at him or saw the direction he went in?"

He shakes his head. "The perp was long gone by the time we got to the scene. The receptionist at the clinic called it in. Miss Da Rosa was a client, and she'd just left after an appointment when a car pulled up to the curb and fired at her. She was shot where she was standing. A man jumped out of the car and grabbed the baby."

"Did the receptionist give a description?"

"Yes, but she was in too much shock to give us much. All she could say was he had dark hair, looked to be late thirties or early forties, and he had a limp."

If the situation wasn't so grave, I'd laugh and fist pump the air. Gia got the bastard good. "Definitely Cruz." I look around, scowling when I spot a couple of news vans pulling up. "I've got to get out of here. Keep this contained. We'll handle telling next of kin, and we'll find the bastard. If you get any leads on his whereabouts, call it in."

"You can count on it, Don Accardi."

"Good man." I clamp a hand on his shoulder and disappear through the front door of the clinic. I approach the front desk where a traumatized older woman is talking to a lady policewoman. "You got a back door?" I ask, removing my cell to call my brother with an update.

"Did we get any leads from surveillance cameras?" I ask a few hours later when we are all congregated around the conference table at Commission Central. Volpe and Mantegna are dialed in from Florida and Vegas respectively.

"We were able to track him leaving the city, but there are a few camera black spots, and we lost him after that," Ben says, pressing a button to pull up a report on the large screen.

"Motherfucker," Cristian growls when his brother's image

loads on the screen. There are cameras all over Fifth Avenue, so we have a perfect view as he hops out of a blacked-out SUV and hobbles across the sidewalk. Bettina is bleeding out on the ground, blood bubbling from her mouth, but he doesn't even look at his baby mama, making a beeline for the stroller. We watch in tense silence as he snatches his five-month-old son and cradles him to his chest, limping back to the car with a smug grin. Before he climbs inside, he thrusts his middle finger into the air.

"His arrogance is astounding," Agessi says. "To pull this off in broad daylight in one of the busiest areas on a Saturday is either ballsy or reckless."

"Where were her bodyguards?" Joshua asks, claiming the attention of every man around the table. "Don't look at me like that! She was my past. I wouldn't have wished her to die like this, but that's as far as my concern extends. I want to know where her protection was?"

Although Cruz had shown little initial interest in his newborn son—before he took off after the battle in February—we still suspected he'd come for him. It's why Massimo personally spoke to Bettina's father and demanded she move to one of the high-security *mafioso* apartments and accept protection. She wasn't supposed to go anywhere without her assigned *soldati*.

"Captain Hayes called an hour ago. They found the four men's bodies in a dumpster a block away," Ben explains. "I'm not sure how Cruz lured them away from their posts outside the clinic, but they all received a call at the same time and then took off."

"Fucking imbeciles," Fiero says.

"Someone got to them." I tap my fingers on the table.

"And Cruz took them out before they could talk," Pagano adds.

"We didn't weed out all the traitors," Cristian says over a sigh. He has taken this hard. None of us had any love for Bettina, but killing a young mother in cold blood, in broad daylight, in front of her baby, is evil personified.

"Keep the surveillance going within your *famiglie*," Massimo instructs. "And continue to build loyalty on the ground. We will weed out the last few rats."

"This seems very coincidental the same week Puccinelli identifies himself and requests a meeting," I say.

"He told me he has broken ties with Cruz, and I'm inclined to believe him," Massimo says. "But we can't rule anything out. It's possible he's lying."

"Are we sure it's wise to meet him next week?" Cristian asks. "What if it's a trap?"

"We're meeting on neutral territory, and O' Hara has reached out to his contacts in Ireland," our president says. "We'll have additional resources at our disposal when we land in Dublin. Something the Italians won't be aware of and won't have. Should they try anything, they'll be outnumbered."

"It sounds like they're most concerned with ensuring we don't tarnish the name of the *mafioso* in the city," Ben adds. He was involved in the call too. "Maximo and Primo fed them a ton of bullshit to get their support."

"Maybe we should lay a trap for them in Ireland and take them all out," I suggest. "Reduces the risk."

"They're part of the *Camorra*, Caleb," Fiero says, grinning. "As much as I love your lust for bloodshed, the last thing we want is to bring the entire *Camorra* down upon us. They'd wipe us out."

"Maltese is right," Agessi says. "Brokering a peace deal is our best option."

"You're all no fun." I smirk as I swivel in my chair.

"No one wants another bloody battle so soon after the last one," Ben says.

"Speak for yourself. I'm always down to gut a few mother-fuckers."

"Maybe I'm getting old," Ben continues. "But I'm voting for peace. I want my kids to be able to return to school. I want to watch Rowan walk across the stage at his graduation ceremony."

"I want that too. Leif and Rosa are going stir crazy being home schooled. Just watch your backs. I don't trust these fuckers."

"None of us trust them," Joshua says. "It's why we're not all going to Ireland for the meeting. If they try to double-cross us by making a play for The Big Apple while you're gone, we'll be ready for them."

"Let's hope it doesn't come to that," Pagano says.

"Where are we at with Gino's files?" Massimo asks, looking between Ben and Joshua.

"Ben, Gia, and I have thoroughly reviewed the files, and we didn't find anything," my twin explains.

"Gia suggested we scan all the paperwork and ask Philip to devise an IT program to look for patterns or anomalies," Ben says. "I think it's worth a shot, so we're putting that in place now."

"Let me know if it delivers any results," Massimo says. "For now, ensure the files are secure."

J nods.

"What about Anais?" Massimo asks, eyeballing me.

"She's still under full surveillance. Apart from trips to the salon and the odd shopping trip, she's holed up in her new apartment. She calls or texts multiple times a day to irritate the fuck out of me. So far, Cruz hasn't attempted to reach out to her. They haven't been in contact."

"She showed up at my office this afternoon," Joshua says, and it's the first I'm hearing it. "Her bodyguards were with her, and they gave me a heads-up," he adds. "She saw reports on TV and figured it out."

"Why did she go to you?"

"You weren't home or answering your cell, and apparently I'm a good substitute," he drawls. "Man, you deserve a medal for putting up with her shit for years. Five minutes in her company and I had a pounding headache and an almost over-riding urge to toss her off the roof."

"I'll drop by her place on my way home," I reluctantly concede. I've been avoiding her like the plague, but I get why she's furious today. Her husband risked everything to grab his baby when he hasn't made any effort to contact her. At least she didn't end up with a bullet in her skull like Bettina. Can't find it in me to feel too sorry for Ina though. She made her bed and paid the price.

"Has Sinaloa backed down?" Massimo asks Fiero.

"Yes, but it was touch and go for a while."

"Told you it was a bad idea," Cristian says. "Thank fuck, we didn't actually go ahead with the deal. If they're this pissy over a failed opportunity, imagine how bad it would've been if we'd reneged on an actual deal."

"We were under pressure, but it was a bad call," Massimo agrees.

"O'Hara came through for us again," Joshua says. "He's a solid ally."

O'Hara had initially suggested a Sinaloa contact, but after thinking about it, he expressed concerns, and then he pulled out all the stops to find an alternative option in Europe. Our new ally covered the gap in our supplies for the couple months it took to get the Cali operation back on track, the Rinascita building repaired on Staten Island, and our product back on the streets in the quantities needed. To avoid a future issue, we are now sourcing twenty-five percent of our needs through this European partner. They're happy to have a new supply chain in the city, and we have a backup in case of future production or shipping issues.

Our new commercial liner arrives next month, and we have another one ordered. By year-end, the cruise liners will have nothing to do with narcotics shipments. We are alternating shipments by sea and air now, using the contact Joshua sourced last year.

Things are finally getting back to normal after a stressful few months, and everyone is relieved.

Chapter Twenty-Two
Elisa

"**W**hat the fuck is he doing here?" Seb snarls, scaring me a little with the venom in his tone.

"I don't know," I truthfully reply as Caleb saunters toward us. Shea, Seb, and I are seated at an outdoor table at the coffee place on campus, grabbing an early lunch.

Heads turn as Caleb approaches, carrying a large, gift-wrapped box and wearing a flirty smile. He pays no attention to the drooling, fawning women though, and that's new. Gia told me he hasn't been with anyone in ages, and he seems honest about proving he's serious about me. Deep down inside, a little kernel of hope is mushrooming, but I stamp it down anytime it attempts to resurface.

I'm with Sebastien now. He's a good guy. Hot and sweet and romantic.

"So why haven't you given him your V-card?" an inner voice asks. I shut that meddling sucker up as Caleb reaches us.

"Hello, Lili." He whips a pink rose out from under the box he's carrying and hands it to me. "You look beautiful today."

He's full of shit. My hair is up in a messy bun. I have zero

Siobhan Davis

makeup on. I'm wearing skinny jeans, an oversized sweater with an obvious coffee stain, and ballet flats.

I take the rose in a bit of a daze. Butterflies are going haywire in my chest, and when his fingers brush mine in the exchange, delicious tingles zip over my hand and up my arm like always.

"Fuck off," Seb hisses as he stands, reminding me I'm not alone.

"Sebastien!" I chastise, climbing to my feet. "There's no need to be rude."

"There is every need to be rude. This is way out of line." He faces off with a smiling Caleb, and I realize Caleb is getting off on this. "She's mine. Fuck off and get your own woman."

"I am my own person, and I don't belong to either of you." I step in between them to defuse the situation before they get into it on campus. Already, we are gathering attention. I push Seb to one side, keeping him close so he can't lunge at Caleb and sign his own death warrant. "Why are you here, Caleb?" I ask because it's been over a year since he showed up on campus.

"I came to ask you to lunch, and I wanted to give you this." He holds out the box.

"That's a very big box," I say. His lips twitch, and I narrow my eyes as heat warms my cheeks. "Mind out of the gutter, Caleb."

"I don't know what you mean, Lili."

I roll my eyes. Seb is practically bristling with anger beside me, and I don't want to cause a scene. "I asked you to stop with the gifts for a reason," I softly say, not wanting to appear unappreciative. Truth is I loved receiving flowers and gifts, but Caleb has stuck to his word, and I haven't received any deliveries since Gia's birthday party. He still sends me daily love letters, and it's getting harder and harder to deny him because

174

he's showing me a romantic side I didn't think existed. Slowly, he is creating cracks in the scaffolding around my heart, and I'm worried I'm not strong enough to resist if he keeps this up.

He'll probably grow tired of waiting and move on, so I just need to hang in there.

"I stopped when you asked, but this is different. It's a study care package. Mom said you were starting to feel stressed, so I thought this might help."

"You bought me a study care package?" I repeat in a robotic voice.

"Yep." His proud grin does funny things to my insides. "I picked out and purchased all the elements individually. I was trying to think of all the things that might help."

"Who are you, and what have you done with Caleb Accardi?"

Caleb emits a booming laugh. "You bring out a side of me I'd kept hidden." His eyes soften. "You bring out the best in me, Lili. You always have."

"Pass me the puke bucket," Seb says before making a gagging sound.

I frown at him. I know this is unfair to him, but there's no need to be so rude.

"Have lunch with me," Caleb says, pleading with his eyes.

"I've already eaten, and I have a tutorial in twenty minutes."

Pain pricks at my heart as his face actually falls.

"No problem." His eyes bore into mine, and my heart stutters behind my rib cage. Butterflies swoop into my stomach the longer he stares at me, and my heart is pounding wildly now. It's like he's reaching inside me and wrapping his essence around my soul. A keening ache builds in my chest, and my fingers twitch with the longing to touch him.

"I've got to go," I say, grabbing my book bag off the ground.

"Give me your keys, and I'll drop this at your place," he says.

"Over my dead body." Seb crunches his knuckles.

What the hell has gotten into him?

"That can be easily arranged," Caleb murmurs in a low voice only I can hear.

I shoot Caleb a warning look as I remove my keys from my jeans pocket and drop them into his palm. "Thank you. This was very thoughtful of you."

"That's me." He leans in and whispers into my ear, "I'm all kinds of thoughtful when it comes to my sweet Lili." He flashes me a wink, and I yank Seb back as he moves to lunge at him.

"Bye, Caleb!" I call out, wiggling my fingers as I get my boyfriend out of there.

"What the fuck, Elisa?" Seb yanks his hand from mine when Caleb is out of sight. "What the hell do you think you're playing at?" he shouts.

"Lower your voice," I say calmly as Shea comes up on my left side. She's stayed quiet through all of that.

"You just gave that fucking asshole keys to your place? He's probably going over to jerk off all over your bed and stamp his mark."

"Firstly, gross, and secondly, Caleb is one of my oldest friends, and I trust him with my life. I get why you're frustrated, but you can't be rude to him."

"He's fucking rude to me every time he pulls this shit, and you're just letting him!"

"It'd be rude to refuse his gift, and it might actually help me." I *have* been stressed about my forthcoming exams. As much as I'm prepared, I'm still anxious. I want to get the best result and leave NYU with my head held high. I want to make my parents proud, and I want to start my new business on the best footing. A lot is going to change in my life in the next few months, and while it's super exciting, it's also nerve-wracking.

"You're unbelievable! I've been so fucking patient with you, and this is how you repay me?"

An icy chill crawls up my spine. "What did you just say?"

"Forget it. Forget all of it. I'm going home." He storms off in a temper.

"What just happened?" I ask Shea.

"I'm just going to say it," she says, walking in front of me. "I don't like that guy. I did at first, but he's all sweet and attentive one minute and angry and controlling the next. I think you can do much better."

"Yeah, I think you might be right."

Gia is waiting in my apartment when I get home later that night, and she opens the door and pulls me into a squeezing hug. "How are you?" she asks, bundling me into the house. "Beatrice is out by the way. She told me to tell you."

"Sorry you got roped into this. I thought I had a second set of keys in my locker, but I couldn't find them. I should have told Caleb to drop my keys back to me."

"It's fine. It gave me a good excuse to come visit."

Her ring sparkles under the living room light, drawing my attention to it. "Wow, that ring is something else."

"It is, isn't it?" She beams.

"Love looks good on you."

"I'm so fucking happy in a way I never imagined. I love him so much it's hard to separate each day to go to work. I literally miss him the second he's gone."

"Aw, that's so adorable. I'm incredibly happy for you," I

add, dumping my bag on the floor and heading to the refrigerator.

"I brought wine," she says, reaching for the cupboard with the wineglasses. "Thought we might need it for the unveiling."

When Gia called to say she was coming over with my keys, I told her about Caleb's gift, and she readily agreed to open it with me. "I'll definitely need it after today."

A frown mars her smooth forehead. "What don't I know?"

I fill her in on the altercation between Caleb and Seb and Shea's confession. "What do you think of him?" I ask as I pour wine into the two glasses.

"I have only met him twice in passing, so it's hard for me to form an opinion yet."

"But?" I ask because I sense there is one.

"I'm not overly keen on some of the things you've told me, but I don't want to be judgmental or biased."

"Biased?" I arch a brow as I hand her a wineglass, and we move to the couch. Caleb's gift is resting on top of the coffee table, waiting to be opened.

She levels me with a look. "Biased about Caleb."

"In what way? You've never been his biggest fan."

"That's before I got to know him and before I've seen him these past couple of months."

"What are you saying, Gigi?"

"I don't want to interfere, because this is your life and I know he hurt you, deeply, but you've loved him for so long Lili, and he's finally on the same page. Would it really hurt to let him in? To give it a try?"

I almost spit my wine all over the place. "You want me to ditch Sebastien and date Caleb?"

"I want you to follow your heart."

"My heart has only ever led me astray," I remind her, taking a big gulp of my wine.

"But has it?" she softly asks. "Maybe your heart was right all along."

"Ugh. Don't say this to me." I lean my head back and stare at the ceiling. "I'm already faltering."

"I know it's a lot to forgive him, but he's trying so hard to be the man you need him to be. I think he really loves you, Lise."

"What if I give in and he decides he doesn't like being in a committed relationship and he dumps me to return to his manwhoring ways?" I lower my eyes as pain spreads across my chest. "It would hurt so bad. Way more than I'm hurting now."

"That is a risk, but I think he's serious when he says he's done with all that. I don't think he was ready to commit before, and it's partly why he was ignoring his feelings for you. But he's ready now."

"What if I'm not enough to keep him faithful?" I brave the question that's most often plagued me. "He's been with so many women, and I'm still a virgin. How could I ever satisfy him? He would stray when I can't give him what he wants."

"He doesn't want any of those other women, and you'd learn what he likes." She reaches over and briefly squeezes my hand. "Of course, you'd be enough for him. You're amazing, and you've got so many good qualities. Caleb would be lucky to have you in his life, and he knows it."

"It's a moot point, anyway." I reach for my wine and knock back a mouthful. "I'm with Seb, and we have a double dinner date on Thursday, or had you forgotten?"

"I haven't forgotten. We'll be there."

"Maybe, I'll see how that goes and then decide."

"I don't want to pressure you. I just want you to be happy, Lise. I don't want you to settle because you think that's the best way to safeguard your heart."

"You think that's what I'm doing?"

She shrugs, casting a glance at the box. "Maybe, but only you can answer that."

Except I'm not sure I can. I'm more than a little confused. "I don't know if I am," I truthfully reply. "Caleb hurt me a lot."

"I know he did, like I know him dealing with those bitches doesn't miraculously heal those wounds, but surely it helped some?"

I nod. "It did." I tuck my hair behind my ears. "Do you think I'm a bad person that I enjoyed what he did? That I don't feel any remorse they're all behind bars now?"

"I think it makes you human, and you don't have a bad bone in your body."

"I liked hitting her. I liked having the upper hand. Those aren't the reactions of a good person, Gigi."

"We're all various shades of good and bad and everything in between. As long as the good wins out more than the bad, I'd say you're okay. And honestly? Look at the world we've grown up in? We've all seen darkness, all been touched by it. It's impossible to walk away unscathed. If you're worrying about your conscience, don't, babe. You're the singular best person I know with the purest heart. Hating on a few bitches who hurt you doesn't change that."

"You're right." I drain my wine for Dutch courage and slide onto my knees on the floor. "I want to open my gift."

Gia kneels beside me, grinning. "Go for it!"

"Did you have anything to do with this?" I ask as the thought occurs to me.

She vigorously shakes her head. "The first I heard of it was when he visited me at work and asked me to drop by with your keys. He would've come by himself, but he had a commission meeting."

"Oh, yes. It's the big meeting in Ireland today, isn't it? Dad told me about it."

"Joshua's on edge. They all are. I'm hoping it goes well and we can put this bullshit to bed. Then we only have Cruz to deal with."

"And his weapon of a wife." I tear at the pink paper, smiling to myself at the haphazard wrapping job. It only makes my heart beat harder for Caleb knowing he did all this by himself. He's crazy busy with *mafioso* shit, so the fact he's making time for me speaks volumes.

"I heard she slammed the door in Alesso's face after he told her he was done."

"Yeah, she was a real bitch." My anger flares as I rip the rest of the paper. "I really want to give her a piece of my mind. Dad has put up with her for years, and she treats him like that? I am praying daily that karma bites her in the ass soon." A gasp flees my lips as I expose the pretty wooden box with the custom engraving. "Oh my god," I exclaim as my fingers trace over the L-I-L-I etched on the lid of the box.

"That is beautiful."

"It is." My voice trembles a little as I raise a shaky hand to the clip to unlock the box. I'm almost afraid to look inside now.

"Holy fuck," Gia says when I pop the lid and the large contents are revealed. "He has seriously outdone himself with this."

My eyes are out on stalks as I examine every item. Hugging the cuddly teddy bear to my chest as I explore my care package, I struggle to contain my tears. Inside is a heavenly scented pillow, a heated warmer to soothe strained muscles, a box of my favorite cupcakes, and French chocolates from The White Plains Chocolaterie, and I bet Caleb grabbed a box for his mother while he was there.

There is also chopped fruit, a couple bags of nuts to snack on, and an aromatherapy roll-on I know came from Sierra because I've used it before. You dab it on your wrists and inhale the scent anytime you feel anxiety, and it helps to calm you. Also included is a heart-shaped smiley-face stress ball, a diffuser set, three scented candles, pens, notepads and other stationery supplies, a travel coffee mug, a box of multivitamins, a lavender eye mask, and a spa voucher for the gorgeous spa three blocks away.

My favorite items are the teddy bear and a rose quartz worry stone. I find running my fingers over the hard smoothness to be soothing in the extreme. I am overwhelmed, and I just sit there with tears in my eyes as I inspect the mountain of stuff Caleb chose for me.

"Wow." Gia looks moved too.

I hug my teddy bear closer. "I can't believe he did all this."

"You can practically feel his love leaking from every item. This is amazing, Lise."

"I know. It's so thoughtful and sweet, and he did all this for me." My vision is blurry as I look at her. "Is it stupid to be most afraid of my dreams coming true? Of finally getting the one thing I have longed for? What if I've built it up to be this big fantasy that just isn't realistic?"

"The best things in life can often be the scariest, and you won't know unless you give it a try."

Chapter Twenty-Three
Elisa

Our double date is an unmitigated disaster, and I breathe a sigh of relief when dinner is over. "I'm so sorry," I whisper to Gia as we hug outside the restaurant. Joshua and Sebastien stand silently on either side of us, not even attempting to pretend they're cordial. To be fair, that's all on Seb. He was ignorant from the outset, clearly holding the fact Joshua is Caleb's twin against him.

"Don't apologize for *his* rudeness. That's on him, not you," she whispers.

I hug her a little longer. "I'm going to end it tonight."

"Good. I don't get good vibes from him."

"Elisa," Sebastien says in a clipped tone. "We've both got early starts tomorrow. I want to take you home."

I shuck out of Gia's embrace, sending my boyfriend a cool look as I step up to Joshua. "Thanks for coming. It was great to see you."

"You too." He presses his mouth to my ear. "Do you want us to drive you home?"

I shake my head as I break our embrace. "I'll be fine." I'm

skilled in self-defense. I know how to shoot a gun and use a knife. I work out regularly to keep fit, and if Sebastien pulls any shit when I break it off with him, I won't hesitate to defend myself. Besides, my bodyguard is shadowing me tonight. He won't let anything happen to me.

"Let's go." Sebastien tugs my hand and drags me away from Joshua.

Gia and her fiancé trade a worried look.

"I'll call you when I'm home," I holler, letting my rude boyfriend lead me to his car.

Sebastien is seething the entire ride back to my apartment. It's only a fifteen-minute drive, but it feels like ten hours. Now that I've made the decision, I'm itching to end things with him.

These past couple of days I have thought long and hard about my motivations for being with him, and they were never right to begin with. I was using Sebastien to try to get over Caleb, and it wasn't fair. He's always been way more invested than me. I'm ashamed of myself because I didn't think I was that girl. The best thing I can do for both of us is to end it. Deep down, I always knew. It's why I didn't ever contemplate giving him my virginity.

All this time, I've still been saving it for Caleb.

All this time, Caleb has still been the one.

It doesn't excuse his sins or mean all is forgiven, but I'm done using Sebastien to distract me from my feelings.

"So," I say when we pull up to the curb at my apartment building, knotting my hands in my lap and drawing a brave breath.

"I'm coming up," Seb snaps, yanking his door open before I've had time to give him my prepared speech.

I race after him. "Seb, wait," I say, cursing as the door opens from the inside, and he slips into the building. He takes the stairs, two at a time, disappearing out of sight. "Fuck it," I mumble. Guess we're doing this upstairs. I take the elevator 'cause there's no way I'm climbing seven flights of stairs in high heels.

When I get out on the seventh floor, he's waiting by the door to my apartment, looking a little red-faced and breathless. Anger eeks from his pores like a tangible substance, and I'm eager to end this now and get him out of my life. I don't know why I ever thought he was sweet when that was clearly a façade. He's been like an angry bear since Gia's party, and I'm done dealing with his mood swings.

We don't speak as I open the door. Seb brushes past me and storms into the darkened room. Beatrice has already gone home for Easter, and the place is eerily quiet. I flip on the light switch and cross my arms over my chest after dumping my purse on the kitchen counter. Sebastien is pacing the floor, clutching handfuls of his hair and looking a tad bit deranged if I'm honest.

"I know why you behaved like that tonight," I say, working hard to keep my voice level. "But it doesn't give you the right to act so rude to my friends."

"He's a prick. Just like his brother."

"That's my best friend's fiancé," I remind him, raising my voice. "You don't get to speak about Joshua like that."

"And *you* don't get to tell me what to do." Stalking to my side, he jabs his finger in my face.

"Back off, Sebastien." I'm starting to feel threatened. "It's obvious this isn't working, so I think we should call it quits."

"What?" he barks, glaring at me.

"I don't want to see you anymore. I want to end our relationship now."

"You little bitch," he snaps, lunging at me and wrapping his hand around my throat.

I act on instinct, lifting my leg and kneeing him in the balls.

Seb roars, releasing me and cupping his crotch. I move to grab my purse, where my pepper spray is, when he shoves me against the door and slaps me hard. Stinging pain rips across my cheek as I lose my footing and tumble to the ground.

A look of horror washes over his face, but I'm not buying it. "Oh my god. Elisa, I'm so sorry." He hovers over me, extending his arm.

"Get out!" I scream. "Get out, or I'm calling the cops!"

"I didn't mean it." He grabs handfuls of his hair, looking panicked, as I scoot back along the kitchen floor.

"Leave, Sebastien. We're over." Scrambling to my feet, I snatch a kitchen knife. "Get the fuck out of my apartment." I brandish the knife in front of him when he doesn't budge. "I know how to use this, and I won't hesitate to protect myself."

"You don't need protection from me." He holds up his palms. "I won't hurt you. I swear."

"You already did!"

"That was an accident. I didn't mean for it to happen. Please forgive me. I'm really sorry, Elisa. I feel awful. Please give me another chance. I know I've been a prick all night, but it was a onetime thing."

All night? Try the past two weeks.

Sebastien is clearly psychotic, and I'm ashamed I fell for the ruse and didn't see his true colors until now. "There are no more chances. I don't want to date you any longer, and I don't want you to come anywhere near me on campus. Leave now, or I'm calling for backup," I say, swiping my purse.

"I fucked up," he mutters.

"I won't tell you again." I pull my cell from my purse as I keep the knife pointed at him.

"I'm going. I'm going." Defeat surges through his tone. "This isn't how I saw the night ending."

It wasn't quite how I saw it ending either, but I definitely saw the writing on the wall of our relationship. "Goodbye, Sebastien."

He mutters something I can't hear as he walks out the door, and I dart forward, slamming it behind him and quickly locking it. My heart is pounding in my chest, and adrenaline is racing through my veins as I slump against the door and slide to the floor. I carefully set the knife down beside me as I raise a hand to my stinging cheek.

That bastard hit me! Mom would be so upset if she knew what went down here tonight, which is why I can never tell her. She has done so much to ensure I never get into a position where any man can hurt me, and I was a stupid fool who didn't see the red flags. I was too hung up on my guilt over using him to realize the kind of man he is underneath that handsome, kind façade.

I'm shaking all over as I press the call button on my cell, hoping my *soldato* bodyguard doesn't hear my voice trembling when I ask him if Sebastien has left the building. Some stress seeps from my tense limbs when he confirms he's gone. Explaining we have broken up, I ask him to ensure he doesn't come near me again.

Ending the call, I feel a little better knowing I have protection. Sebastien spooked me that much. I inhale and exhale deeply, forcefully calming myself down as I prepare to call Gia. I know she'll be worried after tonight, and I need to let her know I got home okay. I want to tell her what happened but not when she's in a car with Joshua. He'll only tell Caleb, and I don't want Seb's murder on my conscience.

He freaked me out. He physically hurt me. He tried to control me. All are justifiable reasons to hate him and want nothing more to do with him, but it doesn't mean he deserves to die.

When I'm sufficiently calm, I call Gia. "I did it," I blurt when she picks up.

"Thank fuck. How did he take it?"

"He wasn't happy, but it's done now, and he's gone."

"Are you okay? You sound a little off."

Gigi has superhero-level powers of observation.

"I'm fine. Just relieved. I was a little on edge doing it. I'm so sorry you guys were forced into sitting through that tonight."

"Like I said, you have no reason to apologize. He's the jerk, not you."

"I'm beat," I lie. "I'm going to grab a shower and crawl into bed."

"I'll swing by for you at ten," she reminds me.

"I'll be ready." I can't wait to go home for Easter. This apartment feels tainted now.

After I hang up, I grab a hot shower, trying to scrub all memories of Sebastien's touch from my flesh and my brain. When I'm dressed and my hair is blow-dried, I crawl into bed with my teddy, curl up in a ball, and attempt to push the horrible events of tonight from my mind.

Chapter Twenty-Four
Elisa

"Okay. That's it." Gia pulls over onto the shoulder and kills the engine. The leather squelches as she turns to face me. "I know something happened. 'Fess up, right now, Lise."

A resigned sigh flees my lips as I swivel in my seat to face my best friend. We're only twenty minutes into our journey to Greenwich, and honestly, I'm surprised she lasted this long before cornering me. "I was going to tell you when we got to my house. I didn't want to explain while you were driving as you're liable to drive us into a ditch."

"What did that asshole do? I know this has to do with him."

I fill her in as succinctly as I can, giving her the CliffsNotes version.

"He *hit* you?" Alarm mixes with fury on her face.

"Yeah, but he won't be doing it again."

"You should have stabbed him." Her eyes flash maniacally, reminding me there's a whole side to my bestie I don't really know.

"He's not worth doing time over."

"Puh-lease," she scoffs, rolling her eyes. "You know we'd make his body disappear, and no one would ever point a finger at you."

"That's exactly what I'm afraid of and why you can't tell anyone, Gigi. Especially not Joshua."

Her eyes pop wide in shock. "You can't be serious, Elisa! You need to at least tell Caleb what's happened."

"Are you kidding? He'd kill him!"

"I don't see the issue." She shrugs like casually discussing murder is no biggie.

"Sebastien is an asshole, but that doesn't mean he deserves to die. It's over between us, and he won't get the opportunity to get to me again. I'd rather just draw a line under the whole thing and forget I ever dated him."

"I think that's the wrong call, babe." She appeals to me with pleading eyes.

"I made a mistake with him, but it's done now. It's in the past. I don't want to make this into a big drama with everyone involved and freaking out. Just let it go."

Her features soften. "Does it hurt?" Her eyes drift to my cheek.

I shake my head. "It's not sore anymore, just a little bruised."

"Now the makeup makes sense."

"You can't see it, can you?" I ask, briefly touching my skin.

She shakes her head. "No, you camouflaged it well."

"Then that's that. Let's go home."

She starts up the engine before turning to look at me. "Just promise me if anything else happens you'll tell me and you'll tell your father or Caleb."

"I promise I will." I'm not stupid, and it's an easy promise to make. If my ex refuses to accept we're broken up, I won't put up with any crap from him. I have enough on my plate with my approaching finals, and he's not going to add to my stress.

"Okay." She leans over and hugs me. "I'm glad he's out of your life."

"Me too."

She puts the car into gear and glides back out onto the road. "What are you going to do about Caleb?" she asks a few beats later.

I lean back in my seat and nibble on my lip for a second. "I don't know. I guess I'll just wait and see."

"Is this seat taken?" Caleb asks, looking down at me with a familiar charming grin. Easter dinner is at Ben and Sierra's this year, and everyone is here now. I've had a nice chill couple of days at home, but I knew all that would change today. The twins only arrived late last night from the city along with Ben, Leo, and Alesso, who returned from the big meeting in Ireland. Sierra already laid down the law, insisting there is no *mafioso* talk today. Today is for family, and business can wait. The long table is rapidly filling as our families claim seats while our moms ferry heaped plates of meat and vegetables to the table.

"It is now." I smile softly at him. We always sat beside one another at family events, except for the last few occasions when I was mad at him and keeping my distance.

Caleb slides effortlessly into the seat beside me, flashing a signature grin. Around us, the rest of our families are getting settled, talking, laughing, and catching up. Rowan pretends not to look from his position on the other side of me as Caleb leans his mouth in close to my ear. "Word on the street is you're single again." His eyes come alive as his gaze devours my face. His lips brush against my earlobe, sending delicious tremors skating over every part of me. "But not for long if I have my way."

"Caleb." I pin him with a "behave" look.

"What?" He shrugs, smiling like he just won the lottery. "Don't act like this is a surprise." He leans in close again, lowering his voice so only I can hear. "You're mine, Lili. Always have been, always will be. Concede defeat because I'm not backing down."

I shove at his chest. "I only just broke up with my boyfriend," I whisper.

"So?" He plays with my hair. "I don't see the problem. There is nothing standing in our way now." His fingers leave my hair and move to my chin, gently tipping my face back. "God, you're so fucking beautiful, Lili, especially when you're stubbornly proud. I—"

He stops speaking the same second I realize the room has gone deathly silent. Caleb releases my chin, and we turn to face the table. Every set of eyes is watching us, and my cheeks instantly heat. I squirm on my chair, hugely uncomfortable with all the attention.

Mom and Natalia are beaming like all their wishes just came true. Sierra and Frankie are smiling. Gia is trying—and failing—to give me a subtle thumbs-up. Rowan's ear-splitting grin is all up in my face. Joshua's stare is pensive, and he's not giving much away. I'm afraid to look at my brother because he's already made his feelings clear about Caleb. The younger kids wear expressions ranging from confused to amused to bored. Uncle Ben is studying us with a serious expression. Leo's gaze is inquisitive, and my dad. Oh boy. Dad is staring at Caleb like he's imagining ten different ways to murder him.

Caleb grins wickedly as his arm slides around the back of my chair. "I have an announcement to make," he says, sounding as cool, calm, and collected as he looks. "I'm in love with Lili, and she's in love with me."

"Caleb!" I hiss, glaring at him.

"Are you denying it?" His eyes twinkle with mirth, knowing I won't lie in front of my family.

I bury my face in my hands, mumbling, "I can't believe you just did that."

"Everyone, eat," Sierra says, taking pity on me, I'm sure.

"This is wonderful news," Mom says, and I lift my head. "Isn't it, darling?" she adds, fixing my stepfather with a look Voldemort would be proud of.

Alesso clears his throat and pins me with a look full of potent emotion. "I think Elisa and Caleb clearly have things to discuss in private, and we should all respect that." The ire has faded from his face replaced with some indecipherable emotion I can't place.

His words help, and everyone goes back to their own conversations, and some of the stress eases from my shoulders. "I am feeling very stabby right now." Gripping my knife and fork, I look at Caleb. "I suggest you don't test me any further."

"Everyone knows now. What other objections do you have so I can quash those too?"

Beside me, Rowan chuckles. "I'll say this for you, cuz, once you put your mind to something, you go all in."

"There is no point in doing anything half-assed in this life, Rowan," Caleb says, setting some meat down on my plate before adding a few slices to his own. "When I see something I want"—his eyes bore into mine—"I go for it with zero regrets, and I hold nothing back." He tweaks my nose. "I have never wanted anything or anyone as much as I want Lili."

"Stop, please," I whisper as warmth crawls up my neck and onto my cheeks. "Everyone gets it now."

"Do you?" He quirks a brow.

"I'm not discussing this at the dinner table any longer. We'll talk later."

"It's later," Caleb says, poking his head into the living room where I'm currently fending questions from Mom, Nat, Frankie, and Sierra. Gia is sitting on the couch on my other side, but she's of no help. She's as giddy as the rest of them.

"Sweetheart." Nat rushes to her son's side and drags him into the room. Gia giggles, and I glare at my bestie. "You need to tell us everything because Elisa is giving us nothing."

"Because there's nothing to tell!" I protest, grinding my teeth to the molars.

Caleb walks over and pulls me from the couch, bundling me into his arms. "There isn't much to tell yet because I'm trying to convince Lili I'm serious. She doesn't quite believe it, but I'm on a mission to prove to her that she's the only woman for me."

A chorus of aws ring out around the room, and I'm officially done. "Get me out of here," I whisper, looking up at him.

"Gladly." He presses a lingering kiss to the top of my head as I gently lay my head on his chest and give in to the comforting feel of his warm body and strong arms cocooning me. "Excuse us, ladies, I have some wooing to do," Caleb says, steering us toward the door with his arm firmly around me.

"Barf," Gia says, but she's grinning. "That was cheese on top of cheese, Accardi."

"Bite me, Bianchi."

"Soon-to-be Accardi," she purrs sweetly, flashing her ring.

"Don't remind me," Caleb says, but we all know he's joking. Those two are close now in a way no one could've predicted.

"Wrap it before you tap it!" Gia calls out as we walk out the door, and I am going to string her up later for this.

"Oh my god." I bury my face in Caleb's chest. "I am going to die of embarrassment before this day is out!"

Caleb chuckles. "They're happy for us."

I lift my head and peer deep into his eyes. "There is no *us*, Caleb. Just because I've broken up with Seb doesn't mean I'm instantly going to fall into your arms."

"I know, Lili, but I'm confident in my wooing skills." He waggles his brows, and it's so hard to stay mad at him. "Let's walk and talk," he says, taking my hand. His large, callused palm is strong and warm in mine as he leads me toward the coat closet, and I already know resisting is futile.

"I know it's warm, but showers are predicted," he says, taking my light jacket off a hook and helping me into it. His fingers brush against my body as he pulls the zipper up, and I'm like an inferno, my body doused in heat from my head to my toes. His eyes never leave mine as he puts his black jacket on, and the intensity of his attention is melting the last of my reservations.

The truth is, as embarrassed as I was by his outburst at the table, I can't deny there's a part of me swooning at this newer romantic side to Caleb. I'd challenge anyone to deny he's sincere. For the first time ever, the prospect of loving him and being loved by him in return is a very real possibility. It is something I have prayed and hoped for, for years, and though it's scary, because he could completely decimate my heart this time if he decides to change his mind, I know I owe it to myself to at least hear him out.

Chapter Twenty-Five
Caleb

"**T**his brings back memories," I say as we swing side by side in the playground on the grounds of the estate.

"It does." Elisa looks less troubled out here, kicking her legs out in front of her and grinning as she soars through the air.

"You used to beg me to push you," I tease.

"You spent ages out here with me," she remembers with a fond smile. "You were very patient with me when I was a kid."

"You made it easy, Elisa." I slow down, figuring she's relaxed enough now to have the conversation we need to have. "There were times I sought you out because you were the only one who could ever bring a smile to my face." I plant my feet on the ground as she slows down too. "I didn't think of you as anything more than a little sister back then, and even when you got old enough, I still wouldn't, couldn't, go there."

She comes to a standstill, and her eyes probe mine.

I reach out and thread my fingers in hers. "But somewhere along the way, that changed. I can't pinpoint exactly when it was because I was in denial, but the way I love you is nothing new, Lili." I tuck a stray piece of hair behind her ear, silently fist pumping the air when a shiver visibly ghosts over her body. "I was a coward because I didn't confront my feelings. You have always been the brave, confident one between us."

Disbelief washes over her face. "You are the most confident, some might say arrogant, person I know, Caleb." She shoots me a cheeky grin, and I have a sudden urge to toss her over my lap and slap her insolent ass. My dick stirs in my pants, loving that idea.

"In all aspects of my life but this. When it comes to affairs of the heart, I'm the furthest thing from confident."

"That's not how it's coming across." Her thumb sweeps the underside of my hand, shooting tingles up my arm.

"Because it's you and loving you is as natural as breathing to me. It's why I never realized I was already doing it." I angle my body, and our knees brush. "What I'm trying to say is I know I have no experience of relationships or love, and you have every right to feel hesitant, but I'm telling the truth. I could never lie to you." I stand and pull her to her feet, gently reeling her into my arms.

Her head tilts back as she looks up at me. Her cheeks are flushed, and her eyes are bright. "I love you, Lili. I love you so much, and I want to be with you. I promise if you give me a chance you won't regret it. I won't let you down." I softly clasp her face in my hands. "I can't live without you, and our time is now. Haven't we waited long enough for this?"

"Caleb." Her voice is choked with emotion as she rests her palms on my chest. "I'm scared."

"I get that. I'm terrified of failing at the one thing that is most important in my life, but if we don't try, we won't ever know."

"What if I'm not good enough for you?" She bites on her lips in an obvious tell.

"What?" Shock echoes in my tone. "Why would you ever think that? I'm the one who isn't good enough for *you*."

"I'm not like all those other girls you've been with. I don't look like them, and I...I—" She cuts herself off and lowers her eyes.

"Lili, look at me." I drop my hands to her back, holding her close as she lifts her gaze to mine. "None of those girls meant anything to me. Harsh, but it's true. You're perfect, Lil." I brush my thumb along her lip. "Every single part of you is perfect. There is nothing I would change. You and I were made to fit together."

"I'm still a virgin," she blurts, and her cheeks stain fire-engine red.

"Thank fuck for that." I rest my brow against hers, and we stare at one another with barely any space between us. "I was praying you hadn't given it to that piece of shit."

"I couldn't do it. I was always waiting for you."

I ease back and cup her face. "It's a gift I probably don't deserve, but I won't lie and say I'm not pleased when I am."

She chews on the inside of her mouth, gulping and looking incredibly nervous, and I couldn't love this girl any more if I tried. I wait her out, watching as thoughts churn in her mind. "What if you grow bored with me or I can't please you?"

This girl. She slays me in all the bests ways. "Angel." I softly caress her beautiful face. "You're a blank canvas, my love. I will teach you what I like, and we'll explore your desires together. You can show me what you like, and I will ensure you feel loved, cherished, desired, and wanted every second of every day for the rest of your life. But there is no rush. We will go at your pace, and I can wait until you're ready."

Tears glisten in her eyes as she stares at me in slight shock.

"You have enchanted me, Lili. I'm forever under your spell." I press light kisses to her cheeks. "And you please me just by breathing, Lili. You could never disappoint me, and I will never grow tired of you." Elisa is usually self-confident, and I curse my stupidity at helping to plant these doubts in her head. My messing around with other women has hurt her and left her feeling inadequate, and it's my job to show her that is furthest from the truth. "You're my soul mate, Lili. You're the woman I was always destined to be with. I'm sorry it took me so long to realize it, but I'm all in now. I am yours, and only yours, forever."

"Caleb," she chokes out over a sob as silent tears stream down her face. "This feels like a dream, and I'm scared I'm going to wake up."

I wrap my arms around her and hold her tight, breathing in her sweet scent and enjoying the feel of her soft curves against the hard planes of my body. "It's not a dream. I'm real. We're real, and I'm going nowhere." I tip her face up so her eyes are locked on mine. "I meant it when I said I'd be patient. You don't need to worry about anything. Let me carry the weight, and I will wait until you are ready. Just give me a shot, Lili. Give us a chance to see how incredible we can be."

"Okay." She's smiling through her tears. "I have wanted this my entire life, and I'm done waiting."

Thank fuck.

I hold her precious face in my hands, and my heart is bursting with joy. I peer deep into her gorgeous eyes, hoping she sees and feels the truth behind these words. "I love you."

"I love you too," she whispers as a beatific smile graces her lips and her tears dry.

My eyes drift to her tempting mouth. "I really need to kiss you."

Trusting eyes pin mine in place. "I really want you to kiss me."

Without wasting another second, I lower my mouth and

brush my lips against hers. Her hands grip my waist as she tilts her head and sweeps her mouth against mine. My hold on her face is tender as I slant my mouth more firmly against hers and kiss her deeply. Her body presses against mine as she meets me kiss for kiss, and I'm drowning in euphoria and the best fucking kiss of my life. My arms band around her body, trapping her against me as we pour years of pent-up longing into every glide of our mouths.

Her lips part eagerly, and my tongue slides into her mouth, tangling with hers in a sensual dance. Every nerve ending in my body is alive, and my cock is solid as a rock, pressing against her stomach in a way she can't ignore. That thought has me pulling back to check she's okay.

"Why'd you stop?" she pants.

"Just checking you're okay?" My eyes scan her face for signs of discomfort, but I find none.

"I'm more than fine." A flush crawls over her face, and I'm very partial to it. She grabs the front of my jacket and pulls my face down to hers. "Keep kissing me, Caleb. I don't want you to stop."

I don't know how long we stay kissing because time seems to have lost all meaning, and we only break apart when Rosa and Aria show up with our moms.

"You were kissing Caleb," Aria says, giggling.

"I was." Lili snuggles into my side, and my arms automatically wrap around her.

"Are you going to marry Elisa?" my sister asks.

"Someday," I reply, tweaking Lili's nose when she stares at me in shock.

"Oh my god!" Mom squeals as if she's five. "You could have a double wedding with Joshua and Gia!"

I narrow my eyes in suspicion. "Were you talking to Cristian?"

"What?" Her brow puckers. "No. Why?"

"Nothing," I mumble, not wanting to admit our friends have placed bets on a double wedding by year-end.

Lili's cheeks are flushed, and she hasn't said anything. Interesting.

"You two look so good together," Serena says, and her genuine joy is easy to see.

"Y'all need to calm down," Elisa says, coming out of whatever place she went to in her head. "We have only just agreed to give things a go. Talk of a double wedding is very premature."

"We're just really excited for you," Mom says with tears in her eyes. "Now both my boys are happy." She plants a hand over her heart as emotion crests over her face. "It's all I've ever wanted." A sob rips from her throat, and Lili instantly shucks out of my arms to hug my mother.

Serena sidles up to me. "Look after my daughter, Caleb," she says as we watch my mom and Lili hug and whisper. Our sisters have long since grown bored and ditched us for the climbing frame.

"I will take care of her. I promise."

She pats my arm. "Alesso wants to speak with you," she adds, and I work hard not to roll my eyes. "You are Elisa's choice. He just wants to know you'll love her and protect her. Reassure him, and he'll back down."

I doubt it'll be that simple, but there's no point in worrying Serena. "I'll talk to him later."

"Also, Sierra said to tell you the west wing is vacant, and you're welcome to it tonight."

"That's kind of her." It feels good to have so many people rooting for us. Honestly, I'm surprised, but I'm not going to knock a gift horse in the mouth. It would be nice to spend tonight with Lili, curled up on the couch, watching a movie, and getting better acquainted with her exquisite mouth. I've never been more turned on just from kissing, and it's further proof of how we have always been meant to be. I don't care what anyone says, Lili is the one, and I'm determined to make that reality a permanent reality in the very near future.

Chapter Twenty-Six
Caleb

"He's got that goofy grin on his face again," Cristian says, yanking me out of the delicious daydream playing on a loop in my head.

I'm reliving Sunday night on repeat because it was magical. Who'd have thought a night in front of the fire, sharing a bottle of red wine, and binge-watching some popular historical romance show, would turn out to be one of the best nights of my life. But it was, and it's all because of Lili. Holding her in my arms and getting to kiss her at will is something I've only dared to dream about, and now it's my new reality.

Lili turns the mundane into the surreal, and suddenly life has new meaning. The restless unfulfillment that has plagued me the past year is a diminishing sentiment now I have the woman of my dreams in my life.

Everything makes sense with Lili, and nothing seems insurmountable. I've been walking on a cloud since Sunday, and I didn't even get laid. Didn't even sleep beside her because we slept in different bedrooms in the west wing, and I was A-okay with that. I meant it when I told her she will set the pace. I don't want her to feel under pressure to have sex. My blue balls can wait until she's ready.

"He's had that look on his face constantly the past two days," Joshua replies, handing me a cup of coffee as we wait for the rest of The Commission members to arrive for the meeting.

"You're in no position to throw shade." I jab a finger at my brother.

"Truth." Cristian grins, slapping me on the back. "I'm looking forward to a nice payout come year's end." He rubs his hands with glee.

"I'll gladly double the pot if it means I get Lili up the aisle this year."

"You might want to keep sentiments like that to yourself around Alesso," Ben says, entering the room and overhearing.

"We're cool," I say. "As long as I don't hurt her and never ever make her cry," I add, repeating the words Alesso said Sunday night when we spoke. Despite what Serena said, I was expecting a brutal lecture, but he didn't go there. He simply told me to take care of her and to not hurt her or I'd have him to deal with. I can respect that.

"I hope it works out," Ben adds, squeezing my shoulder. "Elisa is a sweetheart."

"She is, and I'm a lucky bastard."

The others arrive, and Massimo calls the meeting to order. Pagano and Agessi dial in from Florida and Vegas, listening attentively as Mazzone, Maltese, and our president give us an update on the meeting in Ireland with Puccinelli and the Naples *Camorra* crew. It was a rousing success, and a peace deal has been negotiated, meaning there are no more threats to our families or our businesses.

"Are you sure they weren't yanking our chain?" I ask, not sure if I'm buying it.

"As sure as we can be. They have never wanted war.

Maximo Greco led them to believe we were all corrupt power-hungry animals and we were sabotaging the name of the Italian mafia in the U.S."

"And they just accepted him at his word?" Cristian asks.

"Not at all," Fiero says. "It took years for Maximo to convince them they needed to intervene. At first, they sought refuge there, claiming it wasn't safe after the bombing, and the *Camorra* welcomed them and ensured they were cared for. They didn't ask for anything but shelter, biding their time. It seems Maximo and Primo spent years building a tangled web of lies behind the scenes and gradually pulling others into their net. They timed it perfectly, only approaching Puccinelli when they believed they could convince him they had to intervene. They played up what happened with DeLuca and suggested we were targeting them next, wanting to wipe out any competition in Italy from coming after our territory. Cruz and Marino supported those claims, stating it was why there were traitors willing to go against *omerta* to save the sanctity of the organization."

"I can't believe they fell for it," Volpe says.

"They weren't fully sold," Ben says, "but this is the clincher." He sits up straighter. "Greco told them he had evidence that would prove we were all corrupt. Puccinelli attacked on the basis of seeing that intel once they made it to the U.S."

Joshua and I trade looks.

"That's what they think is in the files?" I ask.

Massimo nods. "If what my father told them is true, and that's a big if, Gino gathered information on all the families as insurance in the run-up to the warehouse bombing. I am guessing some are legit records of illegal activity, but other intel is fabricated to present every *famiglia* in the worst possible light."

Ben clears his throat and cracks his knuckles. "Gino knew

207

the screws were turning, and he didn't trust Maximo even if they had allied behind The Commission's back. He would have turned us all in if we turned on him and taken control, with or without Greco. He must have threatened Maximo with revealing it should he double cross him. That's how he knew it existed."

"But it doesn't," Joshua says, scratching the back of his neck. "We have gone over those files extensively, and the software program Philip set up didn't find anything either."

"Because we were looking for the wrong thing." Fiero's eyes light up. "The intel is in a lockbox in a bank somewhere. Gino stored the key in those files."

J and I exchange another look. "It's hidden in one of the folders," I surmise because it's the only thing that makes sense.

Ben nods. "As soon as this meeting is finished, we are heading to your office, Joshua, to find it."

"So, Maximo wanted the Barone to find the intel first to fully lock down the Italian's support, presuming they would have lapped up that shit."

"Exactly. When the Barone failed in their mission, he convinced Puccinelli to go ahead with their planning. They had already purchased the sub and had men lined up here. He promised he'd provide the evidence once they landed in New York."

"What does this peace deal entail?" Agessi asks.

"We agree not to bring the *mafioso* into disrepute and to meet annually with our Italian compatriots to discuss mutual business interests. As long as we keep our noses clean, they will stay out of our territory, and we'll stay out of theirs," Massimo says.

"What about Cruz?" I ask. "Did they help him to escape?"

"Puccinelli said they argued on the sub about the next course of action. The Italians wanted to adopt a cautious approach and to reach out to us to talk, but Cruz flew into a rage because they wouldn't back him to take control in Maximo's place. They cut all ties when they dropped him and his men off in Delaware and there has been no contact since."

"He's coming for us," Cristian coolly replies in between sips of water. "My brother is a stubborn prick, and if it's power he wants, he won't stop until he gets it—"

"Or he dies trying," I add.

"He has no allies," Pagano says.

"That we know of," Mantegna replies.

"Cruz is stubborn, but he's not stupid. He's got something up his sleeve," I say.

"Until we know what it is, everyone remains on guard," Massimo advises. "For now, let's find this key and get our hands on the intel before someone else does."

The doorbell chimes as I'm finishing getting dressed later that night for my first official date with Lili, and I glance at the time on my watch, wondering if it's my twin with an update on the key. Tucking my shirt into the waistband of my pants, I leave my bedroom and pull up the lobby cameras, cursing when I see who's at my door. I do not have time for her shit today.

"What do you want, Anais?" I ask when I yank the door open.

"Jeez, what flew up your butt?" she inquires, strolling into my apartment like she owns it. She's wearing a flimsy robe that barely covers her semi-naked body and high-heeled slippers. Wine fumes tickle my nostrils as she brushes past me, and it's clear she's pretty trashed. "What the fuck is going on?" Her eyes are out on stalks as she skims her gaze over my pristine apartment.

"I'm going out, Anais. What do you want?"

She scowls and narrows her eyes. "I left some of my products in your bathroom, and I need them."

"Then be my guest but make it quick."

She totters off upstairs, and I follow her movements on my cell through the camera feed, watching as the lying little bitch rifles through the drawers in my bedside tables before wandering into my closet. She's clearly looking for something, but what?

I'm tempted to haul her conniving butt out of my place, but I have more to gain from pretending I don't know.

"Time's up, Anais," I holler up the stairs after a couple of minutes. I watch her scowling and cursing me under her breath on the feed. She stalks into the bathroom, returning a minute later with a bottle of shampoo and conditioner.

She clomps down the stairs, swaying and almost losing her footing. "Where are you going anyway?" Her gaze rakes over me with a pout.

"None of your business."

"You're no fun anymore," she says, putting her hands on my chest and pressing up against me.

"For the last time, I'm not interested." I remove her hands from my body and step back. "Go call your little fuck buddy on the third floor if you're bored and horny." *Yes, Anais, I am watching you.*

"Jealous, baby?" she purrs.

"Never."

Her eyes flare with murderous intent. "I don't know what I ever saw in you."

"Ditto." I point toward the door. "Now, leave."

"You can't keep me locked in this building forever, Caleb," she calls out as she walks off.

"No one is keeping you here, Anais. You are free to leave

whenever you like." I flash her a grin as I slam the door in her face. I chuckle as I watch her flip me the bird repeatedly on camera.

On my way out to pick up Lili, I call the twenty-four-seven team watching Anais for updates. "There are none, Don Accardi. The only time she ever goes out is to the salon, and man, is that bitch vain. She goes at least three or four times a week. Apart from that, she orders groceries and food deliveries, and her only visitor is Giotto."

"She was just snooping in my place. I don't trust her. Make sure someone has active eyes on her at all times."

"Will do, boss."

Chapter Twenty-Seven
Elisa

"**F**or you," Caleb says, producing a massive bouquet of pink, peach, and white roses from behind his back when I open the door to let him in.

My mouth is almost trailing the ground as I drink him in. He is hotter than Hades in a black shirt, open at the neck, and black pants. His gorgeous blond hair is artfully styled, and he's sporting a thin layer of designer stubble. He smells as divine as he looks, and I seriously have to stop myself from pinching my arm because this still seems like a dream. I can't believe he is mine and I'm his. I've been giddy as a schoolgirl since Easter and wearing the most ridiculous grin on my face the entire time.

"Lili." His lips tip up at the corners. "Are you going to invite me in or leave me hanging at the door?"

"Sorry. Come in." I step aside to let him enter. "And thank you for the flowers. They're beautiful."

"Not as beautiful as you," he says, leaning down to kiss me. His arm goes around my back to hold me up when I sway, almost dropping my flowers.

"Is this okay?" I ask, gesturing at myself. I don't know where he's taking me for dinner. I didn't want to go too overboard, but if he's taking me to some super swanky place, I may be a tad underdressed in my navy knee-length dress. It's fitted at the top and ties at the front with sheer lace sleeves and a full skirt that swishes as I walk. I'm wearing silver peep-toe high heels and a matching purse. Beatrice reluctantly helped to curl my hair and do my makeup. Thankfully the bruise on my cheek has gone and no one noticed over Easter weekend. Which is a relief because I was worried Mom might discover it, but she was suitably distracted by Caleb and me.

"You're perfect." Caleb kisses me again, pulling me in close to his body. "I missed you," he murmurs in between kisses.

"You saw me yesterday," I remind him. We spent the day in Greenwich, and I drove back to the city last night with him. He wanted to come in, but I made him leave as I had to study. My exams are only two weeks away, and my downtime is limited. All my clients are aware I'm not available for commissions for the next month, so at least it means I have a little time to see Caleb but not a lot. Which sucks because now we're officially together I want to spend every spare second with him.

"I was so distracted all day thinking about you. About Sunday night," he says, tugging on my earlobe with his teeth and causing a flurry of excitement in my panties.

I swear I've been in heat since Sunday. All our kissing has me turned on in ways I have never experienced before.

"Best. Night. Ever."

"It was pretty perfect," I agree, smiling as I reluctantly break our embrace.

"You're too far away," he says, pouting, as I walk into the kitchen.

I cast him a flirty glance over my shoulder. "I'm putting the flowers in a vase before we leave."

"Hurry up. I'm already suffering withdrawal symptoms."

A laugh bubbles up my throat, and I'm indescribably happy. So happy I could burst.

After I put the flowers in water, I call goodbye to Beatrice and take Caleb's arm as he escorts me out of the building.

"I wish you'd keep your protective detail," he says, steering me toward his Lamborghini.

"There's no need now the threat has passed."

Dad spoke to me before I left Greenwich, explaining about the deal brokered with the Italians and how the threat has passed. He wanted me to keep my bodyguard, but I don't see the need. All the kids have returned to school, and things are getting back to normal.

"What about fuckface? Has he contacted you?"

I shake my head as Caleb opens the passenger door for me. "Nope, and I saw him at school today, and he blatantly ignored me." It was a huge relief because I was afraid he'd try to make me change my mind, but Seb seems to have accepted it.

"I know you like your privacy, but it'd put my mind at ease knowing you had someone shadowing you."

"I'll think about it," I say, sliding into the luxury car.

"You look good in my car," Caleb says after climbing behind the wheel. He leans over and kisses me passionately. "You look good in my life."

"You're so sweet." I run my fingers along the bristle on his chin and cheeks.

"Lili," he growls. "Do not ever call me sweet." He playfully tickles me. "At least not in public."

"But you *are* sweet, and you know I can't lie." I bat my eyelashes, and he chuckles.

"You're trouble, Ms. Salerno." He pecks my lips softly. "My favorite kind of trouble."

"You make me so happy, Caleb." I've got zero chill, but I

don't care. We don't have to stand on ceremony around one another because we have known each other for years. There is a comfort and a familiarity that makes all of this so natural and seamless.

"I'm so gone for you, Lili. I love you so much, angel."

My heart beats frantically every time he says those words. "I will never tire of hearing that."

"I'll never tire of saying it." He takes my hand and brings it to his mouth, kissing my knuckles. "And happiness goes both ways. I've been acting like a lovesick goon all day. Joshua and Cristian are having a field day with it."

"Well, Joshua cannot throw shade!"

"Damn straight." Caleb starts the car and reverses out of the parking space.

Thirty minutes later, after a companiable ride where we talked about everything and anything, he pulls into a side street in Lower Manhattan, in the district known as Little Italy, parking in a small parking lot at the back of a quaint Italian restaurant. "Leo used to take Mom here back in the day," he explains, helping me out of the car. "He told me the food is to die for and it's old-school ambience." He shrugs, looking a little vulnerable as he leads me to the front door with his arm around my back. "I thought you might like somewhere a little cozier than one of the trendier restaurants."

"You thought right." I link my fingers in his as we reach the front desk. "This place is gorgeous." Lighting is low and romantic, and the circular tables are covered with pretty tablecloths and flickering candles. Unlike some more modern places, the tables are positioned well apart for privacy. A gray-haired man plays the piano in the corner, and the garlicky scents twirling through the air have me licking my lips in anticipation. My tummy rumbles appreciatively as a waiter leads us to a nice table tucked into the back.

After ordering, we sip our glasses of complimentary prosecco.

"To us." Caleb clinks his glass against mine. "To forever."

Be still my beating heart. Caleb is so romantic, and he's everything I ever wanted. "Amen to that." I agree, enjoying the bubbly liquid as it fizzes in my mouth.

He tips his head to one side.

"What?" I ask, knowing there's a question.

"You don't balk when I say stuff like that now."

"We're officially together, and I've been on that page way longer than you." I shrug and sip my prosecco.

"You didn't say anything when Mom mentioned a double wedding." He scoots in closer, putting his arm around my shoulders. "Is that something you'd like?"

"I've been imagining marrying you since I was eight, Caleb."

"I could get on one knee now." His eyes twinkle with mirth.

"Don't you dare." I level him with a look. "You propose in Paris. I even drew it for you for one of your birthdays. I think I was eleven or—"

"Twelve," he replies with confidence. "You drew us in front of the Eiffel Tower, and I was on one knee handing you a pink flower."

I arch a brow. "You have a very good memory."

He shrugs, smiling into his glass.

"Is that why you have been buying me some variation of pink flowers?"

He nods, reaching out to thread his fingers through my hair. I left it down and wavy because he told me he loves my hair like that. "Thank you for taking a chance on me, Lili. And forgiving me for breaking my promise to you."

"Except you didn't." I put my glass down, not wanting to drink it so fast. It's the only alcohol I'm allowing myself tonight as this is my last week of classes before we have a study week and then my finals start. I need to have a clear head in the morning. I hook my pinkie around his. "You didn't consciously break your promise to me. I see that now, and I'm not letting what those girls did come between us ever again." They're all behind bars awaiting trial.

"You are too good for me, angel." He leans in and kisses me. "And I think I'm addicted to kissing you." He punctuates the statement with a slew of drugging kisses dropped on my lips and along my jawline, gathering us our fair share of side-eyes. But I don't care. I have dreamed of this, and nothing or no one is taking it from me.

A throat clearing breaks us apart as the red-faced waiter stands awkwardly at the table holding two large bowls of pasta.

"Can I get you anything else to drink?" he asks after depositing pasta, bread, olive oil, balsamic vinegar, and a bowl of freshly grated parmesan on the table.

"I'm fine, thanks." I still have some of my prosecco, and we have a large jug of water on the table.

"I'll take an Italian beer," Caleb says, and the man walks off.

We chat and laugh as we eat, and I've never felt more comfortable with another living soul. We feed one another forkfuls of our dishes, in between kisses, and I'm so deliriously in love I feel like shouting it from the rooftops.

After, we take a stroll through Little Italy to walk off some of the food before Caleb drives me back to my apartment.

"I'd invite you to stay, but I have an early start in the morning, and we both know what'll happen if you come in," I say at the door.

"This next month is going to be hell," he says, tugging on some of my curls.

"I know, but then I'm free!"

"I can't wait." He lifts me up and spins me around.

"Caleb, you're making me dizzy," I giggle, planting my hands on his shoulders.

"What are you doing to me, my Lili, hmm?" He nuzzles his lips against that sensitive spot under my ear. "You've cast a spell on me." Slowly, he lowers my body to the floor, ensuring I feel every hard inch of his magnificent body on the way down.

"It must be the same spell you've cast on me because I'm equally enchanted."

"You own me, Lili." Taking my hand, he places it on his chest in the place where his heart beats. "You own me so completely."

"The feeling is definitely mutual." I stretch up and peck his lips. "And I love I can kiss you and touch you anytime I want."

He spreads his arms out. "I'm all yours. Take your fill." He waggles his brows and I dissolve into laughter.

He pulls me into his arms. "Parting is such sweet sorrow that I shall say goodnight till it be morrow."

"Oh my god. You cannot quote Shakespeare to me and then leave." My heart is a pile of gloopy mush in my chest, and every part of me has this man's name stamped all over it.

"Then let me stay." His eyes bore into mine. "Just to sleep. I swear I won't touch you or expect anything else. Just let me hold you, and I'll drive you to campus in the morning."

Gawd, it's so tempting. I really want him to stay, but will I sleep if I'm in the same bed as him? "I've never slept with any man before."

"Fuckface never stayed over?"

I shake my head. "He wanted to, but I always said no."

"I love I get to have all your firsts, and you get to have all my lasts."

How can I say no in the face of that. "You promise it's just to sleep?"

He offers up his pinkie. "Pinkie promise, angel. Just like when we were kids."

I curl my finger around his before pulling him into my apartment, hoping I won't regret it.

Chapter Twenty-Eight
Elisa

I use the bathroom first, purposely dressing in pajama shorts and a matching top rather than one of the silky nightgowns I normally prefer to sleep in. Butterflies swoop into my stomach as I emerge from my en suite bathroom to find a shirtless Caleb sitting on the edge of my bed, flicking through one of my art-history books. "Bathroom's free," I say, gulping back nerves as I pad in bare feet toward the bed. I dump my clothes on the chair and try not to gnaw off the inside of my mouth.

"Come here, Lili." Caleb's deep voice does all kinds of twisty things to my insides. I turn and face him with a flaming face. Pulling me between his parted legs, he peers up at me. "You set the pace, angel, remember?"

I just know my vulnerability is playing across my face as I stare into his stunning big blue eyes. Caleb is so undeniably beautiful and I'm so, so in love with him.

"We're just going to sleep, and you don't need to be nervous." He plants a soft kiss on the underside of my hand. "I promise. Okay?"

I nod and stand back as he rises to his feet. "You're so precious to me, Lili." His fingers sweep across my cheek. "And you're just too fucking adorable." His lips fight a smirk as his gaze rakes over my sleepwear. "Climb in and make yourself comfortable. I'll be back in a few minutes."

Crawling under the covers, I scoot over until I'm facing the wall, trying to talk myself off a ledge. I'm being ridiculous. He's only sleeping beside me. I'm twenty-two, almost twenty-three-years old, and it's crazy to be this nervous about a guy just sleeping beside me. And it's Caleb. I trust him with my life. He won't force me to do anything. He's already promised. Rolling some of my aromatherapy stick on my wrists, I inhale deeply, forcing myself to calm down until I'm relaxed.

The door to the bathroom opens and closes, and the bedroom light goes out. I hear him dropping his clothes on the chair over mine, and then the covers are peeled back as he gets in. Heat immediately warms me from behind.

"Lil," he whispers in a soft seductive voice. "Can I hold you?"

"Yes," I whisper back, barely breathing.

His body glides up against mine from behind, and his bare chest presses into my back. He keeps his groin away, and it only makes me love him more. This is so far removed from what he is used to, but he's not complaining, only accommodating. Taking his arms, I wrap them firmly around my waist and hold on to them.

"I could get used to this," he murmurs against my ear, making me shiver all over.

"I love you," I tell him, lifting my head and turning around so I'm looking at him. I can just make his features out in the dark room. "Thank you for tonight. I had the best time."

"Me too." He brushes his lips against mine. "Love you, Lili."

We kiss softly for a few minutes, and he breaks our lip-lock first. "Sleep, angel." He presses a kiss to the back of my head. "I've got you."

I'm not sure how it happens, but I fall asleep almost immediately, and I don't wake at all during the night.

My eyes pop open five minutes before my alarm is due to go off, and I suck in a gasp when I find myself facing Caleb with my head on his bare chest and my leg thrust in between his. His arms are still around me, and he's sound asleep, his face peaceful in slumber. Shutting off my alarm, I bask in the warmth of his embrace for a few minutes, slyly checking him out.

His upper body is a work of art and an ode to regular sessions in the gym. His shoulders are broad, his chest smooth, and the dips and curves of his abs almost look painted on. He's all silky tan skin, and I'm tempted to lick him all over. My eyes widen as I lower my gaze down his body, my mouth forming an O. The covers have drifted down the bed, revealing the very large bulge straining against his designer boxers.

Holy Hades. That thing is a giant, although I've only seen one other penis in comparison. I stare at it in fascination, wondering what it looks like without anything covering it.

"Liking what you see, Lili?" Caleb asks in a sleep-drenched voice, and I hear the humor in his tone.

"It's so big," I blurt, and he chuckles, pulling me in closer to his chest.

"You do wonders for my ego." His eyes blink open, and they're instantly adoring.

"Just stating the truth."

"You can touch it if you like," he says, taking my hand and hovering it over his groin.

Propping up on one elbow, I lower my hand and tentatively

223

touch him, feeling the weight of him through the material. "And thick."

He smothers a groan by burying his face in the pillow as his cock jerks under my palm. I run my fingers up and down the length and sides of his cock, tracing the outline through his boxers. It jerks a few more times as I stroke it, and my pussy clenches with need.

"What time do you need to leave?" he asks, snapping me out of the lusty daze I'm in.

I look at my phone. "Shit. I need to leave soon." I bite on my lip, wishing I could stay and explore his naked dick, but I've got a tutorial to get to.

"Take a shower, and I'll make you something to eat," he says, lifting me off the bed and setting my feet on the ground.

"What about you?" I eyeball his erection. "Does it hurt?"

He chuckles as he adjusts himself before climbing out of the bed. "I'm okay. It'll go down." He chuckles again as he watches me in amusement. "But not if you keep looking at it like that."

"Sorry." My cheeks inflame.

"Don't apologize. You're perfect, Lili." He presses a kiss to my cheek. "So fucking perfect you have no idea." He swats my ass. "Now go and shower. You're not being tardy on my account."

The next few weeks fly by in a flurry of activity. I'm in the throes of exams but managing to keep my stress levels down, thanks to Caleb. His study care package helped a lot, and he surprises me with impromptu lunches and takeout dinners. He even helps me run through my study notes, and he stays over some nights. It's still strictly PG, and I still ogle his morning wood like it's my favorite popsicle. I'm pretty sure he drives me to school with the biggest blue balls.

"Will you be home later?" Beatrice asks on Saturday evening when I call time on studying. I have two exams left next week, and then I'm home free. I'm as prepared as I can be, so when Caleb offered to cook dinner, I jumped at the chance.

"Not tonight, no. I'll be back sometime tomorrow."

"Enjoy." Her smile seems insincere, but I accept it at face value. Beatrice is a bit of a strange one. She can be friendly and helpful, and then it's like a switch flips, and she's a little catty and jealous. I've seen how she looks at Caleb sometimes, and I don't like it, but I'm not going to say anything because our lease is up in a month, and we won't be roommates for much longer. No point creating tension when I most likely won't see her after we move out.

I'm still wondering what her deal is when I slip out of the building, heading toward the road. Caleb sent a driver to pick me up because he doesn't like me walking the city streets alone. Especially not after pictures of us have appeared online and people are gossiping over the nature of our relationship.

I grasp my bag tighter as I walk toward the car in the near distance. All the tiny hairs on the back of my neck lift, and I glance around as prickles of apprehension wash over me. I pick up my pace, hurrying toward the car as the sensation of eyes on my back follows me all the way. It's not the first time. Recently, I've had the feeling someone is watching me, but there is never anyone there.

"Good evening, Miss Salerno," the driver says when I all but fling myself into the back of the car.

"Hi. Thanks for coming to pick me up, Roberto."

"It's my pleasure, ma'am."

I scout the area outside as we drive off, looking over my shoulder and back at my apartment building, but there is no boogie man watching me from the shadows. Putting it down to my overactive imagination, I settle in with my Kindle as we make our way through the usual busy traffic toward Caleb's penthouse.

———

Caleb is waiting for me at the door when I exit the elevator at the top level. "Hello, beautiful," he says, instantly pulling me into his arms and slamming his lips down on mine. I melt into his arms and his kiss, soaking up his scent and the feel of his body against mine. "Come," he says when we finally surface for air. He grabs my bag. "I made a prawn curry with fried rice, and it's just now ready."

"Sounds yummy, and I'm starving. Studying always make me ravenous," I admit as he leads me into his place. I've only been here one other time, and it was a complete mess, but today it's like a different apartment. "I see the cleaners were here," I tease.

He pins me with a look. "You'll pay for that sass." He sets my bag on the ground and gently squeezes my ass. Based on how often he fondles my butt, I'm going to hazard a guess he's an ass man. Given my rather modest chest, that can only be a good thing. "I'll have you know the cleaners have not been here since Wednesday. This is all me."

"I'm impressed."

"Good," he says. "I cleaned up my act for you."

I burst out laughing, faltering when I see his serious expression. "For real?"

"Yes. I'm trying to be a better man for you. Plus, Joshua has been busting my balls for years over the state of the place."

"I'm flattered, Caleb, but you don't need to change for me. I love you just the way you are."

"Perfect," he mutters before swooping in to steal another kiss. "You're just so fucking perfect."

"Now you're the one feeding *my* ego."

"It's all true. Take a seat." He pulls out a chair at the dining table propped against the floor-to-ceiling window.

"You look pretty, by the way," he says, leaning down to kiss my cheek after I'm situated.

I'm only wearing a casual dress and tennis shoes, but I took some time to fix my hair the way he likes it and I'm wearing a little makeup. "Thank you." I beam up at him, and he winks as he moves over to the kitchen to plate our food.

I admire the view of the city and the park through the window before my gaze trails over the rest of the open-plan space on this level. "I can actually see what your place looks like now. I like it." It's expensively decorated but still homey. He has family photographs pinned to the walls along with some impressive, framed artwork. Rugs soften the dark wooden floors, and colorful cushions brighten the white leather sectional.

"When you move in, you can redecorate if you like." He just casually throws it out there as he sets a bowl of delicious coconut-scented curry in front of me.

I blink repeatedly as I stare at him, and he chuckles as he slides into the seat beside me. "We're inevitable, Lili. You don't need me to tell you that." He lifts a forkful of curry. "Eat before it goes cold. I spent ages cooking everything from scratch."

"I love that you still love to cook," I say before groaning as I swallow the first delicious mouthful. "Wow, this is so good."

"Good." He pecks my lips. "It's a new recipe I got from Mom."

"I find it so funny that you caught the cooking bug from her, yet Joshua is practically allergic to the kitchen."

"Not totally." He waggles his brows and grins. "He can boil water."

I throw back my head and laugh.

Caleb plays music low in the background as I try not to shovel the food in my mouth like a greedy pig.

"I meant what I said," he adds in between mouthfuls. "You haven't found anywhere to live yet after your lease is up, right?"

I shake my head. "I haven't had time to look. I figured I'd probably stay in Uncle Ben's penthouse until I found office space and a new apartment."

"Move in here. You'd have Gia right next door, and it's central and secure."

"You're really serious?"

"As a heart attack."

"We've only been dating three weeks."

"Who gives a shit?" He shrugs. "We've known each other for almost fifteen years, Lili, and we're endgame. You know it as well as I do."

"I don't know what to say."

"Say yes." He lets his vulnerability shine through for a minute while I try to work out if this is crazy or inevitable.

"I got us a new bed," he adds, rubbing the back of his neck. "And sleeping beside you is the best sleep I've ever had in my whole entire life."

"I sleep great with you too," I admit, stuffing another mouthful of curry into my mouth while I contemplate doing this. Excitement fizzes in my veins, and when I see the raw need on his face mixed with sheer terror, I know what I need to do.

"Okay." A wide smiles races across my lips. "I'll move in with you after graduation."

Chapter Twenty-Nine
Caleb

"What's in here?" Lili asks, frowning as she turns the handle to my special room, finding it locked. "Is this the room you don't let anyone into?" She quirks a brow as she glances at me over her shoulder. "Gigi said it's some kind of sex den. Is it?"

My lips tip up. "That girl has her mind in the gutter." I walk forward and stretch my arm up, pressing my thumb into the little lockbox over the door. "No, it's not a sex den." The lock pops open, and I extract the key. "You are the first person I'm letting into this room," I truthfully admit as I turn the key in the lock.

"Joshua hasn't even seen it?"

I shake my head. "When I set this up, a couple months after we moved into this building, I made a vow that the only person who would ever enter this space was you."

Her entire face lights up. "Now I'm really intrigued."

I open the door and switch on the light, stepping back to let her enter first. "After you."

Her eyes almost pop out of her head as she surveys the

small square room, taking in all the framed pictures on the wall. Crystal lilies in vases are dotted on display tables around the room, surrounding the small two-seater couch with a coffee table situated in front of the open fireplace. A shelving unit on the right stores books, boardgames, and framed photos of Lili and me taken over the years. There are pictures ranging from when we were kids right up to today.

"Oh my god, Caleb." Her voice comes out all breathy, and it instantly stirs things down south. I quickly adjust myself while I watch her reaction. I have imagined it many times, and now the moment is here, it's a little surreal. Her hand covers her mouth as she walks to the left wall. "These are...this is..." She's all choked up, and emotion glimmers in her eyes.

Walking up behind her, I wrap my arms around her waist and rest my chin on top of her head. "Every picture and hand-drawn card you have ever given me."

She trails her finger over the little raised tabs underneath each frame. It's stamped with the year she drew it. Air trickles out of her mouth in rattled spurts as we move silently down the wall while she inspects every piece of her custom artwork. "You planned ahead," she whispers, skimming her fingers over the empty space above last year's tab.

"It was clearly presumptuous of me." I attempt to make light of it, but looking at the empty space where last year's birthday drawing and card should be always brings a painful lump to my throat.

"No." She turns around in my arms, fixing me with glassy eyes. "That's on me. I'm so sorry, Caleb. I should have spoken to you about those girls at the time it happened instead of freezing you out." Pain flares in her eyes. "It killed me avoiding your birthday party, and I..." She reaches up, dragging her fingers through my stubble, and I barely manage to stifle a moan. "I still have them."

"Have what?" I ask, struggling to focus on the conversation with the way her soft fingertips are caressing my face.

"Your birthday card and drawing." Steely reserve is etched across her face. "Come up to the apartment tomorrow, and I'll give them to you." She turns back to the wall, lowering her hands from my face, and I try not to pout. "I can't believe you did this, Caleb. I'm in shock."

I hug her closer to my body. "I told you it's always been you. This is my special space. When I'm feeling low or in need of cheering up, I come in here and play music or read as I look at every piece of art you've ever given me, and it has always soothed my soul. You're my happy place, Lil. My home. My comfort. My joy."

"Caleb." She spins around again, throwing her arms around my neck. "I am so incredibly, deeply in love with you. I have never been so happy. I pinch myself every day when I wake because I wanted this for so long and now it's happening and some days it all feels like a dream."

"It's real, angel. We're the real deal, and I'm going nowhere."

We spend a couple of hours drinking wine and reminiscing over old times while Nat King Cole, Frank Sinatra, and Elvis Presley play in the background. Having her in here feels like everything has come full circle. It feels like I'm exactly where I belong, and my life is finally complete.

I cannot wait to make Elisa Salerno my wife, and I vow to begin planning a Paris trip so I can propose and finally see the lily ring I bought for her on her finger.

I turn on my bedside lamp and switch off the main lights in my bedroom as I wait for Lili to emerge from the bathroom. It's the first night she is staying over at my place, and I'm more excited than a kid on Christmas morning—at the prospect of just holding her in my arms. I'm not expecting anything. I'm letting her set the pace, and I refuse to put her under any pressure, especially when she's taking exams.

The bathroom door opens, and I peel back the covers making room for my love. Elisa pads toward the bed, and my eyes widen as I drink her in. She's wearing a thigh-skimming silk and lace nightie that glides over her gorgeous body, leaving little to the imagination.

My cock instantly springs to life. "Fuck." I rub at my lips as I watch a pretty flush stain her cheeks. "Are you trying to kill me, Lil?"

She giggles as she climbs into the bed and crawls over my lap. "That's not what I had in mind." Leaning down, she kisses me passionately, and I grab her ass through her nightie, groaning as she grinds shyly on top of my erection.

"What are you up to, angel?" I ask, nuzzling my lips against her neck.

"I'm ready," she whispers, placing her hands on my shoulders and peering at me with lust-drenched eyes.

"Ready for what, Lili? I need you to say the words."

"Make love to me, Caleb. I want to know what it feels like to have you moving inside me." She rocks her hips, and her panty-covered crotch slides against my dick making me painfully hard.

"Could we compromise?" I ask, running my fingers up her bare thighs. I can't believe I'm going to say this, but my gut hasn't led me astray yet. "I think we should build up to sex until I know you're definitely ready. We don't need to rush into it. We can do other things first. I want to plan something special for your first time so it's a memory we always cherish."

"Oh." Her blush deepens. "What other things?"

"Take your nightie off, and I'll show you." My hands glide under the silky material, and my fingers brush against her crotch. My dick is like steel behind my pajama pants, and I'm liable to come from just having her sit on me.

She audibly gulps as her fingers move to the hem of her nightdress, and she's trembling a little.

"Lili." I gently grasp her wrist and sit up straighter with her still in my lap. "You set the pace, my love. Remember?" She nods. "We don't have to do this now. We can just sleep. There is no ticking clock."

"I want to progress things, Caleb, and maybe you're right. Maybe I'm not ready yet for sex, but I need you. I ... you make me so horny, and I know you're horny too, and I want to take care of you."

Gawd, this girl. She's unbelievably sweet, and I don't know what I did in life to deserve her, but I offer up thanks every day.

"Do you trust me, angel?" I ask before leaning in to press a tender kiss to her soft lips.

"With my life, Caleb."

"Then trust me to know what you need and to give it to you." Tension lifts from her gaze as she nods. "Good girl." I claim her lips in a deep kiss, holding her body close to mine as our mouths take and take. I don't push, content to kiss her without urgency until she gradually loosens up in my arms. Then I up the ante, kissing her more passionately and driving my tongue into her mouth. Lili moans, pivoting her hips on top of me as my arms tighten around her back, and I thrust my dick against her soft place.

Moving fast, I flip us so she's lying flat on the bed underneath me. Nudging her legs wide, I settle in between them, gently thrusting against her as we continue kissing, silently rejoicing when she writhes against me, pressing her pussy into my dick and whimpering into my mouth. Slowly, I lower the

233

straps on her nightie, continuing to kiss her as I reveal her bare breasts. Without breaking our lip-lock, I cup her boobs. Both are a perfect handful, and I marvel at her soft silky flesh and the feel of her nipples pebbling beneath my touch. My mouth glides from her lips, down to her neck, her collarbone, and lower as I move my body down the bed. My lips close over one nipple as my fingers toy with the other.

"Oh god, Caleb." She arches her back as I alternate between both tits while dry humping the bed and leaking precum like a reborn teenager. "That feels so good."

"I love these," I say, kneeling between her legs and fondling her tits in my hands.

"I know they're not very big, but—"

I cover her mouth with my hand. "Nuh-uh." I shake my head. "You're perfect, Lili. Every single part of you is perfect. You were made for me."

Whatever fleeting self-consciousness just reared its head disappears in her happy smile, and I breathe a sigh of relief. "I want to see the rest of you. May I?" Gripping her nightie, I wait for her consent, which she readily gives. I shimmy the material down her body and toss it aside, leaving her in flimsy lace panties. "Trust me, angel?" I lift her legs and spread them before planting her feet on the mattress, exposing her to me.

"Always, Caleb."

I press a kiss to her mound through her panties, smiling as her hips jerk and a small "oh" leaks from her lips. "Has anyone ever kissed you here?" I inquire, chanting "please say no" over and over in my head.

She shakes her head, and I silently fist pump the air. "He never did that, just with his, um, fingers, and I, um, I sucked his dick."

I'm instantly seeing red imagining her lush mouth anywhere near that asshole's cock, but I force my anger aside

234

because I can't use it against her. Lili isn't the one I'm angry with. "He's a selfish prick," I say, rubbing her through the lace. "But it's good news for me because I get to claim this first."

"That feels good," she whispers as I push down on her clit with my thumb while my fingers glide up and down her slit. Lili throws her head back, and she's like a goddess with her gorgeous hair fanned out on the pillow, her flushed cheeks, swollen lips, and chest arched, nipples taut and standing at attention. Hooking my thumbs in the sides of her panties, I watch her face as I slowly lower her legs to the bed and drag them down her body. Elisa lifts her head, her heated gaze meeting mine as I discard her panties and stretch her legs wider, pushing her knees up toward her chest.

I lie on my stomach in between her legs staring at the holy grail. "Look at you," I say before blowing on her glistening pussy. "You're so fucking beautiful." I part her folds and stare at her virgin cunt with possession and dark desire. The animal inside me wants to conquer and devour, but I keep that beast caged, knowing Lili deserves the gentlest touch.

"Are you going to look at me all day or kiss me like you promised?" she asks, and my chest rumbles with laughter.

I fix her with amused eyes. "So, it's gonna be like that, huh?" I slowly glide my finger up and down her slit. She almost lifts off the bed and her arms collapse onto the mattress as she moans loudly. "Be as demanding as you like, Lil. Tell me what you want," I say before licking a path through her folds. Her whimpering response almost has me coming on the spot. My dick is rock hard and oozing precum, dampening the front of my sleep pants.

"More, Caleb," she pants, thrusting her hips as I leisurely roll my tongue up and down her slit.

"Yes, ma'am." I drive my tongue inside her tight walls, groaning as her taste explodes on my tongue like the sweetest nectar. I'm dry humping the bed as I plunge my tongue in and out of her innocent cunt while my fingers lightly play with her swollen clit. Lili's head is thrown back in passion, and I reach a hand up, flicking one nipple and then the other with my thumb and pointer finger.

"Caleb!" she screams, arching her back more as I pick up my pace, thrusting my tongue in and out with fervor. "That feels so good. Don't stop, baby. Please don't stop."

I add a finger to her pussy, driving it inside her in sync with the thrusts of my tongue, and then I rub her clit harder, pressing down as I feel her walls clench around me. Her legs press against the side of my face as I work her harder, and then she cries out, moaning and screaming my name as her thighs almost strangle my face. Her hips buck up, and her body wriggles and writhes as she shatters on my tongue. I stay with her through her climax, lapping at her juices until I've sucked her dry.

When she's finally sated, I crawl over her body and plant my lips on hers, letting her taste herself on me as my fingers thread through her hair. "How was that, my love?" I purr, trailing my lips down the side of her gorgeous face.

"The best goddamned feeling in the entire world." Lili grins at me before shoving me down on the bed and flipping on top of me.

My eyes drink in her naked body with raw hunger. "You're so beautiful, Lil." I squeeze her ass cheeks as I lick my lips, imagining them wrapped around her nipples. "You're perfect."

"I want to see you," she demands, shimmying her way down my body.

"Go for it, angel." I tuck my hands under my head and lift my hips, letting her pull my sleep pants down my legs.

"That will never fit inside me," she says, examining my dick up close and personal with a look that is part intrigue and part horror.

A laugh bursts from my chest. "Trust me, angel. It'll fit, and you'll love it."

Tentatively, she touches my cock, and I jerk against her hand. Her fingers curl halfway around the base of my shaft. "You're beautiful." Her gaze is full of awe, and it does wonders for my ego.

Despite the torture, I let her explore my cock and my balls, groaning loudly when her fingers rub against my taint.

"Do you like that?"

"I like everything you do to me," I pant as my hips jerk when her tongue touches the tip of my dick. She gives a few exploratory licks, and it's part heaven, part hell. She begins tentatively stroking my shaft, and I place my hand over hers, moving faster and showing her how I like it. Lying back, I let her work me over, fighting the urge to come because I want to savor the moment.

"Aagh," I call out when her mouth closes over the tip of my cock, and she slowly glides her lips up and down my erection. I show her how to hold my skin tight at the base and stroke me up and down while her lips work their magic. Lili is an eager student and a fast learner, and watching her head bob over my dick is all it takes to feel a familiar tingle in my spine and a tightness in my balls. "I'm going to come. Pull back if you don't want me to come in your mouth." That's a lot to ask of a virgin, and I don't have any expectations.

Her mouth suctions harder on my shaft, and she relaxes her jaw, swallowing me farther. I roar her name as my dick spurts in her mouth, ejecting ropes of salty cum down her throat. She stays latched on until I'm spent before releasing me from her mouth with a pop. She sidles up beside me, propping up on one elbow and peering down at me with bright eyes and flushed cheeks. "Was that okay?"

"It was more than okay." I clasp the nape of her neck. "You're a natural, Lili, and I love you so much." We meet halfway as our lips collide and our limbs tangle, and I decide I never want to get out of this bed.

Chapter Thirty
Caleb

"Caleb!" Elisa shrieks, shoving my shoulders as I lower to my knees in the elevator and push her dress up to her hips. "The cameras!"

"I turned them off," I confirm as I push her panties to one side and plunge two fingers into her pussy. "You're fucking drenched, Lili."

"What'd you expect?" she murmurs, gripping the railing to hold herself steady as I rip the panties from her body and attack her with my mouth. "You got me all worked up in the restaurant."

We've just come from dinner with her family in the city after celebrating her graduation. I might have been feeling her up under the table any chance I got. From the looks Romeo was giving me across the table, I'm sure he had an inkling of what was going down, but he was never going to say anything in front of Serena and Alesso.

In the two weeks since we first had oral sex, we've both become insatiable for the taste of one another, spending every night together either at her place or here at mine. Lili is open to try anything, and I'm quickly learning what she likes and what gets her off. She's so responsive, and I've given her multiple orgasms at a time with just my fingers and my tongue.

I glance at the display on the wall, determined to rock her world before we reach the top floor. Adding another finger inside her tight walls, I pump them faster as my lips suction over that swollen bundle of nerves.

"Oh, fuck, Caleb." Lili grabs chunks of my hair as I ravish her pussy. "You are sooo good at that."

I grin into her cunt as I curl my fingers deep inside her, hitting her G-spot as I lightly graze her clit with my teeth.

An earth-shattering scream bounces off the walls of the elevator before she shouts my name and convulses on my mouth, bucking her hips and riding my face. The elevator slows as we reach the top, and I stand, quickly fixing her dress over her body just in time. The elevator pings, and the doors glide open, revealing a scowling Anais on the other side.

Holding Lili's hand tight, I pull her out into the lobby, tucking her protectively into my side, as Anais enters the elevator. "What do you want, Anais?" I glare at her when I see the way she's looking at my love.

Anais thrusts her foot into the elevator, keeping it open. "To ask if you had any update on my husband."

"There have been no sightings since he kidnapped his son. You'll be the first to know when he surfaces."

Anais glances at the torn lace shreds littering the elevator floor with poisonous eyes. "I guess the rumors are true." Hurt flares in her eyes as she looks between me and Elisa. "Why her, Caleb? What does she have that I don't?"

"She is everything you are not, and it's one of the many reasons why I love her and why she'll one day be my wife."

"Caleb!" Elisa chastises me with her tone and her look, but

I won't apologize for speaking the cruel truth. Anais needs to understand Lili is my endgame.

"She'll never keep you satisfied," she hisses.

"She already does in ways you couldn't even begin to comprehend."

Something flashes in her eyes, but it's gone before I can read it. "Then I guess it's truly over between us."

"It's been over between us for years, Anais, not that it was ever anything more than sex."

"For you maybe." Sadness veils her eyes as she lowers them to the ground. When she lifts her head, a weird expression is on her face. She turns to face Elisa. "I know I've been a bitch to you, but you won him fair and square."

"He's not a prize, and it was never a competition." Lili softens her tone, and she's looking at her cousin with compassion Anais doesn't deserve.

"I just want you to know I won't cause any trouble."

My eyes narrow in suspicion. This is not Anais. What the fuck is she up to?

"Uh, okay." Lili doesn't know what to make of it either.

"I hope you're both very happy," she says before the elevator doors close.

We stand outside it for a few seconds in silence.

"That was weird," Lili says.

"Extremely, and I don't trust her." I scanned my place after her snooping visit, figuring she might have planted a recording device, but I didn't find anything.

"Maybe she has finally seen the error of her ways," Lili says, pressing her finger to the keypad at my door. I had her added to the security system so she can come and go as she pleases.

"Perhaps," I mumble as I reactivate the camera in the elevator. Anais has already gotten out on her floor. I shoot off a quick text to the surveillance team, reminding them to continue watching her closely.

"I take it she doesn't know about the lockbox or the trap?" Elisa holds the door open for me, and I lean down to peck her lips as I walk into the penthouse.

"No. We would never trust her with that intel."

Gia found the lockbox key embedded in the side of one of Gino's old folders, but there was no information pertaining to which bank or financial institution housed the lockbox and no identifying markers on the key. It was my idea to set a trap. To stage a false fire at the Accardi Company and leave the door to the filing room open with the key in plain sight. We figured whoever was staking out the place for Cruz wouldn't pass up the opportunity to slip inside the building while all the employees congregated on the sidewalk outside.

It went down earlier today, and it worked like a charm. Two men broke in and stole the key, and we've had them shadowed ever since. As a precaution, we had copies made of the key because we need to hold on to the original. The copy we planted contains an embedded tracker so we can monitor its movements even if we lose sight of the thieves. Now we just wait and see which bank they go to, and then we'll ambush them and steal the contents before it falls into the wrong hands.

We don't expect Cruz to show his face. It's too risky, and we're banking on his goons being goons.

"Has Joshua or Gia called yet?" Elisa kicks off her heels and dumps her purse on the island unit.

"No." I loosen my tie and lift it over my head, depositing it beside Elisa's purse. "I'm guessing there's no update yet."

We have men stationed in hidden vans and locations around the area where the key is, waiting for something to happen. Gia and Joshua are at Commission Central along with most of the other dons, awaiting news. As soon as there's a location, everyone will swing into action. I bailed because it's Elisa's graduation and I'm not needed. We have enough resources on this, and the other dons can handle it without me.

I walk to the refrigerator and remove the bottle of Cristal champagne I stashed there earlier. Grabbing a couple of flutes, I follow Elisa into the living area, setting the glasses and champagne down on the coffee table beside the large envelope I put there earlier.

"I have a graduation gift for you," I say, batting my nerves away as I hand her the envelope and sit beside her on the couch. I hope she appreciates the gesture and doesn't think I'm overstepping the mark.

"You didn't have to get me anything," she says over a wide smile.

I place my hand over hers on the envelope. "Before you open it, know nothing is set in stone. I hope you don't think I have interfered. I just wanted to help, but you can say no if you like."

Her brow puckers. "Okay." She draws out the word as I remove my hand and let her open the envelope and remove the contents. "What is this?" She flips through the impressive glossy brochure.

"Your new office space." She gives me a wide-eyed stare. "It's only three blocks from the Accardi Company building, so it's in a good part of town and easily accessible from here. It's owned by Caltimore Holdings, so if you don't like it, I can get out of the lease. The rest of the space on that floor is rented by other small businesses, and they have a communal hub with a coffee dock, a cafeteria, a gym, and various sized meeting rooms you can book when you want to meet clients."

"How did you find time to do this?"

I brush her hair off her shoulders. "You're the most important person in my life, Lili. I will always make the time for you.

I wanted to take some of the pressure off you. You were busy with exams, so I talked to your mom about the kind of office space you might need and then I spoke to Ben." I shrug 'cause it really wasn't a big deal, and I didn't invest too much time or energy.

"You are so good to me." Flinging her arms around my neck, she plants a firm kiss on my lips. "Thank you so much."

"We can take a tour of the space tomorrow before we pack up your stuff if you like."

"Sounds like a plan though it might take more than a day to box up all my things at the apartment."

Lili is moving in tomorrow, and I've been on a countdown ever since she agreed to share the penthouse with me.

"There's one other thing," I add, picking up the second brochure. "This PR firm came highly recommended by the VP of marketing at our company. The owner is a friend of hers, and they specialize in small businesses and start-ups. I made an appointment for you, and the owner is personally going to handle your account. They will help you with brand manage-ment and marketing and publicity."

She stares at me like I hung the moon in the sky. "You are the best boyfriend, Caleb Accardi, and I'm so lucky to call you mine." She jumps onto my lap and peppers my face with kisses. "I love you."

"Love you too." I squeeze her ass, relieved she took the gesture at face value and didn't get upset. "More and more with every passing day."

"Well," she says, lowering herself to the ground. "Today's your lucky day." She kneels between my legs and grins as her hands reach for my crotch. "You deserve a reward, and I know just the thing."

Chapter Thirty-One
Caleb

T he girls disappear into the bedroom with a bunch of bridal magazines, giggling excitedly, and I wish Lili was also looking at dress ideas. The more I think about the double wedding suggestion, the more I like it.

"So, you set a date?" I ask, pouring two cups of fresh coffee and handing one to my brother.

He nods and smiles. "Gia wants to get married on New Year's Eve."

That gives me plenty of time to propose to Elisa. Propping my elbows on the island unit, I eyeball my brother. "Would you be opposed to a double wedding?"

He arches one groomed eyebrow. "Have you proposed and forgotten to tell me?"

"Not yet, but I'm planning to do it on Lili's birthday. I'm taking her to Paris."

"Canada and now Paris? You're turning into quite the romantic, little brother."

I shove my middle finger up at him. "I'm making Lili's

dreams come true, and you can't throw shade because you're as gone for your woman as I am for mine."

His features soften. "I'm happy for you, Caleb. Elisa is good for you. I have never seen you so at peace within yourself."

"She was the missing piece, J." I sip on my coffee as I consider how the answer to my unhappiness was always right under my nose.

"I'm not opposed to a double wedding," he confirms, "but it'll be up to the girls. Whatever they decide is fine by me."

"It'd be cool to get married together though, right?"

"Seems fitting because we've always pretty much done everything together."

"Love you, broski." I round the island unit and pull my brother into a hug.

"Love you too."

We separate, and I return to my side of the counter. "Tell me about last night." I was in bed, doing all kinds of naughty things with Lili, short of full sex, when everything went down.

"The lockbox was at Barron Financial and Investment."

I roll my eyes. "Typical. We should have just called Charlie Barron and asked him to check." A friend of a friend introduced us to the CEO of the bank years ago, and though he's older than us and married with a family, we've become good friends. Charlie is based in Boston, where the bank HQ is, but he would have made arrangements to get us into the branch here.

"It's a moot point now. We have the box and the goons Cruz hired. They were saying jack shit when we ambushed them, so they were taken to the bunker. Ben and Massimo are going to question them today."

"What was in the box?" I ask, peeling an orange from the fruit bowl.

"A USB key. It's password protected, so Fiero took it to see if he can crack it."

"I'm sure it's only a matter of time. I doubt the tech Gino used is anywhere near as sophisticated as the tech we have now, and Fiero keeps his skills updated." I pop an orange segment into my mouth.

"Agreed. It must be something special if he went to so much trouble to hide it."

I shrug, not really caring now it's safely in our grasp. "Cruz must know by now we've thwarted him. What's his next move?" I muse out loud.

"Nothing good, I'm sure. But one thing we definitely know is he won't back down."

We're two blocks from Lili's apartment when her cell pings, cutting us off mid-conversation. I'm keeping one eye on the road and one eye on my sweet, sexy girlfriend so I see the moment all the blood drains from her face. "What's wrong?"

"Pull over." Her voice trembles, and her hand is shaking around her cell.

I spot a loading bay parking space on my left, outside, ironically, a bridal dress store, and I flick the blinker and drive into the spot. As soon as I kill the engine, I unbuckle my seat belt and swivel in my seat. "You're scaring me, angel. Show me."

She hands the phone over without hesitation, and my blood instantly boils when I see the threatening text message. *Sluts deserve to die* is the caption beside a montage of photos of Lili and me. One was taken last night as we exited the restaurant where we had dinner with the Salerno family.

"Who sent this?" I ask though one suspect instantly springs to mind.

"I don't know the number."

"This reeks of a spurned ex, and considering you only have one, my money's on Sebastien. He's a fucking dead man." I forward the text to Fiero and ask him to trace the number. I was going to send it to Philip, but he's Ben's guy, and word may get back to Alesso. I want to gather all the facts before I call Elisa's father because he's going to go crazy, and he'll want to take immediate action. I need to be sure my personal bias against fuckface isn't clouding my judgment in case something else is at play here.

"I had a feeling someone was watching me," she admits in a quiet voice.

"What the fuck, Lil?" My eyes dart over her face. "Why the hell didn't you say anything?"

"I thought I was imagining it because there was never anyone there!"

"Has anything else happened I need to know?"

She knots her hands in her lap and wets her lips.

"Spit it out, Lil."

In a quiet voice, she tells me what went down the night she broke it off with him.

"He *hit* you?" It takes huge effort not to raise my voice. "That fucking degenerate raised his hand in anger toward you, and you told no one?" I slam my hands repeatedly down on the wheel, wishing it was Sebastien's neck so I could wring it.

"Don't be mad, Caleb. I didn't tell you because I knew you'd kill him, and I didn't want his death on my conscience."

"Of course, I'd kill him! He fucking hit you, Elisa!" I take her hands in mine and force myself to calm down, remembering I'm not angry with her. I'll reserve my rage for fuckface. "How badly were you hurt?"

"I had a bruise for a few days, but I was fine."

"I'm going to kill him for daring to put his hands on you in anger, and you're not going to stop me." I drill her with a challenging look because I'm not backing down from this.

"If we find evidence he's behind this, I won't stop you."

"Good." Her words take the edge off my rage. I gently clasp her face and kiss her softly. "Promise me if anything like that happens ever again you'll tell me immediately and trust me to handle it the right way. If someone hurts you, they deserve to die, Elisa. End of."

"Okay."

I thread my fingers through her silky hair. "I know you have the best heart, Lili. I know you want to see the good in everyone, but not everyone is good. You need to trust me to take care of you and know that I will do whatever it takes to ensure your safety."

"I trust you, Caleb. I'm just not a fan of slaughtering everyone in cold blood unless it's warranted. Then I'll cheer you on from the sideline."

"Good girl." I crash my lips onto hers. "Let's get you packed up and moved out. You're not spending another night in that apartment."

I go to take a piss in the bathroom while Lili heads into her bedroom to begin packing. I am lowering the zipper on my jeans when a loud scream rips through the apartment, and I rush out of the bathroom, racing to Lili's bedroom with panic blaring in my ears. "What the—?" I stumble over my words when I see the mess waiting on Elisa's bed.

"Oh my god." She's visibly shaking, and I pull her back, bundling her in my arms and pressing her face into my chest.

"Son of a bitch." Blood is all over her pink and white comforter, but it's the picture of Lili with a bullet hole in her head stuffed in the dead pig's mouth that sends chills racing up my spine.

"What's—" Beatrice screams, and I turn around with Lili in my arms, narrowing my gaze on her roommate.

I make a split-second decision and dart toward the girl, grabbing her by the throat and shoving her against the wall. "Who the fuck did you let in here?"

Her eyes pop wide in fear as she grabs my wrist and tries to free herself. "No...one," she croaks.

"Caleb." Lili comes up to my side and touches my waist. "Let her go so she can speak."

Reluctantly, I loosen my hold on her throat while still keeping her pinned to the wall. "Talk," I snap.

"I didn't let anyone in, I swear."

"You're lying." I dig my thumbs into the side of her neck as a tear spills from her eyes. "I will give you one last chance, Beatrice. Lie to me again, and I'm throwing you out the window."

"I'm not lying," she says, sobbing as she peers deep into my eyes. "I wouldn't lie to you, Caleb. I love you!"

"What?" Lili says, sounding as dumbfounded as I feel.

"You think you were the only little girl with a crush?" she hisses, glaring at Elisa.

"Look at her like that again. I dare you." I squeeze her throat for extra measure as Lili pulls up my zipper.

"Please." Her voice is strangled as I choke the air from her lungs.

"Let her speak, Caleb." Lili tugs on my arm. "She knows something. I'd prefer we find out what it is before you toss her out the window."

I let go, and she slides to the ground, gasping for air and clutching her throat. Draping my body around Lili's, I hold on to her to stop myself from making good on my threat.

"I didn't let him in," Beatrice says in between sobs, "but I saw Sebastien leaving as I was coming back from the grocery store. He didn't see me, and I just presumed he'd come looking for you and left when no one was home."

"How did he get in if you didn't let him?" I growl, not trusting this bitch one little bit.

"He stole my spare keys." Elisa turns to look at me. "I kept a spare set in my locker at school, and they went missing months back."

"He's a dead man when I get my hands on him." I clasp Lili's hand in mine before shooting daggers at the bitch cowering on the floor. I jab my finger in her direction. "And if I find out you had anything to do with this, you're dead too."

"Get out," Lili says, pointing at the door. "I don't want to see or speak to you again."

Beatrice scrambles to her feet, sniffling and wiping her eyes with the back of her sleeve. I feel her eyes glued to me as she leaves, but I ignore her. I hold Lili's face in my hands. "Are you okay?"

She bobs her head. "I'm fine. I just got a fright when I first saw it." She grinds her teeth. "Now I'm just mad. Fuck that asshole."

Lili rarely curses, and it shouldn't turn me on, especially in this moment, but it does. Then again, everything about her turns me on these days. "I'm going to make him pay."

"Good. I won't lose any sleep over it."

"Grab enough stuff for a few days," I tell Lili. "I'll send someone over to pack up the rest of your things. We're not staying here any longer than necessary."

Elisa removes a bag from her closet and begins throwing clothes into it. I snap a pic of the pig's head on the bed and repocket my phone.

"I'm done," my girl says ten minutes later, and I grab the large duffel bag from her hand and sling it over my shoulder.

Chapter Thirty-Two
Caleb

"R eady?" My gaze dances between Joshua, Alesso, and Cristian as we wait outside the two-story cabin nestled in the middle of a forest in the Hudson Valley where fuckface is hiding out. It didn't take long to pinpoint his location or prove he's the one who was stalking Lili. As soon as I had proof, I dropped in to see Alesso at the CH building where he works because I knew he'd want in on this. To say he was enraged is an understatement.

"Let's get this fucker," Cristian says as the three of them slide their hands into black gloves.

The property is owned by a friend of Sebastien's, and we don't want to leave evidence of our crime.

"We'll take the rear," Joshua says, and I nod as he and Alesso take off for the back of the property, keeping hidden between trees.

Cristian wears an orange lightweight mesh jacket and matching cap we stole from the delivery driver when he showed up ten minutes ago. The dude is currently taking a "nap" in the trunk of his Prius. I shove the takeout bag in my buddy's hand and flash him a devilish grin. "Showtime!" I flex my hands, enjoying the glint of silver glimmering under the moonlight from the brass knuckles I'm wearing.

I creep up behind Cristian as he advances toward the door, keeping behind his back so I'm not seen if fuckface looks out the window.

I stand to one side with my back plastered against the wooden structure as my buddy rings the bell. As soon as the door is fully open, I reach around, grab fuckface by the shirt, and ram my fist into his face. He screams like a bitch as blood gushes from the cuts I've just opened, stumbling back as we push our way inside. Cristian shuts and locks the door as I thrust my fist into the other side of Sebastien's face, relishing the spurt of blood that splatters over my shirt.

He doesn't put up much of a fight as we drag him by his arms across the lower level of the cabin toward the back door where Alesso and my twin are waiting. I slap a piece of tape over the asshole's mouth as Cristian opens the door to the others. Alesso grabs Sebastien outside and goes to town on him, pummeling his face repeatedly while I kick him in the ribs, his stomach, and between his legs.

J disappears inside the house to take care of the cameras while Cristian, Alesso, and I drag him farther into the woods and away from the cabin. Alesso dumps the bag with supplies on the forest floor while I get to work stripping the bastard who hurt my girl. He's whimpering and clutching his stomach like the pussy he is.

When he's naked, we tie him to a tree and douse him in ice-cold water. Joshua shows up a few minutes later, nodding to confirm the cameras are dealt with. I calmly remove the baseball bat I customized earlier from the bag. Sharp nails protrude from the tip and the sides, and I pin him with a malicious grin as I approach. I rip the tape off his mouth and hover over him. "Any last words, fuckface?"

"Yeah, asshole," he pants, spitting blood onto the forest floor. "I fingered her first."

Alesso rams his fist into the dick's stomach before shooting his kneecaps. Blood gushes from the gaping holes as Sebastien howls in pain.

"Not so brave now, dickwad." I bury the end of my bat into his left knee and twist.

Anguished shouts pepper the air, but there's no one around for miles to hear him. Tears stream down his face as he loses control of his bladder. We hop back, chuckling as he pisses all over the place. "Please," he says, finally realizing the gravity of the situation he's in. "I'm sorry. Just let me go, and I won't tell anyone."

"You think you can hurt the girl I love and live?" I swing the bat at his groin, reveling in the animalistic sounds lacing the air. "Fuck you, fuckface. You were never going to live." I bring the bat down on his body, raining vengeance on every inch of him as I swing it over and over, ripping skin and pounding bones. Every cry of pain is music to my ears, and I zone out, going into that dark place in my head, as I make this fucker pay for hurting my Lili.

Blood covers me as I continue beating the fucker until he's an unrecognizable pile of broken limbs and shredded skin.

"Enough, Caleb." I come to as Alesso and Joshua are trying to haul me back. "He's dead," Alesso says. "He can't hurt her or threaten her again."

Throwing the bloodied bat away, I breathe deeply as I watch Cristian and Alesso untie what's left of Sebastien from the tree and toss him to the forest floor. Cristian adds his hat and jacket to the pile with my bat. Joshua dons a full plastic face mask and he's wearing protective gloves as he carries the empty barrel over to the bloody pile. Cristian and Alesso help him to put Sebastien's remains and the other evidence into the drum, and then they back away, coming to join me as we watch my twin work magic.

Joshua carries the vat of hydrochloric acid over to the container where he carefully pours it inside. We watch in morbid fascination as it literally melts away skin and bone until fuckface is nothing but chemical soup. Joshua seals the drum with a secure lid, and then we carry it to the truck we came in, depositing the drum and truck at the chemical plant we stole it from on our way back to the city.

I'm covered in dried blood as I step foot in my penthouse sometime later. I disposed of my brass knuckles, socks, and shoes in the incinerator on the ground level before coming up in the elevator. I don't want to trail muddy, bloody footprints across my pristine hardwood floors.

The lights are out downstairs, but I'm guessing Lili is still waiting up for me. She knew we were going after her ex, and I doubt she could sleep knowing I wasn't home. When I step into our bedroom, I see I'm right. Shock splays across her face when she sees me. Setting her book down on the bedside table, she slides out of bed and comes over to me. She links her fingers through mine. "I don't need to ask how it went," she adds, pulling me into the bathroom.

The monster residing inside me still wants to play, but I ball my hands into fists at my sides, working hard to leash the beast. In the past, I'd have gone to Club H and fucked my way through the orgy room to expend the remaining aggression. Lili turns the shower on, and steam begins filling the room. Her hand darts out to remove my shirt, but I hold her wrist, stalling her. "Don't." I step away, willing the adrenaline racing through my veins to calm down.

"You don't scare me, Caleb."

"I should." My entire body is trembling from sheer blood-lust. "I'm not fully in control now, Lili. Go back to bed. I'll join you in a while."

"I want to help," she says, moving a step closer.

"Don't come any closer, Elisa," I warn, sidestepping her. "I just need some time to calm down."

"What do you normally do?" she asks, standing before me in a pure angelic white silk nightie.

I bark out a laugh. "You don't want to know."

"I do." She juts her chin up as steam swirls around the room.

"I'd go to a sex club and fuck, angel. Hard and fast for hours and hours until it was all gone from my system."

She gulps. "You can fuck me. You know I'm ready."

"Hell no." I vigorously shake my head. "I'm not doing that to you."

Hurt flares in her eyes. "Because I don't know what I'm doing?" she asks in a timid voice, and my protective side surges to the fore.

"No, Lil. That's not it. It's because you're too good to be fucked like a whore."

"What if I want you to?" Her chin juts up again. "What if I like it?"

Jesus Christ. She's really not helping. "If that's what you want, we can do it." She moves toward me with her lips curling into a smile. "But not tonight. I'd traumatize your pussy for life if I fucked you raw your first time, and it wouldn't be enough. I'd want to do it all night."

She steps right up to me. "I want to be good enough for you, Caleb, and I don't want you holding back."

"I'm not fucking you tonight, Elisa. I'm saving your first time for Canada." I hadn't told her yet. I was keeping it as a surprise, but I need her to leave this bathroom before I lose my control and pounce on her.

"Canada? What's in Canada?"

"The royal suite in a fabulous hotel in Banff, surrounded by mountains and forest and a lake. We're going there next weekend, and I'll make love to you the right way. The way you deserve. Now, please, be my good girl and go back to bed. Let me handle this myself tonight."

"Okay, but we're talking about this again."

I slump against the wall when she finally leaves, thankful I didn't give in to my pleading dick and ruin all my carefully laid plans for a romantic first time.

"Morning, babe," Elisa says, walking into our bedroom carrying a tray. I'd only just woken up and reached out for her, frowning when my hand touched cool sheets. She was still awake when I finished fucking my hand repeatedly in the shower last night, and she'd opened her arms for me offering silent comfort. Finally exhausted, I'd curled up against her slim body and instantly passed out. I fully expected her to still be sleeping when I woke.

"What time is it?" I ask over a yawn, pulling myself up against the headboard.

"Late." She places the tray table over my lap, and the scent of creamy scrambled eggs, crispy smoked bacon, and buttery toast tickles my nostrils and tempts my taste buds.

"This smells delicious. Thanks." I stretch up and kiss her lips.

She slides onto the bed beside me, wearing a green silk

patterned robe that ties at the middle and rests at her knee. "Are you okay now?" she asks as I take a drink of freshly squeezed orange juice.

"Yes. I'm sorry if I scared you last night."

"You didn't."

I raise one brow as I shovel bacon and eggs into my mouth, moaning as the delicious taste explodes in my mouth.

"I know who you are, Caleb, and I know what you do. The blood and violence don't scare me. I've grown up surrounded by it even if my parents shielded me from a lot. What scares me is not being able to be there for you. I understand why you didn't want to fuck me last night, but I need you to understand I'm not some precious princess. I can handle rough sex."

"Angel." I sweep my fingers across her cheek. "I love you for accepting me, faults and all, but you don't yet know what you like or don't like, and I refuse to pressure you. We'll take things a step at a time, and after you've experienced sex, if you want to try it hard and rough, we can, but I never want you to feel like you have to be a certain way to be with me."

"I know you have needs, Caleb," she says as I shove more food in my mouth. "I know you are used to sex a certain way and I just want you to know that I can be who you need me to be in the bedroom."

"Lil, I just need you to be *you*. The rest will take care of itself." I don't know how to say I don't want her to be like the other women I've been with without hurting her, but I've got to try because she's getting hung up on things that really don't matter to me, and I don't want her stressing out. "I don't want things to be the way they have always been because this is different." I cup her face. "Everything we have done so far is different and infinitely better because I love you and I'm so hot for you. I've never had that level of intimacy with anyone else before, and I'm loving it."

I lean in and kiss her tempting lips. "I've been happy to wait to have sex because the anticipation is exciting for me. I know when we make love for the first time it's going to change me. It's going to undo everything I thought I knew about myself, and I want to prolong that feeling." I rub her lower lip. "Please don't compare yourself to others or think that you are somehow failing me because you are not."

"I love that you're so considerate of my needs and so gentle with me, but I'm not breakable, and I want to explore everything with you, Caleb. Just promise you won't treat me with kid gloves. Let me decide what I like and what I can handle, and I'll only know if we try everything."

"Okay. Just don't push me or tempt me to do something until you are ready. I couldn't forgive myself if I hurt you in the name of my pleasure."

"You wouldn't do that. You couldn't." She places the fork back in my hand. "Eat. You must be starving."

"I am." I take a large bite out of my toast.

"I just want to say one more thing, and then we'll table this discussion."

I continue eating and slurping my coffee as I watch her work her way up to saying whatever is on her mind.

"I'm not opposed to going to Club H with you."

I almost spit coffee all over the comforter. "What?" I splutter, sure I must be hearing things. There is no way my pure innocent Lili wants me to take her to a sex club. My ears must be playing tricks on me.

"I'm not a prude. I'm just inexperienced, and I want to experience everything with you."

I shake my head. "I'm not taking you there. I won't share you, and your naked body is for my eyes only."

She rolls her eyes. "Do you realize how sexist and hypocritical you sound right now?"

"Don't care," I say before shoving the last of the bacon in my mouth and chewing. "Unless you want me to slaughter every fucker in the place for even breathing the same air as you, we're not ever stepping foot in Club H." I canceled my membership months ago, and I have zero interest in taking my woman there. Unless she's curious and she wants to look, and then we can fuck in one of the private rooms. I'd be down for that, but all this talk of sex clubs is premature until we've had sex and she learns what she likes.

I can't wait to teach her.

"Those are famous last words, Caleb," she says, waggling her brows and swaying her ass in my face as she slides off the bed and saunters into the bathroom.

Chapter Thirty-Three
Elisa

"The views are truly stunning. This must be the most beautiful place on Earth," I say, letting the awe I'm feeling filter through my tone as I sit on the window seat in the luxurious suite Caleb booked in the plush hotel set in the middle of Banff National Park in Alberta, Canada. Snowcapped mountains rise majestically outside the window, looming over the crystal clear smooth waters of Moraine Lake. Bordering the lake and surrounding the hotel, which has been built to resemble a sprawling castle, are copious trees and dense woodland. According to the concierge—a friendly older woman from the local area—the trees over on this side of the park are mostly made up of Douglas fir, white aspen, lodgepole pine, white spruce, and balsam poplars.

"Is it romantic enough for you?" Caleb asks, wrapping his strong muscular arms around me from behind. He nuzzles his nose in my neck before grazing his teeth against my earlobe, sending heady shivers cascading across my sensitive flesh. "I want this weekend to be special."

"It's perfect, Caleb." I turn around and snake my arms around his neck. "It couldn't be any more romantic."

"That sounds like a challenge." He waggles his brows, and a smile grows on my lips.

"I can't believe you haven't had a relationship before because you're a natural boyfriend. You make me feel so loved."

"It's because it's you. Everything is natural with you, Lili. Only you." His lips descend in a tender kiss that turns my insides to mush. I pout when he pulls back, and he chuckles. "As much as I'd love to stay here and get lost in you, you have appointments at the spa."

"I do?"

He nods. "I'm going to check out the gym and the pool while you get pampered." He threads his fingers through my hair, tilting my head back a little. "Then we have a private dinner at the rooftop restaurant."

"You are really spoiling me."

"You deserve it." He pulls me back in flush with his body. "I want our first time to be spectacular. I want this to be a weekend we look back on forever with fond memories." His adoring gaze melts me into a puddle of goo at his feet. "I know you're nervous, but you should know I am too. I have never had this, Lili. It's all new for me as well. I'm experienced in fucking not making love. I'm as much a virgin as you are."

Not technically, but I get the point he's making, and it helps to settle my nerves to know he's nervous too. That this is as much a big deal for him as it is for me. I trace my fingertips through the stylish stubble on his cheeks. "I'm nervous, but I'm excited too. I can't wait to be intimate with you. To feel a part of you and to know this is what it'll be like for the rest of our lives."

"I'm glad you have come around to the inevitability. I'm

glad we're on the same page." His eyes shine with some indecipherable emotion.

"I was protecting my heart and ensuring I didn't set myself up for a fall, but you have more than proven how serious you are, Caleb. But know one thing, my love." I stretch up and kiss his gorgeous mouth. "I always believed we were inevitable." Even during those rough months when I believed he'd broken his promise to me, I couldn't dispel the sense of rightness I felt whenever I considered us together.

"I love you, Elisa Salerno." Caleb hugs me close. "So fucking much. You are my world, and I will do everything to make you happy and keep you safe. I promise."

After a manicure, pedicure, facial, and massage, I'm brought back to our suite where a hairstylist and makeup artist are waiting to do my hair and makeup. Caleb is nowhere to be seen, but he's clearly been back here if the gorgeous green and gold dress waiting on the bed is any indication. Exquisite gold strappy sandals and a designer purse complete the outfit.

Caleb shows up just as I'm ready, displaying perfect timing. He looks good enough to eat in a custom-fit black suit with his signature black shirt and a gold and black tie. "You take my breath away, Lil. Look at you," he says as I twirl for him, feeling like a million bucks.

"I could say the same to you. You're gorgeous."

"I love you." He reels me in, pressing a light kiss on the end of my nose.

A photographer arrives then to take photos. "We need to capture every moment," Caleb whispers in my ear as he holds me close while we pose for the man.

The private dining area of the rooftop restaurant is tucked

into a corner, shielded by an ornate patterned foldable room divider. We can still hear the patrons in the main part of the room, but we can't see them, and they can't see us. Our table is pressed up beside the large floor-to-ceiling window offering the most incredible view of the landscape spread out below us. Twinkling lights shimmer from the trees surrounding the hotel, and they join with the moon in casting shimmering rays across the placid waters of the massive lake.

"You couldn't have found a more romantic place in the entire world," I say in a breathy tone, completely bowled over by the location and all the trouble Caleb has gone to. "I am the luckiest girl in the world to be here with you."

"I'm the lucky one." Caleb hands me a flute of champagne after the server has left with our order. "To us," he says, holding up his flute for a toast.

I clink my glass against his. "To the future."

We enjoy a sumptuous meal, and the atmosphere is romantic and relaxed. Conversation flows easily, and I'm floating on a cloud as we make our way back to our suite a couple of hours later. I'm relaxed, but excited nervousness lingers in my veins at the thought of finally knowing what it feels like to have Caleb inside of me.

A gasp escapes my lips when I enter our room to discover the rose petal path leading from the door to the large four-poster bed. Lit candles surround the perimeter of the room, and the curtains have been left open to maximize the beautiful backdrop. "I thought we might take a naked dip in the hot tub," Caleb says, circling his arms around me and kissing my cheek. I look outside to our decked balcony where a large hot tub waits. Beside it is an ice bucket with more champagne chilling.

"Okay." Nerves thread through my tone.

"Lili." He turns me to face him. "It's okay to say no. I just thought it might help to relax us and help to get us in the mood."

"It's a wonderful idea. Let's do it."

"Are you sure?"

"Yes." I place my hands on his chest and stare into his gorgeous eyes, showcasing every emotion racing through me. "I trust you, and I want this with you."

He kisses me softly and sweetly before silently turning me around and helping me out of my dress.

"You're so beautiful, Lili." He scans the gold and black lace bra and panties set I'm wearing with clear admiration.

Gia dragged me to La Perla to shop for the trip, and I'm glad she did. "Do you like it?" I ask, batting my eyelashes.

"Love it, though I'll love it more when you're out of it." His eyes flash with heat.

I unclip the bra and fling it aside, keeping my eyes trained on him as I shimmy the panties down my legs, leaving me standing in just my heels. I hold my head up, feeling confident and powerful as his gaze roams every inch of my body. Caleb's words and constant reassurance have helped to erase any lingering doubts. I know he wants me, and I don't compare to anyone else. I know this night is as new for him as it is for me.

"Your turn." I challenge him with my eyes.

"You want me naked, angel?" He smirks, loosening his tie and lifting it over his head.

"Yes, please."

Caleb flashes me a flirty smile as he shucks out of his suit jacket, draping it on the back of the chair. "Your wish is my command."

I lick my lips as I stalk forward to help him. I unbuckle his pants while he unbuttons his shirt. Lowering to the ground, I untie his shoes, remaining on my knees as he gets rid of all his clothes until he's standing before me in glorious nakedness.

My gaze trails over him from his feet to his head, loitering on the hard length jutting out from his body, already leaking precum, and my pussy is soaked as potent need whips through me.

"I need to taste you," I say, sliding my palms up his thighs and licking my lips again. "I need your cock in my mouth so bad." I am addicted to sucking his dick. Watching him fall apart as I work him over is one of the best feelings in the world. To know he is putty in my hands, that I, an inexperienced virgin, can give him that much pleasure and have him worshiping the ground I walk on is an incredible high.

"You know I won't say no. I'm addicted to the feel of your mouth on my dick."

"I'm addicted to your dick, period," I say, and he chuckles.

Wrapping my fingers as far as they will go around the base of his erect cock, I begin stroking him as my tongue darts out, licking his crown. Caleb's groan is my own aphrodisiac, and I open my mouth and suck him down, greedily running my lips and my tongue up and down his throbbing erection, loving the sounds pouring from his mouth.

"Enough, angel," he says a few minutes later, pulling out of my mouth and helping me to my feet. "I want to come in your pussy." He looks out the window. "What about the hot tub?"

"It can wait." I press my body all up in his. "I need you now, Caleb. Make love to me."

He carries me to the bed like I'm precious cargo, laying me down gently before he dashes outside to grab the champagne, setting it beside the bed. Then he spreads my legs and buries himself between my thighs, sucking and licking and fingering me until I shatter on his tongue. It doesn't take long because I'm already so horny and dying to feel his cock inside me.

"Condom?" he asks, lifting a brow as he kneels between my legs.

I shake my head. "I'm safe, and you know I'm clean. I'd rather feel all of you inside me."

"I've never had sex without a condom, and I got tested recently. I'm clean too."

"Okay."

He covers my body with his, careful to keep his weight off me. "I love you, Elisa. For always."

"I love you too." I drag my fingers through his gorgeous hair before letting my hands explore his muscular back.

"Are you sure you still want to do this?" he asks, pushing my thighs apart with his knees.

"I have never been surer of anything."

He plants his lips on mine before lifting his head. "If you want to stop at any time, tell me. I'm going to go slow, but it will still hurt a little."

"I spoke with Gia and my mom. I know what to expect."

"I will take care of you, Lili." His fingers dance a slow dance across my collarbone.

"I know you will. Now stop stalling and make love to me."

He chuckles before leaning down to kiss me again. Positioning himself at my entrance, he keeps his eyes locked on mine as he slowly inches inside me. The feeling of fullness is almost instantaneous, and I part my legs more, wincing at the sharp stab of pain when he pushes through my resistance.

Caleb stalls, his gaze running over my face. "Do you want me to stop?"

"No way." I cup his face. "Keep going, my love."

Caleb's body is straining with the effort involved in going so slow, and it only makes me love him even more. He continues pushing and I bite on the inside of my cheek to avoid crying out. He is so big, and I feel so incredibly full. My walls are hugging him as he carefully eases inside me. When it feels like he can't possibly go any farther, he stops, looking down at me with so much love and lust I feel like crying. "You're my beating heart, Lili." He holds his body still as he leans down to kiss me. "You feel so incredible, and I'm feeling so much. God." He rests his head on my shoulder, and I hug him to me, circling my legs around his waist, ignoring the stab of pain the motion produces.

"I love you. I love you. I love you," I say, my heart as full as my body. I dot kisses over his face and run my hands up and down his back. "You can move, Caleb."

His head tips up. "Are you sure?"

"Yes." My lips curl in amusement, but I love how careful he is being with me. "I want to feel you moving."

Caleb maintains eye contact with me as he begins moving in and out, very slowly at first until he feels me relaxing. We kiss and caress as he makes love to me, and though there is pain mixed with the pleasure, this is the singular most incredible moment of my entire life. "Go faster," I request when the stirrings of lust twist in my core. I pivot my hips and angle them to meet him as he picks up his pace.

"Fuck, Lili. This is too good," he pants in between rolling his hips and hitting some magical place deep inside me.

"Oh!" I rasp as pleasure surges through my veins. "Do that again."

Caleb angles his hips and hits that spot inside me over and over, and I'm digging my nails into his back, arching my spine, rolling my hips, and claiming his lips in greedy kisses as he thrusts deep and hard with precise careful movements. "I'm going to come," he pants. "I can't hold back any longer," he adds, trailing his fingers between our bodies to find my clit.

"I'm close too." It's almost miraculous. I really didn't think I could come from sex my first time, but I feel my orgasm building as he rubs my clit and drives his erection deeper inside me. I fall off the ledge first, crying tears of joy as my body drowns in the most blissful sensations. Caleb follows me over the ledge a couple of seconds later, shouting my name and gazing at me with shock and so much love as he spills his hot seed inside me.

After, we lie wrapped in one another's arms without speaking for a few minutes. I snuggle into his side as his strong arm holds me close. "Are you okay?"

"I'm peachy." I can't help giggling as I lift up and peer down at him.

"Was it good for you?"

"It was amazing. It was everything I had hoped for and more." I trace circles on his chest with my finger. "Was it good for you?"

"Incredible. Best experience of my life." He holds my face in his firm grip. "I have never felt anything like that before, Lili. Being inside you with no barrier is the most indescribable feeling. I have never felt closer to another living soul, not even my twin."

Tears prick my eyes, but they are joyous ones. "I love you so much, and I want to do that with you every single day for the rest of my life."

Chapter Thirty-Four
Elisa

We don't make love again because I'm sore, and Caleb refuses to hurt me, but we sleep contentedly side by side, and we have oral sex when we wake. After a gorgeous breakfast on the balcony followed by a dip in the hot tub, we get dressed and head out to explore the area, hiking one of the lower trails before making our way into the town where we find a cute diner for a late lunch. When we return to the hotel, we take a swim together in the pool before enjoying a couple's massage. Dinner is at a different restaurant within the hotel tonight, and it's no less spectacular.

By the time we make it back to our suite, we're both ravenous for one another, and we collapse into bed in a heap of tangled limbs. Caleb makes love to me again, and it's even better this time. The following morning, I surprise him with a morning wake-up blowjob before I climb on top of him and ride his cock. We don't bother getting dressed, spending the day between the hot tub and the bed, having sex all over the suite and in the shower.

I'm almost crying when Monday morning rolls around and

reality comes calling. The Accardi Company private jet is waiting to take us back to New York, but I truly don't want to leave.

"We can come back," Caleb says, tucking me into his side as we exit the hotel and walk toward the car.

"I would love to buy a place here," I say, daydreaming out loud. "A cabin in the woods overlooking the lake with a hot tub and a roof garden to admire the stunning views."

"Leave it to me," my boyfriend says with a glint in his eye. "It's my job to make your every dream come true, and you won't find me lacking."

The next three weeks fly by, and we're both busy. I'm setting my business up with the help of the PR firm Caleb hired for me and a new PA I recruited via Uncle Ben. Amie is a godsend, and together we are fitting out my new office, setting up a new website, and getting promotional material together for our launch campaign. I have settled into Caleb's apartment like I always lived here. I'm adding a few personal touches to the place, and we even had my family over for dinner last weekend. I think Caleb and Dad bonded over the Sebastien situation and they are getting along, which is a huge relief. I knew once Dad saw how happy Caleb makes me he would come around. It helps that Mom is on our side. Even Romeo is thawing.

Life is good even if Caleb has been busy with *mafioso* shit and I haven't seen him as much as I'd like. They didn't get any useful intel out of the thieves because Cruz is smart enough not to give his location away. All contact between them was via an intermediary who stayed hidden behind the scenes. They have no clue where he's hiding out, and The Commission is growing increasingly frustrated.

Fiero cracked the password on the USB key, and we discovered damaging intel, both real and fake, on every family except for the Accardi *famiglia*, naturally. If Cruz had gotten his hands on it, it would have spelled the end of The Commission and the Five Families. Everyone is hoping there isn't a copy of the files out there somewhere, but for now, the threat seems to have ended. Finding and dealing with Cruz is the last item to be fixed. Everyone is keen to return to peace and prosperity.

It's Saturday, and I'm in the laundry room when Caleb sneaks up behind me, making me scream and jump when his hands land on my bare stomach under my crop top.

"Oh my god." I playfully push him away. "You almost gave me a coronary!"

"Your powers of observation suck, angel. You make it too easy to sneak up on you."

"Not that I'm complaining, but why are you home? I thought you had a meeting at Commission Central?"

"I did. Cruz has been spotted in Vegas, and the word on the ground is he's planned a big takeover. It's all-hands-on-deck, and I'm flying there with the other dons in an hour. I just stopped by to grab a bag. We might have to stay overnight."

"At least it means the end is in sight." My arms go around his neck. "I'll miss you. Please be careful."

"I'll miss you too and always."

I narrow my eyes at him because everyone knows Caleb has a reckless streak. "I mean it, Caleb. I know how badly you want to end Cruz. Promise me you won't take any crazy risks. I can't bear the thought of anything happening to you."

"I'm not the same man, Lili. I have you to come home to now, and that means more than revenge. I promise I'll be careful. I won't take any stupid risks." He offers his pinkie. "Pinkie promise."

I curl my pinkie around his, and then we kiss. It quickly

turns heated, like always, and we strip in record time. My hands are on the top of the washing machine, with my ass in the air, as Caleb drives into me from behind, and I moan in appreciation. I love making love with him. We have so much sex, and every time is better than the last. We're having fun learning how to turn one another on and exploring different positions. I can't believe I have gone twenty-two, almost twenty-three, years of my life without experiencing the joy of sex, but I'm definitely making up for lost time. I'm insatiable, and my man can't get enough either.

Caleb's fingers creep around my body to my clit, and he rubs me fast in sync with his thrusts. My inner walls grip his cock as I get close to the promised land. "Now, Lili. Come now!" Caleb commands, pinching my clit as he rams inside me, and I shatter all over his dick. Caleb covers my body from behind as he comes while my body shakes and trembles from a powerful orgasm.

"Fucking hell, Lil." Caleb hugs me from behind. "I'm addicted to making love to you."

"Good, 'cause I demand it multiple times a day."

"Perfect," he murmurs, tracing my earlobe with his tongue. "So. Fucking. Perfect."

He pulls out and cleans me up with some tissues before helping me back into my clothes. "I'll text you when we arrive," he says, grabbing his bag from the floor.

I walk him out to the door, peppering his handsome face with kisses while he lingers in the doorway. The two *soldati* on guard at the door are new, but I'm not surprised he's taking precautions. I'm sure all the dons are. It could be a trap because you never can tell with Cruz DiPietro. The men pretend not to look as we make out like we're never going to see one another again. We can't ever say goodbye without overdoing it because we're just that gone for one another. "You better go, or you'll miss your flight."

He kisses me one final time before walking to the elevator. "Oh," he adds, turning around to look at me. "Don't plan anything the week of your birthday. I have a surprise."

My heart turns somersaults in my chest, and I wonder if it's a trip to Paris. Caleb hasn't hidden his desire to marry me sooner than later, and I can't think of a single reason to wait. He has always been it for me, and he's an amazing boyfriend and partner. Even better than anything I ever imagined. "I look forward to it." The elevator doors glide open, and I blow him a kiss as he steps inside. "Love you. Be safe."

He flashes me a signature grin before blowing me a kiss just as the door closes.

I return to my laundry, and when it's done, I make a chicken salad for lunch. I have just opened my laptop to do some work when the doorbell chimes. I don't bother checking the camera feed because there are bodyguards on the door today, and they wouldn't let anyone get close if they were dangerous. Still, I check the peephole before opening the door, inwardly groaning when I see who it is.

Anais has kept a relatively low profile of late, and she hasn't bugged Caleb or me, so I don't know what she wants. She presses the bell again, and I sigh. She won't back off, so ignoring her isn't an option. Opening the door, I instantly frown at the panicked expression on her face. "Thank fuck." She grabs my arm and yanks me out into the hallway.

"What the—" I cut myself off when I spot the slumped forms of my bodyguards on the ground. "What's going on?" I wrench out of her arm, immediately suspicious just as an alarm goes off, shrieking a high-pitched tone and sending red flashing lights darting across the private lobby.

"We're under attack. There's no time to explain," she says,

grabbing my arm and dragging me toward the door to the stairwell.

"Stop." I grip her wrist and dig my heels in, not going anywhere until I call Caleb. This smells off.

"There isn't time, Elisa!" she screams. "It's Cruz. He's come for me, and he's coming for you too."

"No." I shake my head. "He's in Vegas. He's—"

"He's not!" she roars, tugging on my arm. "It's a trap to get all the dons out of the city. I knew he'd come for me, and I know the way his brain works. He won't leave you here, Elisa. He'll take you as payback."

"I need to call Caleb." My cell is on the island unit in the kitchen.

"You can call him from my cell," she says, dragging me toward the door. "We need to get out. I think this building is going down."

The door to the stairwell opens, and a somewhat familiar guy pops his head in. "Come on! We need to get out of here stat."

"I'm trying, Giotto!" Anais says, and I remember the name. He's the *soldato* from the third floor she's been fucking.

"He's in the building, and he's coming for you now, Elisa," Giotto says, stalking forward. "Caleb will pump me full of bullets if I don't get you to safety."

I stare at his face, and there's something off about it and him and the entire situation. Nerves fire at me from all angles as goose bumps sprout on my arms. "I'm just getting my cell, and then we'll leave," I say, shucking Anais's arm off and backing up.

They exchange a look, and all the hairs lift on the back of my neck. Adrenaline courses through my veins as my fight-or-flight response kicks in. I turn and run, but I'm too late.

Giotto tackles me from behind, taking me to the ground.

"You just had to make this difficult, didn't you, *Lili*," he says in my ear in a completely different voice. "It doesn't matter anyway because very soon there won't be anyone left to stop me."

I kick and fight as he manhandles me to my feet.

"Shut up, bitch," Anais says, lunging at me.

I scream as pain pierces me in the side of the neck, staring in shock at the large empty needle she's holding in her hands. "What did you do?"

"Don't worry, *Lili*," the man in front of me says. "You're just going to sleep for a little while."

I sway on my feet, and my vision turns blurry, but I see enough as he peels the mask off his face revealing his identity. "No!" I gasp, staring at Cruz in horror right before I pass out.

Chapter Thirty-Five
Caleb

My cell beeps just as I'm about to board the plane en route to Vegas. I step to one side to check the message I've just received, earning a frown from my twin. All the blood leaks from my face when the picture loads. It's Lili. She's stripped to her underwear and tied to a chair in a dingy room. Her head lolls forward, her hair hanging in strands around her face. Panic sluices through my veins as I read the accompanying message with location coordinates.

TELL NO ONE OR SHE DIES. I WILL KNOW.

I take off running as Joshua calls after me.

Elisa

Pain-filled grunts fill the air as I come to, disorientated and confused. Hair curtains my face as I lift my head, moaning at

Siobhan Davis

the ache in my neck and the throbbing pain in my arm. My vision is sketchy when I open my eyes, and I have trouble focusing. A rotting stench filters into the air, and my nostrils twitch. The floor under my bare feet is cold, dirty concrete, and the raw stone walls are covered with stains. The air is frigid, lifting all the hairs on my body and hardening my nipples behind my flimsy bra.

But that is the least of my worries when I hear a familiar voice.

"Lili." His gravelly tone sends icy shards plunging into my spine.

I turn my head in horror, barely able to see him through knotty strands of hair. "Caleb," I rasp in a hoarse voice, hoping the vision I'm seeing is a nightmare and not reality. My love is tied to a chair beside me in only his boxers. Arms behind his back and ankles bound to the chair legs, like me. Blood seeps from the hole in his arm where they hacked his tracking chip out, and blood also covers his face, coats his hair, and drips down his chin and onto his chest.

"The lovebirds are reunited for one final tragic act," Anais says, yanking my head back by my hair and causing me to cry out as splintering pain radiates across my scalp.

"Leave her the fuck alone!" Caleb shouts. "I'll kill you. I'll kill both of you."

Anais tilts my head to the side so I can see everything going down. "Look what your love did to him," she scoffs. "He just raced off without hesitation, leaving his brother and others to their fates."

"Always so fucking arrogant, Accardi," Cruz says before ramming his fist into Caleb's stomach. "But I appreciate your predictable reckless streak."

"Stop!" I scream as Cruz continues beating my boyfriend.

282

"Just tell us what you want, and we'll do it!" Right now, I would do anything, sacrifice anything, to set Caleb free.

Outside, a loud boom claims all our attention, and my eyes widen in horror as I stare out the small window. A mushrooming fireball shoots upward through the sky from the direction of the airport.

"You're a dead man," Caleb says in a fearless tone, eyeballing Cruz with unconcealed hatred. "I'm going to enjoy ending you."

"You and whose army?" Cruz stands, flexing his bloody knuckles and grinning at the fiery sky outside. His phone pings. Removing it from his pocket, he chuckles as he reads the message. "They're all dead, and there's no one to stop me now."

Oh my god! It all snaps into place. It was a trap to get all the dons on the plane and take them out. My eyes whip around to Caleb, and his reassuring gaze meets mine, silently coaxing me to trust him. Caleb wouldn't leave his twin to die. This must be part of some plan, so I force my anxiety aside and concentrate on getting out of here alive.

"Let me see that." Anais lets go of my hair and stalks over to her husband, her heels clicking on the hard ground. She's dressed in a figure-hugging dress with her cleavage hanging out, high heels, and pearls. A fur coat keeps her warm while I'm over here literally freezing my butt off in my underwear. She grabs his cell and smiles. "You did it, baby." She throws her arms around Cruz and kisses him.

Cruz slides his hand under the back of her dress as he devours her lips. I throw up a little in my mouth watching him grope her ass and grind his hips against her.

Caleb looks at me while our kidnappers are busy making out, lowering his eyes to where my hands are tied behind my back over the chair. He is busy at work loosening his binds, and I do the same, offering up thanks that Dad insisted on training me and Romeo when we each turned thirteen. He has no expectation about any of us initiating, but he has always insisted we are well prepared for the world we live in. I might not be a badass like Gigi, but I can hold my own.

Unfortunately, Cruz isn't swayed by his wife's wiles for long. His eyes whip to mine, and I momentarily freeze before slowing my motions so it's not obvious I'm trying to free my hands.

"How long have you two been a team?" Caleb asks, looking unfazed despite our predicament. He's cool as a cucumber as he silently works to loosen the rope around his wrists.

"A long time," Anais coos, snuggling into her husband.

"Did you really think I'd let you fuck my wife and live if there wasn't an ulterior motive?" Cruz shoves his hand down the front of her dress, fondling her ridiculous tits.

"From the start?" Caleb asks, and I know he's feeding their egos and keeping them talking on purpose. They are both narcissists, so it shouldn't be too difficult.

"The first couple of years were retaliation for Cruz fucking that slut Bettina," Anais says, pushing her tits into her husband's hand as he continues groping her.

It's disgusting. They both are.

"Until we realized how alike we are and our goals were aligned," Cruz adds.

"And what now, Anais?" Caleb asks. "You're just going to raise her kid as your own?"

"Yes!" she snaps. "We need to present a family image so the rest of the *mafioso* will fall behind our leadership, and Cruz needs an heir for succession."

"Anais is barren, so there was no choice but to use one of my whores to breed my child," her despicable husband explains. How sad for Bettina. She seems to have had real feelings for him, but she meant nothing to him. She died for

284

her mistakes, and that little boy she gave birth to will pay for them.

"Cruz!" Anais feigns hurt. "A little compassion, please. You know how much it upset me not getting pregnant."

"It's a sign," Caleb says, smirking. "Mother Nature knew you'd make a lousy mom, so she made it so you couldn't have kids."

Anais lets loose a high-pitched screech. Removing Cruz's hand from her chest, she lunges at Caleb, slapping and hitting him while Cruz just laughs.

"What goals?" I blurt, trying to draw her attention away from my love. "What goals were aligned?"

Anais glares at Caleb before tossing her dark-blonde hair over her shoulders. "We both wanted ultimate power. It's our destiny," the delusional bitch says. "We were always meant to be king and queen of New York. It would've happened sooner for me if that bitch Sierra hadn't stolen Ben."

"He was never yours," I say. "Ben would never have married you. You were a spoiled brat then just like you are now. He despises you."

Anais walks forward and slaps me across the face. I knew it was coming, but I still don't regret my words even though I hear Caleb chastising me in my ear.

"Touch her again, Anais. I dare you," Caleb growls.

"Oh, Caleb." Anais crouches in front of him. "Your threats are amusing but empty."

"Get away from him!" I scream when she drives her hand under the waistband of his boxers and touches him.

"Darling. There'll be time for that later. Let's finish story time." Cruz barely looks concerned that she's groping another man. If they have truly been working together for years, they have both willingly fucked other people with full knowledge and permission. I struggle to understand that because I can't conceive ever sharing Caleb with anyone or ever wanting any other man to touch me.

"I do miss your dick." Anais removes her hand, and I work harder to free myself. That fucking bitch is not putting her hands on my man again. The rope is definitely looser, so we just need to keep them talking for a little longer. Anais pats Caleb's flaccid cock over the material of his boxers, and I want to slice her hands from her body. "We'll have one final fuck before my husband kills you. For old time's sake." She pins me with a smug look. "I'm sure you're gagging for a decent fuck. We all know the little virgin can't satisfy you."

"No longer a virgin, and my man is well satisfied," I coolly reply. "More than he ever was with you."

That earns me another slap and another warning glare from Caleb.

"Pity." Cruz grips my chin, arching my neck so I'm forced to look at him. "I was looking forward to deflowering you." His hand slides down my body to cup my crotch, and bile travels up my throat. Caleb is hurling insults at him while bucking on the chair. Cruz's eyes light up. "Bet you're still an anal virgin."

I can't disguise my terror, and he barks out a laugh. "Oh, I am going to enjoy this." He moves his hand down lower, poking his finger into my ass through my panties. He smirks at Caleb. "It's only fair, Accardi. You fucked my woman; now I get to fuck yours." Caleb is going crazy, and that's the only reason I'm able to keep it together rather than freaking out.

"You were spying on him all this time," I blurt, looking at Anais, hoping she takes the bait. "Why? What did you gain?"

My diversion works. Cruz smirks at me as he moves away, walking back to his wife. Relief surges through me, but it's short-lived. We are far from out of the woods. "Anais fed Caleb intel when it suited us," he explains, "and she was able to keep tabs on most of the key players while we plotted in the background."

"Except it all went wrong," Caleb clips out. "We got the upper hand in A.C., and Puccinelli washed his hands of you."

"We didn't need the Italian, and the Grecoes were fools." Cruz puffs out his chest. "Anais begging you for protection was all part of the plan because we needed those files to destroy The Commission and take control."

"You ruined everything." Anais jabs her finger in my face. "I couldn't get close to him to gain access to the file room because of you, and Joshua practically threw me out the day I showed up at his office."

"We know you placed cameras and audio and bugs in her apartment, and you have the building locked up like Fort Knox," Cruz says to Caleb.

"That's why you were masquerading as Giotto," I surmise. Caleb jerks his head in surprise because he wasn't aware of that.

"That was only a recent development when we had to revert to Plan B." A thunderous look crosses over Cruz's face, and he darts forward, punching Caleb in the face.

I scream, shouting at him to let him go. Anais slaps me in the face, and I use the commotion to work faster, feeling the ropes loosen further.

"Cruz has been in the city the entire time." Anais peers at her husband with an adoring look. "We were meeting regularly at the salon." She turns gloating eyes on me. "I was fucking Sebastien there too."

Shock races through me. "He was a spy?"

"A distraction," Cruz confirms. "We wanted to distract Caleb, and we knew a possessive boyfriend would work like a charm."

"Not that it helped much in the end." Anais scowls. "I still couldn't get to that key, and then Seb fucked it all up by getting attached to your little virgin ass." She rakes a derisory gaze over my body. "God knows why. You're nothing special." Her eyes linger on my chest. "A boob job would have done wonders for your sex appeal, Elisa, but you're too timid to try anything bold."

"Elisa has the perfect body, and she's anything but timid in or out of the bedroom. She is worth a million of your lying whore ass," Caleb says.

Both husband and wife attack him, and I use the opportunity he's given me to loosen the ropes more. Not much further and I'll be free. Ideas churn through my mind as I figure out how to play this to our advantage.

"You thwarted our plans to have you all sent down," Cruz adds, straightening up and continuing speaking as if he and his wife aren't two deranged lunatics who totally deserve one another. Anais kisses Caleb on the lips, and I shoot daggers at her back. She flips her middle finger at me as she moves over to her husband, sliding her hand down the back of his pants.

They make me sick, and I can't wait for karma to finally get them.

"So you left us no choice but to kill everyone." Cruz grins as he looks out the window in the direction of the airfield.

"You're an idiot," Caleb says. "You think you can blow up a plane and commit mass homicide and get away with it?"

"It wasn't as neat as handing the files over anonymously to the authorities and letting them do my dirty work, but it's a worthy Plan B. No one paid the price after the warehouse bombing." He folds his arms. "They can't pin anything on me because my planning was exemplary. I bought my own airline to understand the inner workings of the industry, make contacts, and devise a foolproof plan. This was always my backup strategy if I couldn't get my hands on the files."

"So why not kill Caleb on the plane?" I ask, just as the rope fully loosens, and I'm free. I don't know if Caleb has managed to free himself too, but I can't risk looking, so this is all on me.

"Because he deserves to suffer before he dies. It's punishment for daring to taunt me for years." Cruz strides toward me with evil written all over his face. I prepare myself, having decided what I'm going to do. "That's where you come in, sweetheart." He grabs my boob through my bra. "I'm going to fuck you every which way from Sunday while he watches. Then Anais will take what she wants from that cockroach while you watch your love get hard for another woman." He leans in closer to my face. "Then, I'll kill you slowly, making him watch the blood drain from your body. After, I'll keep him alive for a while. A few weeks. A couple months." He shrugs. "I'll prolong the agony for as long as I can before he rots in this cell."

"Fuck you," I say before gathering saliva in my mouth and letting it loose. It lands on his cheek, and he's instantly enraged. I use my body when he slaps me, letting it propel me backward with force. My chair slams to the hard ground, the weathered wood shattering upon impact like I hoped. Ignoring the rattling pain splintering up my back and Caleb's panicked shouts, I wrap my free hand around one of the broken spokes of the chair, feeling the jagged end and smiling internally.

I wait for Cruz to lean down before making my move, praying like I have never prayed before. "Time to lose your virginity, little mouse," he says, reaching for me.

"Time to go to hell." Lifting my arm, I shove the jagged piece of wood into his neck with force. Blood spurts from the wound as I hit the artery, and I hammer the end with my palm, pushing it down and driving it deeper, using all my hatred to fuel my movements.

Cruz stumbles to the side, staring at me with fear-laden eyes as his fingers curl around my makeshift weapon.

Anais screams, reaching for her husband as blood bubbles in his mouth, and he crashes to the ground. I slide out from under him in time, dragging the base of the chair with me. Only one of my legs is free, but the wooden spoke is still tied around my calf. I scramble to untie the last knots so I can help Caleb.

"You fucking whore!" Anais screams, jumping on me just as I've freed my leg. Angry tears fill her eyes as her hands wrap around my throat, and she squeezes. I do the only thing I can think of and punch her in the boobs. Then Caleb surges forward, curling his arm around her neck and yanking her off me.

"I told you not to touch my girl," he snarls, dragging her back a little. "Follow your husband to hell, bitch, and align your goals for eternity." Locking eyes with me, he twists her head and snaps her neck in a lightning-fast move. The light instantly dies from her eyes, and she slumps to the ground, joining her dead husband.

I climb awkwardly to my feet, stumbling toward Caleb, and we fall into one another.

"You're okay. We're okay," he says, holding me close as I shiver all over from the pure adrenaline coursing through my veins.

"The others," I croak, hoping I'm right.

"They're safe. Joshua knew something was wrong when I took off without telling him and refused his calls. I knew he'd jump to the right conclusion. We had suspicions it was a trap, and my taking off confirmed it. J knows the only reason I would ever leave him without a word is because something had happened to you. Like he knows if something had happened to you it was because of Cruz."

"Caleb." Panic jumps up and bites me. "You didn't tell him?! My dad might've been on that plane! Your dad too!"

"Elisa, calm down." He clasps my face in his hands. "I couldn't risk calling him because Cruz threatened me. I wasn't about to risk your life especially when I knew my brother would figure it out. Trust our freaky twin bond. My brother is alive, and I know he got everyone off that plane in time. If Joshua was dead, I would know it." He thumps his hand over his heart. "I'd feel it in here. Trust me, J is on his way now to rescue us."

I rub the back of my neck. "Thank God, they didn't know about the new tracking chips."

He grins. "We were right to keep that news a closely guarded secret."

"So, what now?" I ask, shivering as I glance around the chilly cell. I spare no more than a passing glance at the two dead assholes on the floor. They got what was coming to them.

Caleb swats my ass and reclaims my attention. "You remember the last time I stood before you covered in blood?" He arches a brow as his pupils darken.

Lust coils low in my belly as I quickly catch on. "Oh, yes, baby. You're on," I say, bending down to remove the last tie on my leg.

"I'm not sure how gentle I can be," Caleb says, pushing me up against the wall as his fingers find their way into my panties.

"I'm not sure how gentle I want you to be," I reply over a gasp as he plunges two fingers deep inside me.

"I think we're compatible in more ways than one," he admits over a wicked grin.

I part my legs and push my chest into his as he pumps his fingers in and out of me in a punishing pace. "Only one way to find out, my love," I say, shoving his boxers down and gripping his solid erection.

Epilogue
Elisa – Six Months Later

"**Y**ou look beautiful," Dad says with tears in his eyes. "Too good for that punk." It's said in jest, but I'm not sure he's fully forgiven Caleb for what he walked in on that day when he showed up with Joshua and a team of men to rescue us from the dungeon Cruz and Anais had locked us in. They burst into the room, all guns blazing, to discover Caleb and me fucking in the blood of our enemies.

That story is now legendary in *mafioso* circles, and no one refers to me as the little virgin anymore.

Dad almost killed Caleb, but Joshua managed to wrangle the gun out of his hand before he could pull the trigger.

It was fun times, for sure.

"I love him." I know I have a dreamy look on my face, like always when I think of my fiancé. Caleb took me to Paris for my twenty-third birthday and proposed in front of the Eiffel Tower, exactly how I had drawn it all those years before. It's just one memory, in a long list of memories, I will cherish until the day I die. "I adore him, and I can't wait to start a family with him." My hand gravitates to my stomach, and I smile at

293

the secret I'm carrying. No one knows yet, including Caleb. It's going to be his wedding gift, and I'll tell him after the ceremony.

"You're truly happy, honey?" Dad asks, scrutinizing my face for any signs of cold feet.

"Incredibly so." I take his hands. "You don't need to worry. He treats me like a queen, Dad. I have never felt more loved or cherished."

"I see that. I just had to make sure. I know I bust his balls, but it's mostly for fun. He's a good partner, and he'll make a good husband and father. I wouldn't have given my permission when he came to see me otherwise."

"I'm honestly surprised you didn't try to shoot him again. It wasn't even that long after—"

"Let's not go there, Elisa. I worked hard to scrub that awful image from my brain."

I burst out laughing, but Dad isn't even mildly amused.

"I fail to see the humor. No father should have to witness that."

"You didn't actually see me naked or—"

"I saw his naked butt as he was driving into you, and that was enough to scar me for life, trust me."

"Aw, Daddy." I place my hands on his chest and smile. "You'd swear you never had sex."

A mischievous grin washes over his face. "Did I ever tell you about the time—"

I cover his mouth with my hand. "Point made, Dad." I shiver all over. "Never share sex stories with me."

"Agree not to have sex with your husband while rolling in the blood of dead assholes, and we have a deal."

I giggle again. "Love you."

"Love you too, sweetheart. So, so much." His eyes rake over

my gown again. "You look like a bona fide princess in that dress. You are stunning, Elisa. A beautiful woman, inside and out."

I twirl in front of the mirror, admiring the way the fitted corset top molds to my curves, enhancing my natural assets. Tiny diamante embellishments are dotted over the top before it gives way to a wide satin sash, tied at the back in a bow. The skirt is full-on princess with layers upon layers of chiffon over tulle. I decided not to wear a veil so the dress speaks for itself. Instead, I'm wearing a crown as I prepare to marry my king.

My dress is the opposite of Gia's sleek, sexy, figure-hugging gown. Gigi's dress is also strapless but in an hourglass shape with a fishtail train. She's wearing a long lace veil, and I can't wait to see it on her. We had fun planning our double wedding, and we did everything together, including dress shopping and fittings. In all my childish imaginings, I never factored in a wedding with my best friend, but it couldn't be more magical or more perfect. The twins are close, and it's only fitting they get married together.

"It's time," Mom says, slipping into the room. She had just ducked out to ensure all the guests were seated. We're getting married at St. Patrick's Cathedral, and a bishop is conducting our joint ceremony. It truly is a fairy tale come to life. Over three hundred friends and family members are seated in pews outside, awaiting the brides.

"You and Gia will be the talk of the town," Mom says as more tears well in her eyes. The makeup artist has already had to fix her up twice.

"No more crying, Mom. Ria doesn't have time to fix up your makeup again."

"I'm just bursting with happiness for you, Elisa."

"So smile. Don't cry." I laugh as I pull her into a hug.

Out in the hallway, we meet Gia and Rico. I hold hands

with my best friend as we make our way toward the main part of the cathedral.

"I'm so happy we did this together," Gigi says as we walk side by side talking in hushed voices. Our fathers are conversing quietly behind us.

"It makes it all the more special, sister."

Tears stab her eyes. "In so many ways." Her face is aglow, and her lips look ready to burst with whatever secret she's holding back.

"Spill it, sis."

"I'm pregnant," she whispers in my ear.

I slam to a halt, staring at her in shock.

"Is everything okay," Rico asks.

"Yes." Gia warns me with her eyes not to say anything. She loops her arm in mine and pulls me forward. "You really need to work on your poker face, Lise."

"It's not that." My heart swells behind my chest. I look at her and mouth, "I'm pregnant too."

This time, it's her turn to stop. "Get out!"

"Girls, what's going on?" Dad asks.

"Nothing," we say in unison, sporting matching grins. We lean in to one another, whispering as we walk toward the entrance doors.

"Does J know?" I whisper. She shakes her head, and I giggle. "It's your wedding gift too?" She nods, and I giggle again. We're so in sync.

"How far along are you?" she whispers.

"Seven weeks."

"Oh my gawd." She's practically bouncing. "I'm eight weeks."

Happy tears fill my eyes. "We'll be pregnant together, and our kids will be cousins and best friends."

"I didn't think this day could get any better, but it just did," she says as we walk up to where our bridesmaids are waiting. Shea and Aria are standing with me, and Rosa and her cousin Tosca are standing with Gia.

"You are the most stunning brides, and those twins are lucky bastards," Frankie says, earning a frown from the priest standing to one side of the inside door. The main church doors are locked to keep the large crowd outside from gate-crashing. New York society and the media have had a field day since we announced our engagements and double wedding. Hundreds of well-wishers line the streets around the cathedral, and security has been massively ramped up for the day.

Rico steps around me, offering his arm to his daughter. Joshua is the oldest twin, so we decided Rico and Gia would walk with their bridal party first and then we'll follow. "Ready, *tesoro*?"

"As ready as I'll ever be." She turns to look at me. "See you up there, sister."

Mom and Frankie trade beaming smiles.

"Love you," I say, stepping back as the music starts and Gia steps through the door into the church.

"I'm proud of you," Dad says a few minutes later when we get into position. "I couldn't have asked for a more perfect daughter." He softly kisses my cheek. "Your mother and I wish you and Caleb every happiness for the future, Elisa." Tears gleam in his eyes. "I'm happy you got your man."

"Me too, Daddy."

The orchestra starts up our song and I lift my head, clutching Dad's arm tight as we step through the doors. Our guests are on their feet, every head turned in our direction as we make our way up the aisle, followed by Aria in her pretty pink dress and Shea in a different style dress made in the same material.

The smile on my face is genuine as I walk toward the love

of my life, and even though the walk seems long, because the cathedral is huge, it isn't uncomfortable. I find I don't mind the attention. Seeing so many smiling faces only adds to the surge of emotion bubbling in my chest.

I look ahead, seeing Gia and Joshua watching with large smiles on their faces, before I switch my attention to my beloved. Caleb is wearing his emotions on his face, and I have a sudden urge to lift up my dress and race toward him. Somehow, I compose myself though Daddy chuckles when my steps quicken.

Caleb looks so hot, so fuckable, so gorgeous, in his custom-fit tuxedo. His hair is neater than usual but still in that messy style I love. His eyes twinkle with love and warmth, and he is all I see as we approach. Our eyes remain fixed on one another as Dad guides me toward the other man in my life.

"You are so beautiful, Lili, I can hardly breathe," he says when we arrive.

"Take care of our girl, Caleb," Dad says, guiding my hand to Caleb's.

"With my life, Alesso." They share a nod before Dad steps back to take his seat.

"Hi." I beam at my intended. "You are literally my every fantasy come to life, Caleb Accardi, and I'm the luckiest girl in the world to be marrying you."

"Sure you don't want to ditch him for me?" Cristian grins as he tries to wind my fiancé up.

"Sorry, Cristian. I've only had eyes for this one since I was eight."

"Some best man you are," Caleb teases, pulling me in close to his side.

Cristian had previously agreed to be Caleb's best man, so Joshua asked Vittus to be his. Rowan and Giulio are their respective groomsmen, keeping it all in the family.

"You are breathtaking, Lili. I love the dress." Clear admiration shines from my groom's eyes, and I bask under the glow of his attention.

A throat clearing reminds us of where we are. Holding hands, we turn and face the altar the same time Gia and Joshua do.

"Dearly beloved, we are gathered here today..."

The ceremony flies by, and most of it goes over my head because I'm so fixated on my love, and he is all I see. Gia and Joshua make their vows first, and when the bishop pronounces them man and wife, we join the congregation in applause. Caleb whistles as Joshua dips his bride down low, passionately kissing her as the crowd whoops and hollers.

Then it's our turn.

We hold hands and lock eyes as we exchange rings and recite the formal vows before adding our own. My voice projects around the large cathedral from the small mic attached to my dress as I speak first. "I fell in love with you, Caleb Accardi, the moment I met you when I was eight. It didn't matter it wasn't appropriate for a little girl to daydream about a teenager five years older than her, or to doodle his name all over her schoolbooks, or to paint drawings of Parisian proposals and lavish weddings, because I always knew. In my heart, I always knew you were the other half of my soul." Oohs and aahs ring out around the congregation.

My heart feels so full as I stare at the only man I have ever loved in this way. "I can't explain how I knew, but that truth was always there. It took some time to find our way together, but when we did, it only confirmed what I have known for most of my life. We were always meant to be. You are the man I want to share my life with. The man I want to raise a family with." I almost choke over those words knowing how happy he's going to be when I tell him. "The man I want to grow old with. Being with you completes me, Caleb, and I promise to love you every day for the rest of our lives. I am honored to be your wife."

Ignoring tradition, Caleb leans in and kisses me. It's tender and full of emotion and it melts my heart.

"We haven't gotten to that part yet," the bishop quips, and our guests titter.

We break our kiss, and Caleb stares adoringly at me as he states his vows. "I have adored you, Elisa Salerno, from the first moment you entered my life as a vivacious, inquisitive little girl who loved to follow me around like a faithful puppy dog."

I swat his chest as everyone laughs.

"There were times growing up, and later in life, when I felt lost and alone, and those were the times when I always sought you out because you alone had the power to make me feel like I belonged. Your soul has always called to mine. I couldn't explain it back then and I didn't try because I was a coward." He squeezes my hand. "I was afraid to confront the truth hidden in my heart for fear of failing you. You have always been the braver one of the two of us, and you fought for us when I didn't. Deciding to fully open up to you was the best decision I ever made. I have never been happier, and it's all because of you. You have brought out the best in me, Elisa. I wake each morning with a smile on my face because you are in my arms."

Quiet sobbing breaks out behind us, and I'm guessing Mom and Natalia will need makeup touch-ups several times today.

"I love you, Lili. You are the other half of my heart and soul, and I can't wait to spend every second of every day of the rest of our lives together. I am proud to call you my wife."

Caleb clasps my face gently as the bishop pronounces us husband and wife, leaning in to kiss me as applause breaks out around us. Caleb holds my face tenderly as he kisses me deeply, sliding his tongue against mine, pouring emotion into each sweep of his lips and thrust of his tongue.

The rest of the ceremony goes by in a blur, and then we're walking down the aisle with Gia and Joshua, all of us smiling and laughing and bursting with joy.

We take copious photos in the cathedral and out on the steps, surrounded by armed guards, while news helicopters hover overhead and media vans line the sides of the road. Well-wishers call out and cheer, and by the time we finally crawl in the back of our chauffeur-driven car, my feet are aching, and my cheeks hurt from smiling so much.

"Well, Mrs. Accardi," Caleb says, taking our joined hands and bringing them to his lips. "How does it feel to be a married woman?"

"It's the most amazing feeling in the world, husband." He brushes his lips against my knuckles as he smiles. "How about you?"

"I'm on top of the world." He stares adoringly at me, and I can't wait a second longer to tell him.

"I have news that will heighten that feeling."

"Do tell, wifey."

I scoot closer, fighting tears as I take one of his hands and bring it to my stomach. "We're having a baby."

His eyes widen before filling with emotion. "For real, Lili?" Shock splays across his handsome face. "You're pregnant?"

"Yes." I hold his hand to my stomach. "We created life, Caleb, and he or she is growing inside me right now."

"This is officially the best day of my life," he says, leaning down to kiss my tummy.

"Every day with you is officially the best day of my life." I wind my arms around his neck when he straightens up. "I knew it when I was eight, and I'll still know it when I'm eighty."

"Thank you for never giving up on me, for always believing in us." He brushes his lips against mine.

"Thank you for making my fairy tale a reality."

He holds me against his chest, banding his arms around me in familiar protective strength that always makes me feel safe and loved. "I will always make sure your dreams come true."

———

Type this link into your browser to read the Paris proposal bonus scene: https://bit.ly/CKONYBonus

The next book in my *Mazzone Mafia* world is **Taking What's Mine** – Fiero Maltese's story. Available to preorder now. Check your local store.

Her teen crush is now a ruthless killer and powerful mafia heir. Will one life-altering night unite or destroy them?

Bennett Mazzone grew up ignorant of the truth: he is the illegitimate son of the most powerful mafia boss in New York. Until it suited his father to drag him into a world where power, wealth, violence, and cruelty are the only currency.

Celebrating her twenty-first birthday in Sin City should be fun for Sierra Lawson, but events take a deadly turn when she ends up in a private club, surrounded by dangerous men who always get what they want.

And they want *her*.

Ben can't believe his ex's little sister is all grown up, stunningly beautiful, and close to being devoured by some of the most ruthless men he has ever known. The Vegas trip is about strengthening ties, but he won't allow his associates to ruin her perfection. Although it comes at a high price, saving Sierra is his only choice.

The memory of Ben's hands on her body is seared into Sierra's flesh for eternity. She doesn't regret that night. Not even when she discovers the guy she was crushing on as a teenager is a cold, calculating killer with dark impulses and lethal enemies who want him dead.

Understanding the risks, she walks away from the only man she will ever love, stowing her secrets securely in her heart. Until the truth becomes leverage and Sierra is drawn into a bloody war—a pawn in a vicious game she doesn't want to play.

As the web of deceit is finally revealed, Ben will stop at nothing to protect Sierra. Even if loving her makes him weak. In a world where women serve a sole purpose, and alliances mean the difference between life and death, can he fight for love and win?

———

See where it all began! ***Condemned to Love***, the first book in my ***Mazzone Mafia*** world, is available now in ebook, paperback, alternate paperback, hardcover, and audio.

About the Author

Siobhan Davis™ is a *USA Today, Wall Street Journal*, and Amazon Top 5 bestselling romance author. **Siobhan** writes emotionally intense stories with swoon-worthy romance, complex characters, and tons of unexpected plot twists and turns that will have you flipping the pages beyond bedtime! She has sold over 2 million books, and her titles are translated into several languages.

Prior to becoming a full-time writer, Siobhan forged a successful corporate career in human resource management.

She lives in the Garden County of Ireland with her husband and two sons.

You can connect with Siobhan in the following ways:

Website: www.siobhandavis.com
Facebook: AuthorSiobhanDavis
Instagram: @siobhandavisauthor
Tiktok: @siobhandavisauthor
Email: siobhan@siobhandavis.com

Books By Siobhan Davis

NEW ADULT ROMANCE
The One I Want Duet
Kennedy Boys Series
Rydeville Elite Series
All of Me Series
Forever Love Duet

NEW ADULT ROMANCE STAND-ALONES
Inseparable
Incognito
Still Falling for You
Holding on to Forever
Always Meant to Be
Tell It to My Heart

REVERSE HAREM
Sainthood Series
Dirty Crazy Bad Duet
Surviving Amber Springs (stand-alone)
Alinthia Series ^

DARK MAFIA ROMANCE
Mazzone Mafia Series
Vengeance of a Mafia Queen (stand-alone)
The Accardi Twins
*Taking What's Mine**

YA SCI-FI & PARANORMAL ROMANCE
Saven Series
True Calling Series ^

---

*Coming 2024
^Currently unpublished but will be republished in due course.

www.siobhandavis.com

Made in the USA
Monee, IL
05 July 2024

61235277R00194